TO FILL A JAR WITH WATER

Juliette Rose Kerr

JULIETTE ROSE KERR

Juliette has made Plymouth, MA, her home for the past fifteen years. She holds a BA in English from Pepperdine University, an MLitt in Shakespeare Studies from the University of St. Andrews, Scotland, and an MA in Spiritual Formation from Gordon-Conwell Theological Seminary. When she's not writing, she works as a full-time End of Life Doula and Christian Spiritual Director at The Rose & Poppy. This is her debut novel.

Juliette is available through her website:
theroseandpoppy.com or @theroseandpoppy

This novel's story and characters are fictitious.
Certain long-standing businesses and places are reimagined,
but the characters involved are wholly imaginary.

To

Caleb, Nathaniel, Noah

& Scott

—my bright lights on the way

And to the town of Plymouth, MA,

which is the beating heart of this story—thank you.

Love is the wisest of madness,
able to suppress bitterness,
sweetness able to heal.

—W. Shakespeare

Rose

June 24, 2015

Rose had read somewhere that loneliness hurt more than a broken arm. There wasn't a cast or a pill or surgery that could heal it. Although she'd never thought about it before, she knew what they said was true. And even though there was a cure, everyone walked around like there was no medicine for it. Loneliness felt like the gargantuan shadow of a giant, stalking her, enveloping her—making all the colors around her gray. It swallowed colors whole. And even though they weren't too far beyond her reach, she never seemed to catch up with them.

"Ro-Rosie," Dottie called to her from down the aisle. "I'm gonna need you to restock all the feminine products in aisle nine. After you're through there, be a dear and gather all the electric scooters in the parking lot. Drive them back where they belong."

Dottie was Rose's uber-efficient manager at the big-box store where she'd worked for the past two years.

"And when you're done with the scooters, stop by the employee lounge, pretty please with sugar on top?" Dottie winked and swished back to the stockroom.

Rose caught a glimpse of the back of her t-shirt through her undone apron. It read, "Little Miss Sassy Pants." She smiled.

Dottie had such a carefree way of dressing, but Rose knew it wasn't something she could ever get away with wearing. She didn't have Dottie's natural confidence. Hesitant to put herself out there, Rose often rinsed and repeated the same outfit—a white shirt, a pair of faded, hand-me-down 501s, and a pink zip-up hoodie when the weather got colder.

Today was Rose's seventeenth birthday and she'd already caught wind of the little party Dottie whipped up for her in the break room. She'd organized the "shin dig," as Dottie liked to call it, with some of the girls who worked at the jewelry counter. They'd spilled the beans in the parking lot this morning walking into work.

If this birthday was anything like the last, Dottie would have baked a special cake for her decorated with little pink flowers on top of chocolate frosting. Rose also had a small obsession with Schweppes Ginger Ale. She knew that would be there too. Ginger ale always reminded her of her grandmother who used to give her a glass when she visited after church each Sunday. She would open a can of brown bread and pour baked beans on top, then serve her a glass of Schweppes over crushed ice. They'd sit around her small kitchen table, just the two of them, say grace and talk about the morning's Sunday school lesson.

Rose appreciated Dottie's thoughtfulness and how she made sure to jot down every employee's mentioned preferences in her pocket-sized, polka-dot notebook she kept in her immaculate store apron—the one she washed and ironed weekly. It made Rose feel seen, heard—noticed—like she didn't have to beg for the attention. Dottie's small gestures were always able to create some distance between her and the giant, if only for a moment.

"You never know when it may come in handy someday," Dottie liked to say, patting the cover and placing it with particular importance in her pocket for safe keeping.

Rarely left unattended, Rose spied it in the break room the other day. She turned the pages perusing the dainty notebook. Under her name it read, "Rose = bookworm, church bells, snowmen, and walking." Rose wasn't sure if walking was really a favorite thing of hers or something she did more out of necessity, but for the most part, Dottie was a keen observer of people's interests. Tempted to pencil in additional information like her favorite band or her favorite order at Mamma Mia's, Rose decided against it and placed the notebook at the bottom of Dottie's locker out of the way of other prying eyes.

The parking lot was virtually empty this afternoon. Rose felt the hot asphalt through the soles of her white sneakers. At what temperature did rubber melt? It was brutal weather for a fair-complexioned girl with ginger hair. Last week her freckled shoulders fried under similar conditions, and now her red-peeling skin rubbed against her ivory tank top. The tips of her shoulders, especially the small bone that protruded on either side, would again be bright red by the time she was through gathering them all up. *Why hadn't she worn any sunscreen like Carrie had told her to?*

Strolling through the parking lot, keeping an eye out for scooters, Rose liked to keep a low profile. Naturally reserved, although most people didn't think of her that way, she avoided eye contact with customers. Riding the scooters back to the parking bay always made her feel a little awkward.

Come to think of it, she did a lot of jobs at the store that made her feel uncomfortable. She was self-conscious when she restocked the feminine products, pregnancy tests, and adult diapers. She cringed when she had to clean out the sanitary napkin bins beside the women's toilets. Just thinking about all the times she did awkward jobs at the store made her cheeks flush, although in this heat you'd never notice.

Why wasn't she assigned any of the normal jobs at work? She'd do anything to clean the dressing rooms or collect the empty cardboard boxes by the registers. She'd be happy to oversee cleaning up the break room or wiping down smudged fingerprints from the front windows. But she knew daydreaming about the nicer jobs at work was useless. Rose knew Dottie trusted her. She counted on her to get the job done, even the embarrassing ones, without complaint or push back. Responsible, reliable, steady—Rose did what she was asked to do. She liked being helpful.

Just as she spotted the first scooter, she heard a scream come from the gardening center near the corner of the lot. People were gathering around a spot on the ground. Worried there'd been an accident or a child hurt, she sprinted toward the commotion. Breathing heavily, she saw a dark figure from the corner of her eye.

"Ma'am, I didn't see him. I'm sorry," he said. "One minute I was backing up, and the next minute I felt something underneath my back tire. I had no idea."

Dressed from head to toe in pitch black, except for a tooth of white in his collar, the sun, high in the sky, fiercely beat down on him. Rose worried the priest might pass out from heatstroke or shock. He was an older man, and small beads of sweat formed on his brow and upper lip. Pulling out a dingy handkerchief from his back pocket, he wiped his forehead.

As he leaned over to inspect the injured dog, Rose thought he was most likely pleading with the dog to get back up. He made a half-hearted attempt to wake it by rubbing its side and nudging its shoulder.

Small drops of sweat from his brow fell on the dog, but not even this baptism could help the poor fellow now. A few women in the crowd began to fan themselves with their grocery circulars and glanced uncomfortably at each other.

"Does anyone have a blanket in their car?" Rose asked as she approached the group, snapping them out of their collective helplessness.

She identified the owner because she was the only one who was wiping tears and snot onto her shirtsleeve. Patting the poor dog's back, she kept stroking its face. She called him Patches. Rose assumed the dog must've jumped out of her open window as she backed out of the parking space. He was so quiet, lying on the hot pavement; but Rose was relieved when she saw he was still breathing and opened his eyes.

A few people in the crowd put their hands on her shoulders offering their support. Rose noticed no one touched the priest or made a similar gesture. He stood like an island. A gentleman in a seersucker jacket brought a blue wool blanket from his car.

"Let's get Patches onto the blanket and lift him into the car," Rose directed. "You, sir." She pointed to a man in the front of the crowd. "Can you lift his front legs and can you get his back?" She gestured to another man standing at the back who looked strong enough to carry some weight.

The owner stood doubled over, tipping forward from the weight of her tears and would not let her precious animal go.

"Can someone drive her to the vet?"

The priest held his hand up halfway in the air and the crowd gradually dispersed as the dog was lifted into the car.

Gently lowering the gate of the SUV, Rose locked it into place and tapped the back of the car twice. The priest opened the passenger's side door for the owner and walked around the back of the car to the driver's side. For a moment, they caught each other's eyes and Rose's heart ached for him. She saw his hand slightly shake on the door handle before he opened it.

As the car exited the parking lot, Rose waved goodbye, although she knew they couldn't see her. The thought of something being hurt on her birthday gave her an uneasy feeling in the pit of her stomach.

Woozy from the heat, Rose abandoned her task of finding the scooters and headed back inside. A cold blast of air froze the sweat to her body when she re-entered the store. Her skin was sticky and clammy. She shivered.

With five minutes left until the end of her shift, she remembered the party in the break room and headed in that direction. As she walked down the aisle toward the back of the store, she heard a few distant "happy birthdays" from co-workers who were restocking the shelves or milling about. The sides of her mouth curled up into a smile and she untied her knotted apron at the back.

The break room door was perpetually broken, but Rose managed to jimmy it open just in time to catch Fran, a stockroom assistant, scurry back to her locker at the far end of the room. Rose watched as Fran grabbed her purse.

"How's it going? Stayin' for some cake?" Rose asked the air.

Without replying, Fran made a dash for the door. It creaked open and slammed shut. The slam was forceful enough for someone to lose a finger if they weren't careful.

Fran reminded Rose of a frightened animal that had lost its ability to trust people. All attempts to connect with her were useless. She feared everybody. Like a nervous cat, she bent down when she was touched to avoid human contact.

"Rosie." Dottie popped her head through the door. "I'm sorry, doll, but I just can't stay for cake. I gotta fill out one of those incident reports on account of the dog getting run over in the parking lot. I'm sorr-ry. I'm not sure anyone is gonna make it back here either."

Rose's heart sank a little in her chest.

"The air conditioner is fried in the home-improvement aisle and the crew is crawling around in the ceiling ducts trying to fix it. It's hotter than H-E-double-hockey-sticks out here!"

She was visibly frazzled, but not wanting Dottie to see her disappointment, Rose continued to smile and nod. She gave a big thumbs-up.

"I understand, Dott."

"Go ahead and take the cake home. Share it with your sister. Happy birthday, Rosie!"

"You betcha, I will." Rose playfully mocked Dottie's Midwest expression.

Dottie blew a kiss in her direction and a waft of scented air lingered in the break room when she closed the door.

Rose scratched her head, unsure of how to get the cake home in the blazing afternoon heat. She crossed her fingers, hoping it wouldn't melt along the way, and thought a couple layers of tinfoil should do the trick and keep it contained. Pulling out the sheet and ripping it along the metal teeth, she wrapped the cake, pressing the tinfoil down along the edges. She wanted to make sure she wouldn't get any chocolate icing on her white top, the one she'd worn especially for her birthday.

As she sealed the back of the cake, she noticed a single finger swipe in the icing.

"Fran," she muttered to herself.

She hung up her yellow apron and grabbed her purse. It was a little over a mile walk back to the apartment she shared with her sister, Carrie.

Carrying the cake was more difficult than expected. Using a carriage to transport it to the edge of the parking lot, she secured the cart in a dried-out island and picked up the cake. With both hands underneath it, she kept a laser eye on her shirt and looked down every now and then to make sure it wasn't covered in chocolate.

As she walked, her mind wandered to the dog in the parking lot. It suddenly occurred to her that her father's childhood dog was named Patches too. What a strange coincidence and even stranger that she didn't notice it earlier. But memories of her childhood were always so heavy with pain that she hesitated picking them up. She never had enough strength to carry them for very long, so she mostly left them alone and created a little graveyard for them in the back of her mind.

But her heart ached remembering her father. He was only thirty-nine when he died from a fast-moving cancer last December. From diagnosis to death was only twelve months. It was barely enough time to realize what was happening before they put him deep in the ground.

And sadly, soon after his death, she and Carrie lost their mother too, when she quickly remarried and moved to Florida with a man she'd just met. Barely five months had passed since his death before their mother was married again. Rose knew deep down her mother was the type of woman who couldn't tolerate loneliness, even a passing hint of it.

Rose and Carrie spent much of their young lives parenting themselves, as well as their mother. She was a fragile sort. Their father's quick death was like a tornado, destroying what little foundation she possessed. After he was gone, she was decimated, broken up into a thousand little pieces. She ended up clinging to the nearest man for fear of being swept away by her own sadness.

Fortunately, Carrie was old enough to be Rose's guardian. However, the girls were forced to live on a shoestring budget. Their old house was sold to pay off some of their father's outstanding debts, which didn't leave much left over. There was just enough for their mother to get a long-awaited facelift and for the girls to put down a security deposit on an apartment near town. At seventeen, Rose wondered if she had more wrinkles than her mother now.

Pausing to reposition the cake, Rose's arm was sore and red from the tinfoil rubbing against her skin. Holding it out in front of her, she continued to walk home past the hair salon and dance studio, and the red brick wall she used to sit on while waiting for her mother to pick her up from class.

Carrie supported them by waitressing in the restaurant of a harbor-front hotel. But during the off-season, she was lucky to get a handful of customers a day. If they didn't tip well, it affected their bottom line.

Carrie was allowed one meal per shift, which helped, but she often bagged up half of it to share with Rose when she got home. Their cupboards were mostly stocked with canned food and large bags of white rice. They'd also made use of the town's food pantry on more than one occasion.

On the walk home, the heat started to get to her. She felt dizzy. Invisible waves rose from the pavement like a mirage, and she was sure by now her face was as red as the color of her hair.

The cake was getting too heavy to carry much further. Debating whether to abandon it somewhere before she reached the apartment, she noticed a black line of icing on her new top where the tinfoil folded in.

At a bus stop up ahead, she could catch her breath. The humidity in the air was making it difficult for her to breathe. The air was literally soaked with water. If she'd wanted to, Rose could've wrung it out with her two bare hands.

Needing some energy to walk the last quarter-mile home, she opened the tinfoil and swiped some icing on her finger and licked it clean. Pulling out a crumpled tissue from the bottom of her purse, she tried to wipe the black mark off her top, but it wouldn't budge. Rubbing was making the stain worse. She smeared a charcoal line across the hem.

She decided to leave the cake on the bench. She couldn't dump it. Throwing away good food felt criminal, and she convinced herself that someone would come along and eventually eat it.

Rounding the corner near Bailey's Nursery, she wondered if Carrie would make it home from work before she went to bed, or if she would spend another birthday by herself in the apartment alone.

Carrie

"Where'd you get this?"

He bit Carrie's shoulder hard enough to leave a mark. His rough lips grazed her skin.

"It's a scar," she said under her breath.

A red-orange glow entered from a crack in the blinds and lay like a tangerine blanket on top of tangled sheets.

"And this?"

He pointed to a faint patch of red on her stomach a few inches below her belly button. His fingertip snagged her skin as he tried to scratch it off, plowing red lines into her.

"Will-l…" Carrie pulled his hand away, becoming irritated by all his questions. "It's a strawberry birthmark," she said without looking directly into his eyes, and automatically directed her gaze up to the ceiling.

As they kissed, his stubble scraped her face and neck raw like sandpaper. He crushed her breast with his hand, heavy like a paw, bruising it a little. He abruptly turned her over.

The room was quiet except for the distant hum of a car on a nearby street. She was starting to feel unsettled. Her stomach muscles tightened and the atmosphere in the room shifted. A buzzing noise got louder in her ears. Just as she went to say something in hopes of slowing down the pace, he turned her head away, pressing her face into the sheets.

She tried to ignore the anxiety building inside her. Getting back into the moment, she tuned out the signals her body was giving her. Concentrating on a handful of beer bottles on his nightstand, she willed her mind to wander but found it impossible to let go. Her heart thumped rapidly in her chest. Holding her breath, she knew there was no way to stop it.

"Stop! Stop! Will!"

She quickly turned over, forcefully pushed him away and stood up. Grabbing her clothes off the floor and chair, she ran to the bathroom and locked the door.

"What the—get back here. Where the hell are you going?"

Running the tap water, Carrie looked in the mirror. Black spiders of mascara crawled down her cheeks and formed like ink blots in the sink below. Her tears burned hot, smearing the makeup down her face.

She paced the bathroom floor, then sat naked on the edge of the cold tub. The ceiling fan hummed loudly above her. She pulled out a small red bag from her purse and took out a used, bent spoon and a plastic lighter. She cooked a fine, white powder to the point of liquid brown sugar. With a syringe she took from the bag, she eased the liquid into the tube. Bending her knee, she placed her foot on the tub beside her and spread her middle toes apart. Injecting the warm liquid into a tiny vein between her toes, the light on the ceiling blurred. She slumped her head to one side and her eyes eased closed. Sliding down the side of the tub, she crumpled to the floor and curled up on a moth-eaten bathmat. The buzzing flatlined.

When she eventually opened her eyes, she wasn't sure how long she'd been out. Rolling on her back, she stared up at the popcorn ceiling covered in dusty cobwebs.

"Carrie! Carrie!"

His voice and the cold tiles on the floor woke her up.

"What's goin' on in there? Open the damn door."

He repeatedly banged his fist on the hollow door. She involuntarily winced each time.

"Your car's blocking the driveway."

She heard him barrel his way down the hallway into the kitchen.

"I don't have to put up with this shit," he yelled in her direction. "Let's go!"

Carrie cautiously opened the bathroom door and looked out.

"W-When's your dad coming home?" She used the question to gauge his anger.

Slowly pulling her tank top over her head, she walked quietly toward his voice, carrying her sandals and purse in one hand.

"He's not."

She watched Will grab his keys and a pack of cigarettes from the countertop. His eyes bore holes into the top of her head as he passed her in the hallway.

"Will?"

She weakly tried to stop him.

"I-I'm sorry. I didn't mean to end it so quickly. I don't know what came over me."

She stared down at her chipped toenail polish and kept her head slightly bowed.

"Don't come over here and jerk me around. The money—now this. Shit, Carrie," he seethed behind his teeth and yanked his arm away.

She quickly moved past him in the doorway, and as she did, he raised his hand and slapped her hard on the back of her head.

Carrie slinked to her car and got in. She threw her purse into the back seat and rolled down the window. The air in the car was hot and humid. Her cheeks burned from the heat. She prayed the car would start.

Putting her hands on the hot steering wheel, she briefly looked up to see his eyes glaring at her from his rearview mirror. Forgetting to look back, she put the car in reverse. A passing car honked and startled her. She slowly backed up and decided to drive around the corner, needing a minute to pull herself together before she drove home.

Out of sight of his black truck, she picked at a scab on her left hand and made it bleed. Raising her hand to her mouth, she licked the blood away.

Having an urge to drive somewhere—anywhere, before heading home—Carrie found herself at the waterfront parked next to a tall, decommissioned brick smokestack.

It stood alone, as the rope factory that once bustled near it was now silent. Only the bones of the building were left to crumble in a forgotten parking lot. She examined the shoddy scaffolding, an exoskeleton that was left on the half wall of the building.

Rolling down the window, she listened to the sea water lap, clap against smooth pebbles. Like white noise, it calmed her frayed nerves. And she watched as the golden sunset diffused into soft, pink waves across the summer sky.

A scarcely used, metal-roofed train station sat empty to her left with a lone seagull perched on its rooftop as her car sat idling.

Out in the distance, along the horizon of the steel-colored water, a whale-watching boat slowly made its way into the harbor. It imperceptibly moved in a straight-line past Bug Light. Nicknamed "America's Hometown," Plymouth was unique. It was a place where the old and new, the dead and the living, the ancient and the modern seamlessly coexisted. Its shores were a haven—an opportunity—for any who were willing to come and make it their home.

A picturesque downtown, stately seafront homes, and horse farms in the heart of Chiltonville were some of the reasons why many families stayed and didn't dream of living anywhere else. Now, businesspeople from Boston, willing to brave the longer commute, found a place to raise their families along quiet, tree-lined streets. Locals and transplants lived side by side in a place where salt air and straw alchemized to make a little piece of heaven here on Earth.

A striking totem pole on the side of the highway beckons travelers to slow down. But, like most coastal towns in New England, the waterfront, with its walk-up restaurants, mom-and-pop souvenir shops and penny candy stores, board up their windows at the first signs of winter or when the tourist buses stop coming. Plymouth hibernates until the last hills of black snow mixed with salty grit melt into the asphalt.

The thought crossed Carrie's mind that she could leave tonight. She could drive up heavily forested highways all the way north to Maine and try to start again. But in front of her lay the ocean with its fickle hues she was reluctant to leave. Right now, it looked like a smooth, gray blanket trimmed in white, fluffy foam. She was tempted to lie down in it and pull the water up to her chin and rest, too tired to do anything about her life as it was. Too much about it was broken and she was paralyzed by the weight of the problems before her.

And then there was Rose. She was invisibly tethered to this town, unable to leave, even if she'd wanted to.

Grit and sand crushed under the weight of her tires as she pulled out of the parking lot.

Daniel

It was a warm and cloudless morning when he parked his truck under a shady tree in the corner lot at the counseling center. Creamy white blossoms from a flowering dogwood tree littered his hood, leaving marks. He remembered his mother chaining the blossoms together to make a necklace for him when he was a boy.

The counseling center was a new building in a residential area that had been rezoned for commercial use. It sat along a street peppered with hold-out homeowners not ready to leave just yet, but who were slowly being crowded out. One home now stood next to a Dunkin' Donuts and another sat conspicuously near a dermatology office. They were both across the street from a brand-new county courthouse.

The counseling center made an effort to have discreet signage respecting its neighbors, but that made it virtually impossible for new patients to find. He'd driven past it at least three times before his first appointment.

Today was his third session and although he thought he'd run out of things to say, he discovered his thoughts and feelings dripped out of him like a leaky faucet with no end in sight. After each session, he usually felt depleted—drained—as if he'd been to battle. It wasn't easy telling someone else about his darkness, but he needed to be there. He wanted to come, longing for someone to see him, not look at him, but really see him.

Smoothing his wrinkled khakis down after he closed the truck door, he put his keys in his pocket and slowly walked to the entrance. He went in to register and signed his name, Daniel Goodman, 9:45 AM, and took a seat.

Playing with an unraveled thread on his chair, he bounced his leg to stem his feelings of self-consciousness. He willed himself to relax but couldn't. To the strangers in the waiting room, his fidgeting most likely looked like a tic—his antsy movements a result of something more serious than plain anxiety. He jumped out of his chair, took a stroll around the room, and pretended to admire the bland artwork on the walls—New Mexico sandscapes.

"Daniel," Paul called his name.

He pushed his hands deeper into his back pockets and gave an imperceptible nod of acknowledgment. Keeping a steady eye on the floor, he walked in Paul's direction.

Will it ever get any easier?

"We'll be in here this morning."

Paul pointed to a room on the right with two chairs facing each other. One chair had a side table next to it with a box of tissues. Daniel assumed that was for him and took a seat.

Placing his hands on the armrests, he felt like he was strapping himself into an electric chair. He moved his hands and rested them on his thighs. Wiping his hands back-and-forth on his pants, he heard the tick of the wall clock. The air conditioning blew from a grid near the floor, cooling his ankles between his socks and his pant hem.

"How's it going, Daniel?" Paul sat relaxed. "How are you doing at the sober house?"

Paul slightly tilted his head to one side and pushed his eyeglasses up with his thumb, which tended to slip down the bridge of his narrow nose.

"I've been there about f-five months now."

His voice sounded louder than he wanted it to. He took a few deep breaths and tried to relax...*In....out...in...out.*

His pulse raced despite his efforts to keep calm. Paul wasn't making him nervous, but the gravity of what they talked about did.

"Take your time. There's no rush. Just breathe," Paul encouraged.

Daniel's chest unnaturally rose and fell. Paul's did as well. He exaggerated his breathing too.

"Let's start again, all right?"

Daniel nodded.

"Can you tell me a little bit about your drinking habits?"

"Before the O.U.I.?"

"Yes, let's start there."

"I didn't act out or m-misbehave when I was younger. I just quietly got drunk. I mostly did it alone, sometimes with Will, but I kept it under the radar until my O.U.I. two years ago." Daniel's voice suddenly dropped. "When I almost hit the woman and her b-baby in a crosswalk heading home from school."

He rounded his shoulders and nervously cleared his throat.

"I usually didn't drink at school. I saved it until I got home after my schoolwork was done. I'm regimented that way. H-Homework, then beer or something stronger."

For a moment, Daniel allowed himself to be distracted by the clock ticking on the wall, lulling him away from painful memories, but then forced himself to return to the present.

"There was a balcony outside my bedroom window where I'd sit and stare at the stars. I drank my way to sleep."

As Paul took a sip from a cup of water next to him, the silence in the room nudged Daniel along to say more. He noticed Paul was never overeager to fill the silence. He always looked content to sit and listen. It unnerved him a little.

"M-My father was barely home, and when he was, he just sat in a chair staring at the TV. My brother, Will, is really the only family I have, although we don't talk anymore."

"Can you say more about your home life?"

"Dinner, Will and I used to get ourselves. Laundry, me. Trash, Will. Mowing the lawn, Will. Making lunches, me. We were pretty much alone a lot of the time. O-Orphaned may be the wrong word for it, but I felt like an orphan. At seventeen, it was a lot of responsibility for a kid."

Daniel stopped speaking for a second and felt the chair underneath his legs. He found himself holding his breath again as red blotches tingled at his neck and seeped down onto his chest. The air under his shirt heated up.

Irritated that strong emotions always appeared on his face, he was angry that his blushing allowed the world to be an audience to his deepest feelings. *Why couldn't he feel things in secret like other people?*

"You mentioned your mother last week, can you tell me more about her? Your relationship?"

He swallowed hard.

"My mom, uh, she left when we were young. I was in elementary school. She found another man with more money. I think that's what Will said. I'm not s-sure. She may have wanted more money, but she probably also wanted a husband who was even the slightest bit interested in her." His voice rose.

A strange mixture of anger and sadness swept over him—a swell of tears built up ready to cascade over him. He tried to hold it back, but really, how much control did someone have in a flood?

"She lives in Arizona now, but Will doesn't wanna give me her address. He acts as though she's dead, but she's not. I used to ask for her address, but then I got the hint that Will wanted me to drop the connection."

Daniel pulled out a tissue from the box just in case the dam broke.

"Hasn't she tried to contact you directly?"

He'd never thought of that before.

Why hadn't she called? Why hadn't she tried to contact him herself?

Will and his dad didn't need to be the middlemen.

"Can I be honest with you?" Daniel immediately realized the stupidity of his question. "I sometimes dream I'm with her. I-I have conversations with her in my head. I'm lying with my head in her lap as she strokes my hair. It's crazy, right? But it feels so real. I can feel her hand on my head."

Daniel's cheeks heated up, like he was sitting too close to a campfire.

Paul was quietly engaged in the conversation, but he was making Daniel do all the hard-emotional lifting. He wasn't doing it for him.

"This sounds stupid, but I tell her about my day and how l-lonely I am."

A heavy sob, like a full-rain cloud soaked his cheeks with tears.

"I tell her I miss her."

He looked anxiously over at Paul.

"And the other day, I started shaking after one of my daydreams. I almost couldn't stop."

And just as he was describing the event, his body began to slightly tremble again—a visceral reaction to the memory of his mother. The trauma of her leaving had seeped into his cells.

He'd shared a special relationship with her. She'd treated him as if he were her only son. And although the guilt of her favoritism shamed him when he thought of Will, it also felt good to be held in such high favor. When he was young, he'd noticed her little gestures that told him he was more important than Will or even his father. So, how could she have left him too?

Really, it made sense that she would show him more affection. His father was never home, and Will was unlovable a lot of the time. He had a perpetual chip on his shoulder and constantly rejected any kindness she offered him. He never let her in, but why should he? Most of the time his mother merely tolerated Will. She treated him like a pestering fly and simply swatted him away.

But Daniel knew he loved Will so much that he tried to make up for his mother and father's lack of interest. However, there was only so much he could do. He didn't have the capability or the responsibility of cleaning up his parents' mess. He simply loved Will the best he could. He loved him by never saying no to him, by doing and being whatever his older brother wanted—by lacking any boundaries. Constantly bending to his brother's whims made him a human puppet. Daniel realized this was the very reason why he found himself at the counseling center and in Paul's office today. *Was he born without a backbone?*

Guilt ripped a hole through Daniel's heart—the size of the Grand Canyon. Deep down he knew what his mother was doing but did nothing to stop her. He didn't stand up for Will, mainly because he felt too small and insignificant himself. Instead, he consoled Will by taking another drink with him whenever it was offered.

"The truth is, I'm not sure why I'm crying. It comes up hard from my gut and feels like I'll never stop."

Daniel coughed in an attempt to trick his body to stop crying. He switched his balance in his chair and then happened to notice Paul's diplomas were in the shape of a cross on his back wall.

Was that a coincidence?

The temporary distraction helped. He dabbed a tissue under his eyes, then grabbed another one out of the box.

"I liked me when I drank, and I kinda hate myself when I don't. Drinking Danny was brave and funny. Sober Danny is weak and anxious—scared just about all the time. Sometimes I wish I still drank. I'd have a lot more confidence that way. I'm so tired of feeling exposed all the time."

Anger had replaced his tears. Only a small pile of used tissues on the side table were evidence that it had happened at all.

Jotting something in his notepad, Paul eventually spoke up. "Daniel, what's life like at the house for you?"

Daniel rubbed his hands on his pant legs, and finding a small hole in his khakis, started to pick at it.

"Before going to bed every night, I take a drug test, and I wake up every morning next to men that are, for the most part, strangers to me."

He looked down at the floor.

"I'm there because of the c-choices I've made. It's where I have to be." He cleared his throat and sat up straighter in his chair. "I need to stay at the house. I want the routine—the accountability."

As Daniel finished his last sentence, bright crimson dots began to appear on his lap one at a time. Five large drops of blood collected before he realized what was happening, and for a second, he wondered if they were falling from his eyes.

"I think you need a tissue for your nose." Paul leaned forward, attempting to assist him, halfway reaching for the tissue box on the table.

Wiping his nose, blood smeared the length of his finger. He looked at it, still comprehending what was happening to him, then he reached for a tissue himself. Leaning his head back, he looked at the ceiling.

"I think you're meant to lean forward and pinch," Paul offered.

Leaning his elbows on his knees, he pinched the bridge of his nose and waited. It didn't take long for the bleeding to stop, and he looked up at Paul who was still waiting on the edge of his seat.

"Do you still want to go on or do you need a few more minutes?"

"No, I'm good."

Daniel sat back in the chair holding the bloodied tissue under his nose. He replaced it with a fresh one and added the blood-soaked one to the pile already on the table.

"Okay then, Dan, since we only have a few more minutes, I wanted to ask you about work these days."

"I'm working at a local nursery shoveling manure, watering trees and unloading trucks, whatever I can do to help out around the place."

He was fulfilling the probation requirement for his O.U.I. The officer assigned to him always reminded him to stay focused. So Daniel focused on keeping sober, working hard, and staying out of trouble. He was also attending AA meetings.

Daniel glanced over at the clock behind Paul's shoulder to make sure he wasn't going over time.

"Mr. Bailey, the guy who owns the nursery, took a r-risk on me and gave me a job when no one else would hire me. I got the job just after I dropped out of high school. I've been there a year now."

A warm feeling in his chest stoked when he spoke of Mr. Bailey.

"He's a great guy. I know when you live in a small town, it's hard for some folks to forgive you when you do something wrong. They take it personally, but Mr. Bailey isn't that way at all."

He took a deep breath.

"I never would've thought shoveling manure at the nursery would be my salvation. But working at Bailey's now, even in this sweltering heat, has saved my life. It really has. When I'm not at the house or g-going to night school to finish my GED, I'm at Bailey's Nursery off Searchlight Drive."

"Good, good, Daniel. I think we'll need to stop here for today."

Paul looked at this wristwatch.

"Do you have a trash can I can put these in?"

Paul pointed to a bin in the corner of the room.

Patting his front pockets to make sure he had his keys, he nodded in Paul's direction and turned to leave.

"See you later, doc."

"You got it," Paul replied.

Making a new appointment before he left, he walked out into the parking lot and kicked the dust from underneath his feet. A layer of dirt covered his work boots. Breathing in the warm, sweet air, he bent over and picked up a white flower that had fallen off a tree. Opening his door, he put it on the dashboard, knowing full well the bloom would soon turn brown. Buckling his seatbelt, he turned right onto the road and headed toward the nursery.

☾

In the parking lot, he sat for a second and pulled himself together. Feeling a little lighter, the session had opened some space inside him. He had a little more internal bandwidth. However, he knew it wouldn't take long for the gap to be filled in again, like a hole dug too close to the ocean. Did he have enough power to control the contents going back inside?

From the outside, the nursery looked small. It had a rustic store front with some baskets filled with petunias hanging from the eaves and a couple of wheelbarrows and bunny hutches lining the wall off to the left-hand side. But when he wandered past the koi pond filled with lily pads on the right side of the store, walked down a small path lined with blossoming trees, and made a left at the greenhouses over by the hydrangeas, there were more plants and flowers than he'd ever seen in his life. He didn't know all their names, but thankfully it wasn't a prerequisite for the job. The only flower he could name was probably a rose. The way the flowers smelled out back, he thought he could taste them.

Walking past customers, Daniel heard the low-lying hum of bees darting in and out of pink and lavender bushes and the familiar call of birds perched in tree pots near the side wall. Out in the way back, near the storage barn, a forklift engine sputtered and beeped, moving large pallets of salt bags and wood pellets.

Taking a deep breath, the air around the nursery smelled like sweet earth. And he found it funny that so many of the good memories he was making there were now linked to perfumed air.

He usually ate lunch near the flower stands on an overturned orange bucket leaning against the metal fence, out of view from the customers. At Bailey's, just for a little while, he forgot the drug tests and the noise of the sober house. He forgot about the broken men. He forgot the regret—the fear. Happy working with his hands in the outdoors, he liked building up a sweat and working himself hard. He hoped to release some of the toxins that had built up over the years. He wanted to rid himself of all the crap he'd ingested—all the stuff he'd poisoned his body with. And if he was honest with himself, he was probably punishing himself a little too—paying an unspoken debt he owed the woman and her baby.

Paul constantly reminded him to be gentle with himself, but he wasn't exactly sure what that meant. Gentle wasn't a term he grew up with. Gentle, hell, nothing about his life so far had been remotely close to gentle. How can you do or be something you've never known before?

Grabbing his lunch and a plastic bucket, he sat by the fence. After eating some of his sandwich, he leaned back and closed his eyes, feeling the sun full on his face. The sun's heat penetrated his dark t-shirt, warming up his chest.

With his eyes closed, he was tempted to fall asleep. And he was close to it, but a full-throated crow squawked in a bush nearby interrupting his plans. It wasn't too long before heavy footsteps crushed the seashell walkway in front of him, signaling someone approaching.

"Daniel, what have you done to my peony, son?"

He opened his eyes and saw Mr. Bailey standing in front of him, the sun at his back.

"They look absolutely pa-the-tic! And my geranium pots? Are you overwatering them? My African Violets are on death's door. They look like they're drowning."

Daniel shoved the last bite of sandwich into his mouth and stood up.

"Yes, s-sir." He answered him as best he could, as Mr. Bailey continued his gentle tirade.

"I know you want to keep them alive, but you've got to let them breathe. Let'em be, son. They've got to dry up a little."

They both smiled at each other when they caught on to the unintended double meaning.

"Sir, I thought that's what they needed in all this heat," Daniel said sheepishly, still unsure if he should take Mr. Bailey's chastising to heart.

"Let me tell you a little secret. There's a little something called 'too much of a good thing'." Mr. Bailey counted off on his left-hand. "Too much water, too much sun, and too much plant food can hurt them too. Plants, like people, need to find their own way to survive." Mr. Bailey knowingly poked his shoulder.

Daniel swiped the crumbs off his mouth. Mr. Bailey was good at explaining things. He was good at making complicated thoughts simple.

"I think you get what I'm trying to say." He patted him on the back. "Let's get back to work, son."

Standing with his paper lunch bag in his hands, he watched Mr. Bailey go and tried to imagine having a conversation like that with his own father. His dad was incapable of being present and thoughtful like Mr. Bailey was. Distracted and transactional, his father liked to give commands more than have conversations.

He picked up his shovel leaning against the metal fence and knocked it on the ground a few times to coax off the dirt. It made a sharp noise when the metal accidentally made contact with some concrete. Throwing his lunch away, he dusted off his phone to check for any messages and put it back in his pocket. He breathed deeply, taking in one last smell of the flowers. Resting the shovel on his shoulder, he walked back.

"Daniel?" He heard his name over the intercom.

A customer at the checkout desk needed some chicken coop wire. Since they couldn't find any near the front of the store, he thought to look in a rarely used storage shed at the back of the nursery. If it wasn't up front, that's the only other place it would be. He put his shovel down and jogged over to the shed.

Dark and musty, the only light coming into the shed was through a few cracks and knots in the wooden walls. He left the door open to let in the sunlight. When he entered, he sneezed on account of the dust and dirt. Pulling out a bandana from his back pocket, he wiped his nose, and noticed an old Bailey's Nursery sign in the back corner covered in cobwebs. It'd been years since anyone had been back here.

Looking behind some wood pallets leaning against the side wall, he thought he saw some wire sticking out at the top. Attempting to pull it up, it wouldn't budge. Leaning over, he moved the large pallets to the side and scraped the floor. It wasn't there. An old wood crate was in the way of some large, deconstructed cardboard boxes and he moved them both to the side.

Taking a peek at the other side of the boxes, he slowly moved them. But instead of coop wire, he found three small bottles of vodka—two empty and one full. One full. He automatically looked behind him to see if anyone was coming, then turned back and stared at the bottles again.

Sweat dripped down his face and he wiped his dirty brow with an equally dirty forearm. The discovery caught him off guard, and he immediately felt a burst of anger. He was angry at whoever had left their stash of alcohol here and was equally angry he was the one to find it. He punched the side wall hard with his fist.

"Damn it!"

Part of the skin on his knuckle came off and started to bleed.

It was only one small bottle of vodka, but it didn't take long before he felt himself spiraling inside and slightly starting to shake. Even looking at alcohol made him nervous now and it easily unearthed old feelings he'd shallowly buried.

Rubbing his hands on the side of his jeans, he again turned around to see if anyone was coming. Even though he hadn't done anything wrong, he already felt guilty. Every small creak the shed made got him nervous. It wouldn't be long before someone would be coming to check on him.

At that very moment, it seemed that all the counseling he'd received, all the advice he'd been given, every meeting he'd ever attended, even the jailtime he'd served, all vanished into thin air. He couldn't hold on to any of it.

Slowly, he crouched down to examine them more and leaned over to touch them. Bending forward, he hesitantly reached out his hand.

"Hey, Dan." He heard his name called from a few feet away. "We found it. It was near the greenhouses," Pete called out.

He recoiled his hand and stood up stiffly. Haphazardly leaning the cardboard boxes back where they belonged, he turned toward Pete's voice.

"Great. I-I couldn't find it back here." He nervously laughed.

"Can you do one more thing for me? That customer needs a hydrangea bush too, blue. Bring one up front for me?"

"N-No problem."

Thinking he'd feel relief that he'd been saved from making a huge mistake, instead he felt only shame. What if Pete hadn't come by? What would he have done? The small voice in his head berated him.

He was torn not knowing what to do next. Should he tell Mr. Bailey and have him suspect he was drinking again, or should he pick them up and get rid of them himself? He could get fired or even face jailtime again if Mr. Bailey found out. Or even worse, he could lose Mr. Bailey's respect. *Why did he have such bad luck?*

Looking back toward the shed, he approached the door and decided to secure the wooden latch.

Running over to the potted plants, he picked up a blue hydrangea and brought it to the front of the store. After leaving it on the counter, he wrapped a bandana around his hand to stop the bleeding.

Making his way to the other end of the store, he saw the shed through the backdoor window. He couldn't take his eyes off it.

"Did you see any ghosts in there?"

Mr. Bailey placed a hand on his shoulder.

"Some folks say that shed is haunted. I should take it down. It's getting to be just a massive junk drawer, but it didn't start out that way. Did I ever tell you it used to be Eleanor's? She called it her 'she-shed'." He chuckled to himself.

Daniel continued to stare out the back window.

"She prettied it up and used to take her breaks out there. Spending most of her life surrounded by boys, it was the only place she had to herself. But whenever I saw her out there, I kind of felt sorry for her. She looked lonely. She stopped using it a few years ago and now it's just collecting dust. What do you think, Daniel? Should we get rid of it? Tear it down together? Could be fun."

"I guess. If Mrs. Bailey doesn't need it anymore."

"That settles it!" Mr. Bailey swatted his back.

"You and I are gonna tear down that haunted house once and for all!"

Will

Driving home from work, Will cracked open the window of his truck to cool down. The handle was stiff. He pushed in the lighter. When it popped, he lit his cigarette. The paper sizzled, looking like a small piece of molten lava at the end. He took a long-extended drag and exhaled into the cab of his truck, permeating the air around him. Breathing in the charcoal smoke, he adjusted the sun visor.

He'd been working construction since he left high school four years ago and felt dead tired, like he'd run out of gas. More tired than any twenty-two-year-old should feel. His hands were calloused, and his clothes were always dirty. His skin was dark and leathery, and the cracks around his eyes were filled with small specks of black he could never get out. It hurt to get out of bed in the morning.

He'd worked hard ever since his mother walked out on them on Christmas Day, when he and Danny were little. But what she walked away from, he carried. What she left, he picked up. He felt obligated to clean up her mess, although she'd never extended him the same courtesy. He'd looked after Danny as best he could, but since then, since that very day, he hadn't trusted women very much.

It was never an easy house to grow up in. His parents' relationship was like a pot of boiling water with the lid on, always ready to erupt. But his mother leaving on Christmas Day was inexcusable. He hadn't forgiven her, nor would he ever. She was dead to him, and if he had his wish, she'd be dead to Danny too. She didn't deserve sons, but what she did deserve would only get him put in jail.

The day she left, he remembered cutting her face out of every family picture she was in. When he put the pictures back in their frames, he didn't care about the empty space where her head should be—an obvious void. In every possible way, he tried to erase her from his life.

As he drove to Falls Tavern, Will's mind forced him to remember jagged memories, cutting himself repeatedly on the shards. He didn't want to forget the pain or move past them. By inflicting the pain of memories on himself, he hoped somehow to hurt her too—like a reverse voodoo doll.

The memory of his mother always played in his mind on the same record groove, always scratching the same rut. Even though it happened years ago, it still felt like yesterday. The anger still hot. The rage still raw. The wounds still open and festering.

"Will, can you tell your father I'm just running next door to Mrs. Towns to grab a cup of sugar? I'll be right back."

His mother waved from outside the storm door.

Will watched her walk past the half-melted snowman in the front yard. The sun caught her dress just right and he saw her legs through to the place in the middle. The fabric was bright orange, just like the color of her hair. She forgot her jacket.

She never came back. After months of waiting, she never called. She never wrote. She just vanished, leaving two boys to fend for themselves with a father who was more married to his work than anything else. That day, that damn Christmas dinner sat there. In fact, it sat on a polished, mahogany dining room table for days. Ice melted in the sink. Half-washed lettuce wilted in an oven-heated kitchen. The ice cream melted in a container on the counter. Eventually, a sweet stench wafted from the kitchen into the den as he and Danny watched TV.

They cleaned it up when they couldn't stand the smell of rotting food any longer. Will held a trash bag open as Danny carefully threw the contents of the meal inside. They both carried a garbage can to the curb for pick up. Danny aligned his with the mailbox. Will didn't really give a damn and left it halfway in the street.

"Hey. You comin'?"

A man outside tapped the driver's side window of his truck as he passed by, heading into the tavern. Will sat motionless in his truck, not sure how he'd gotten there. He'd driven without thinking—on autopilot. He concluded having a heartless mother contributed to his absent-mindedness and not his excessive drinking.

Grabbing the keys from the ignition, he lifted his hips to put his wallet in his back pocket. The truck cab lit up with blue light. He glanced at his phone. It was a text from Carrie.

"Can you meet me tonight after work?"

He let the text sit, not answering. Maybe if he made her wait, she'd want him more. But then he realized that type of thinking only put Carrie in the driver's seat and he knew that was no place for a woman.

"Comin'?" The man knocked again.

Will looked up and waved him off.

He threw his phone in the glove box, got out of the truck, and slammed the door shut. Hiking his pants up, he clapped his hands together. It made a small dust cloud in the air.

Before reaching the second step of the landing, the door of the bar flung open and out flopped a regular he'd seen before but had never talked to. He reeked of Captain Morgan and cigarettes.

The old guy fumbled and fell to his knees, like he was praying. He wobbled in place for a few seconds. There was a slight odor of sick on him but no visible chunks. Too drunk to brace his own fall, the old guy started to fall forward like a tower, keeping his arms at his sides.

"What the—"

Will grabbed him before he hit the deck.

The drunk's face was stained with broken capillaries, and he had a dark swollen nose. Will thought for a second the fall may have been an improvement to his appearance. The man's belly stuck out in front of him, making him look nine months pregnant.

Holding him in a kneeling position, Will slapped his face. He was way too heavy to carry anywhere.

"Hey!"

He debated how many strikes he landed on this sorry bastard's face would be too many.

"Hey!"

Will stopped slapping him when he started to wake and watched the man's eyelids open to reveal a light shade of yellow where the whites of his eyes used to be. Up close, he smelled like he hadn't taken a shower in days, and his big red shirt was so dirty it looked like it might crawl off him.

"Bud, what's your name?" Will practically yelled. "Where do you live?"

Slapping him two more times on the cheek seemed to do the trick and revived the old dog for the time being.

"It's B-Bert. I was just headed home. Help me get to my car," he said, and then proceeded to vomit all over the landing only a few inches away from Will's work boots. The splat made Will gag a little and take a step back.

Fortunately for Bert, a small ripple of pity overcame Will's larger wave of disgust. He stood staring at the bar door, wishing he'd been either a few minutes early or a half an hour late to the bar tonight. Either side of this shitshow would have suited him just fine.

"Come on," Will mumbled under his breath. "I'll do better than that, old man. I'll take you home."

Will knew he wasn't going to win any public service awards for it, but that'd probably be him in the next few decades if he kept up his present drinking habits. The way he saw it, he was helping himself out—paying his drunk ass forward. He hoped some kid in the future would slap him silly and help get him home too. He was making a major deposit in the bank of karma this evening. Taking a drunk home who was blowing chunks, that was some serious coinage.

"Gimme your arm."

Will loaded him into the front seat, buckled him in and leaned him forward. Reaching for Santa's wallet, he recognized the street name on Bert's license. It was over by his house.

"You good?" Will asked.

The old man looked over at him but didn't open his eyes.

"Yap."

"If you're gonna puke again, let me know and I'll roll down the window."

There was no response, only a head nod.

"You should probably think about drinking less."

The man briefly opened his eyes. "That's what my daughter s-says."

"You might want to listen to her. There are meetings on the west side of town over at that Methodist church. I think my brother goes there."

"O-Oh, 'kay." The old man closed his eyes again.

Pulling up in his driveway, Will couldn't help noticing the similarities to his own house. They could both use a gardener and a repair man. There was a lot of useless crap in the yard.

Sober enough to walk to the front door alone, Bert got out of the truck slowly. Without saying a word, he steadied his feet before he took the next step. He nodded his head in Will's direction and swayed to the front door.

Will watched him knock at the door but didn't stay. He'd completed his charitable act for the year and wanted to get back to the bar so the night wouldn't be a complete washout. The guy was still knocking when he drove away.

Rose

"**B**aby doll, how was your birthday?"

Dottie greeted Rose in the break room. She had a voice that made Rose feel like the sun had come out on a cloudy day.

"I was just at church this morning and sent up a special little prayer for you." Dottie made the *you* sound sweeter than the rest of the words.

Twirling in her locker combination, Rose opened the metal door.

"It was all right. Quiet. Carrie was home late."

She didn't have the heart to tell Dottie about what happened to the cake, or that she'd spent the evening crying all by herself. Last night, she wished she could've called up her grandmother and poured out her heart to her, but she'd passed away a few years ago. Her grandmother was the one she ran to when she had nowhere else to turn. She was the safe harbor—the lighthouse beaming in the dark. If she were still alive, Rose wouldn't have felt so desperately alone on her birthday. Her grandmother would have waited for her on the front porch, welcomed her in with a hug, and then beat her in a game of gin rummy as they listened to Benny Goodman on the radio.

"What'da think of the cake? Good, hun?" She smiled broadly. "That's my mom's recipe and I knew you'd love it. I knew it was your favorite!" Dottie's voice sing-songed, as she patted the notebook in her apron pocket.

"I've never tasted better, really. Thanks for going to all that trouble. You really didn't have to."

Hanging her purse on the hook inside her locker, she tried to fix her ponytail using a small mirror inside the door. It was a little warped when she looked into it, like a mirror you'd find at a carnival.

As she stood at her locker, there was so much she wanted to tell Dottie. But often when she went to speak, she bit her lip instead. Today was no exception. She leaned against the door and watched Dottie get ready.

As long as Rose could remember, she was an expert at stopping words from escaping out of her mouth. She always spoke carefully, weighing the weight of each syllable. Something about her words made Rose feel like they were poles keeping people away, somewhere off at a distance. And not wanting to give people an excuse to leave her, she kept most things close to her chest and locked away inside. She couldn't bear to be left alone any more than she was.

She forcefully closed her locker door.

"You just gave me the biggest fright! I was in my own little world just then and you went and snapped me out of it!" Dottie patted her chest and then adjusted the glitter headband on top of her head.

"Now, let's get down to business." She winked. "Today, sweetie, I'm gonna need you to restock the pregnancy test bin."

Tempted to roll her eyes, Rose found the inner strength to stop herself.

"Trish has the bin key. She's working behind the snack counter today when you need to find her. Also, we're having the mobile blood bank come to the store today. They plan on parking in the left-side lot, close to the front entrance. When they get here, can you help whoever's in charge get situated?"

"No problem." She gave a quick informal salute.

"Good. Now you go scoot along, doll."

Dreading her assignment, but even more so talking to Trish, Rose slowly made her way to the snack counter via the shoe department and gardening center.

Trish wasn't the easiest co-worker to get to know. She considered herself second-in-command, right after Dottie, although she'd never officially been asked to fill the role. In fact, Trish even had a second set of master keys made for her own personal use. And unfortunately, her ego was inflated beyond all recognition when she was given the store's alarm code. *What was Dottie thinking?*

Trish kept meticulous records as to when employees arrived at work and when they clocked out. She recorded all the information in her notebook which was eerily similar to the polka-dot one Dottie used.

But Rose knew how to get under Trish's skin. All she had to do was swing by the bedding department and unfluff some of the pillows on the display beds. Toss one on the floor, if she really felt daring. Maybe even "accidentally" spill a little coffee on a dust ruffle, just the tiniest splash, so Trish couldn't decide whether it was worth the effort to change it or not.

She'd heard from other co-workers that annoying Trish was considered a perk of the job, although Rose hadn't tried it yet. However, the thought did cross her mind and she was often tempted to, which made her feel a little guilty. Just because Trish's behavior was overbearing and petty didn't mean she had to act the same way. But what astonished Rose the most was that, sometimes, when she was restocking shelves or dusting the display cases, she found herself whispering a prayer for her. Unconsciously, she found Trish's name coming out of her mouth, underneath her breath. Somewhere deep inside, Rose wanted the best for Trish and hoped God would help her, even if she couldn't.

"Hi, Trish. I'm here for the key. Dottie sent me."

"You took your sweet time, didn't you? I expected you five minutes ago. Really, Rose, you should work on being more prompt. You can never go wrong by being on time, I always say. Punctuality is a virtue. Didn't your parents ever teach you that?"

"No, I don't think so. I'll, ah, work on that."

"See that you do," she said and handed her the key.

Rose headed to the feminine-needs aisle. Pregnancy tests were kept under lock and key at the store, mainly because the customers who really wanted them were the ones who had the most difficulty paying for them. Dottie hated five-finger discounts.

"Chop-chop, Rose, no dilly-dallying this time," Trish admonished her from a distance.

Some of the strangest items in the store were stolen, mostly by girls. There were the obvious ones like lipstick and eyeliner, items easily hidden up a sleeve. But lately, Rose noticed there were odd items stolen too, like spoons, lighters, and first-aid kits. Perfumes used to go missing all the time, but now girls were getting caught right and left due to the little RFID tags placed in strategic places on the bottle. They alerted you when something wasn't where it was meant to be.

"Rose—Rose," Carrie whispered loudly from the other end of the aisle.

Rose saw Carrie's eyes wide open, looking desperate. Her tied up hair was loose and spilling down her neck and the sides of her face.

"Carrie?"

"I need a favor." Carrie ran up to her. "I need you to bring me one of those." She nodded toward the bin. "Bring it to the restroom?"

"I'll meet you in there," Rose said flatly.

Locking up the bin and putting the key in her pocket, Rose quietly made her way to the back of the store with the pregnancy test hidden under her yellow apron. Rose knew she was a terrible thief. The carton was obviously visible, even though she'd attempted to conceal it. The contour of the box poked her apron out. It would be a miracle if she made it to the women's restroom without getting caught.

She unconsciously started to whistle, but then realized her poor whistling could have the opposite effect of attracting unwanted attention. She stopped whistling and bit her lip to remind herself not to try again. She would anonymously leave money for the test on Dottie's desk before she left for the night.

Carrie was Rose's older sister by four years. Lately, they hadn't seen much of each other at the apartment, their schedules never quite syncing up. But she had no idea Carrie had a boyfriend or that she was having sex. Rose felt a little betrayed. *Was that the right word, the right feeling?*

As she walked to the restroom, Rose sensed a great distance between her and her sister. While Rose had only been kissed once and never had a boyfriend, Carrie was having sex with a man Rose had never met and was now possibly pregnant. It didn't seem possible. *How could she do this to them?*

Secrets deeply affected her. They always felt like something sneaking up behind her. With her dad's sudden death and her mom's abrupt departure, even the slightest changes to her normal routine felt sudden and alarming. It was hard for her to tolerate most types of change. Change felt like tectonic plates shifting beneath her. Small movements still caused a great deal of damage, much of it that went unseen.

Maybe she was a hard worker and creature of habit to avoid the peaks and valleys of everyday life. Maybe she worked hard, even exhausted herself, to distract herself from things she found too difficult to cope with. If she was being honest with herself, Rose knew big changes made her feel unsteady on the inside, even panicked and unsafe.

It just never occurred to her that people led lives separate from her own. Right now, people all over the world were cooking dinner, bathing their children, holding hands, laughing, and even having sex. Life was being lived all around her, and just because she didn't see it, didn't mean it wasn't happening.

Not everyone went to high school and walked to work. Not everyone was coming home exhausted after a long day and needed to study. Not everyone experienced grief and loss at the same depths she had. People were living lives Rose couldn't even fathom. And as she walked toward her sister, the world was feeling infinitely bigger and more unpredictable. She began to tremble.

Rose couldn't imagine her sister sharing her body with anyone else. She couldn't picture her sister being naked in front of a man. She couldn't visualize her sister exposing all of herself to someone else, especially someone Rose didn't know. Maybe what she couldn't picture was doing the same herself. Maybe what she couldn't picture was being that completely vulnerable with another human being.

"What stall are you in?"

Rose entered the brightly lit bathroom. The floor was partly covered in used toilet paper and balled-up wet paper towels. She resisted the temptation to see whose responsibility it was to clean up the bathroom on the employee work chart behind the door. Was that really so important now? Rose scolded herself.

"Over here. Pass it under."

Rose waited in silence, staring at water intermittently drip from a leaky faucet at the sink.

She walked over to try and tighten the handle. It wouldn't budge. Wiping her wet hand on her apron, she paced the room. It was quiet, except for the buzz of the lightbulb above. Rose stared at her scuffed, white Converse sneakers.

"Doll, you in here?"

Rose stood up stick-straight and smoothed out her apron. Dottie's voice echoed off the tiles in the bathroom, making it sound louder than it really was. The door slowly opened. Rose saw her teased hair before she saw her face.

"Are you feeling all right? I couldn't find you in the feminine-products aisle, so I thought you may be in here."

She walked over to the sink where Rose was standing.

"The blood mobile just pulled up and they're going to need to know where to plug into our electricity and water valves. Do you mind showing them?"

Dottie abruptly stopped speaking.

"What in the world! What in the world is that doing all the way in here?"

Rose momentarily stopped breathing, remembering she'd left the box balancing on the corner of the sink counter only inches away from Dottie.

"How'd that get in here?"

Rose shut her eyes tightly waiting for Dottie's reprimand.

"I've been looking for that high and low. I was wondering what I'd done with my neckerchief! I must've dropped it in here this morning when I came to fluff up my hair."

Dottie walked straight past the counter where the box was sitting next to the hand dryer on the back wall.

"Now doesn't this look better?" she said, making a quick knot and admiring herself in the dryer's nameplate. "What once was lost is now found!" Dottie gave Rose a quick wink in the mirror.

"Rosie, if you're feeling all right, you gotta shake a leg." Dottie tapped her wristwatch. "I think the woman's name is Pam who's in charge of the blood mobile," Dottie said *mobile* as if it was two words. "I'll see you outside?"

Dottie walked past the carton without saying another word.

"Carrie? I've got to go. I'll talk to you when I get home, okay?"

She tried to reassure her as best she could, but at this point, there was very little Rose could say to make the situation better.

Closing the bathroom door, the outside world seemed different to Rose than when she'd first walked in. She couldn't quite put her finger on it. The lights, maybe the people, seemed altered. Walking in the direction of the parking lot, she couldn't feel the floor beneath her feet. Her legs went numb—her mind swimming.

It was as if a switch had been flipped inside of her and she was flooded with a wave of anxiety. She nervously played with a strand of her hair, twisting it on her finger until it turned purple.

What saddened Rose as well was the feeling that she had to keep a secret from Dottie, a woman whom she considered to be a lot like her grandmother. Her stomach churned, worrying whether Dottie knew she'd stolen the pregnancy test—temporarily. Dottie noticed everything. The box was impossible to miss. Why hadn't she said anything to her? *It was right there on the counter!*

"Are you Rose?" An unfamiliar voice caught her attention. "I'm Pam. I think Dottie told you I was coming." Pam fixed the nametag on her white lab coat. "I'm here to set up the blood mobile."

Rose blankly stared at her.

"Can you show me where to hook up to the electricity and such?" Pam balanced a clipboard in one hand and a steaming cup of coffee in a Styrofoam cup in the other. "And before I forget, can you pop inside the mobile and fill out some paperwork for me? I need to grab an employee's signature before we set up the equipment."

Rose stepped inside. The interior smelled of sugar cookies and isopropyl alcohol. There were four large leather seats sitting in front of four different TV screens. They were all tuned to different channels. It felt chaotic to Rose, like four people talking all at once. She tried to concentrate.

Pam fiddled with the paperwork on her desk and found a blue pen in a container next to the stapler.

"They always like forms filled out in blue," she said.

Rose stood patiently and noted Pam was visibly perturbed by the unnecessary request from her higher-ups. Briefly looking out the window of the mobile, she saw Carrie walking slowly to her car. For a split second through the window, they caught each other's eyes, and Rose knew.

Carrie was pregnant.

Without warning, Rose's eyes filled with black.

"Miss, Miss."

Rose woke to Pam lightly slapping her face.

"If you're going to faint, you picked the perfect spot to do it in."

She passed some smelling salts back and forth underneath Rose's nose. The acrid smell woke her.

"No need to worry, you just nicked your chin on my desk on the way down." Pam articulated each word carefully. "You're going to be fine. Does the sight of blood make you wobbly?"

Pam made small talk while applying steady pressure to Rose's bleeding chin. And, for a moment, Rose could've sworn Pam was speaking another language. The words were all jumbled and didn't make any sense. Her eyes wouldn't focus.

Probably sensing her disorientation, Pam started talking louder, like you would to someone elderly.

"COME AND SIT BACK HERE FOR A SEC, OKAY?"

Rose leaned against the back of Pam's desk.

"You know, Connie, this always happens to my Mike. He takes one step in the blood mobile and down he goes like a sack of potatoes. Without fail, he passes out. I think he's scared to come on board now." Pam spoke to another woman sitting at the front of the bus.

"Blood doesn't faze me one hoot. When I was a phlebotomist in the 80s in L.A., we had to collect this one particular blood sample in a glass container. Wouldn't ya know it, but Mrs. Butterfingers here drops the glass bottle. It looked like a regular crime scene, just like the one you'd see on CSI. Blood was splattered just about everywhere."

Rose tightly closed her eyes trying to tune out Pam's commentary. She felt a little squeamish, and Pam's chattering bordered on more annoying than comforting. If Rose was more assertive, she'd have taken her hand and put a finger up to Pam's lips. Instead, she tried to bear the avalanche of anecdotes and prayed they'd soon stop. *Breathe, just breathe.*

Gradually opening her eyes, she looked down at a small, jagged white scar on her left wrist. It crossed deep turquoise veins and sat a few millimeters below a small vein that pulsed with her heartbeat. The line on her wrist was pale, a different color than the rest of her skin. Sometimes she thought it still ached. She clamped down on it with her right hand.

Staring at the scar, she burst into tears. Rose couldn't stop herself from crying. In the mobile with Pam and Connie, an internal dam broke. She sobbed as Pam handed her squares of white gauze to dry her eyes.

"Honestly, dear. There's no need to make such a fuss. It's only a little cut on your chin. Buck up, we'll have this fixed in no time."

"But what are we going to do?" Rose said quietly.

"We'll get you all cleaned up and put back in one piece, that's what!" Pam's nursing skills and encouraging demeanor emerged with a fervor.

"Let me take a quick peek again." Pam gently tilted Rose's chin back to look at the wound. "It's just a graze, dear. It will all be fine soon enough. I promise."

Pam gently patted the top of Rose's hand.

But what if it isn't?

Carrie

Gripping the steering wheel tighter, Carrie drove home in silence. A feeling of dread settled in her bones. She'd made some stupid mistakes in her life, but none that would last a lifetime. She couldn't even say the word out loud. *Pregnant.*

Two tests confirmed it. The first test she dropped into the toilet when she saw the results. Reaching into the bowl, she shook it dry, hoping the cross on the plus sign would fall off. It didn't.

Whatever luck she thought she possessed simply vanished away. Not only was she twenty-one and unmarried, but her drinking was out of control and her using was most likely headed in the same direction. What had she done to the baby already? It was hard not to worry about the potential damage she was doing to it before it was even born.

And what did Rose think of her? That was the barb that stung the most.

Carrie unrolled the car window, breathing in as deeply as she could. Wanting to calm herself down, she felt like using. But now, it was out of the question. She looked over at two small empty gin bottles on the passenger's side floor mats. Self-medicating her anxiety was no longer an option.

She'd seen the devastated look on Rose's face through the window in the parking lot. Rose looked shocked, bewildered. Was she strong enough to bear Rose's disappointment? There was a whole other side of her Rose knew nothing about, and wouldn't have known, if she hadn't needed her help getting a pregnancy test.

Carrie second-guessed her decision to ask Rose for the test, but they were so expensive. She and Rose had difficulty paying their electric bill on time. She could barely afford a pregnancy test, so how would she ever afford a baby? There'd be another mouth to feed and clothe and shelter. The weight of the world on her shoulders threatened to crush her flat.

Pulling to the side of the road, she wept. Heaving sobs came out of her and black spots appeared on her gray t-shirt. Each time she attempted to take another breath, it made her cry even more. Pounding her hands on the steering wheel, she knew there were other options to take care of the situation. She could get an abortion, but was that really what she wanted to do? The unanswered question sent a cold chill down her spine.

Carrie had always protected Rose and she did it long before she could even articulate what it was that she was doing. But Carrie knew she couldn't protect Rose from this, but could she lean on Rose herself? Was she strong enough to handle what was possibly coming her way?

When Rose was born, Carrie considered her her baby. She'd change her, feed her, and sneak into her room at night to make sure she was still breathing by holding a finger up to her nose. She was a little mother to her. When Rose cried or got hurt, Carrie felt it too—deep within her. It was almost as if Rose was a part of her own body. Where Rose began and she ended, she wasn't sure.

And Carrie protected her fiercely, most especially from their own father.

When they were much younger and Carrie saw him approach Rose's room at night, she would purposefully stay awake and desperately try to make him forget her.

"Daddy, I can't sleep," she would say, making sure he gave her his full attention. She had to.

Carrie was in the fifth grade when it started.

The first time it happened, he came into her bedroom to soothe her after a scary dream. That night the room was pitch black, except for the moon beaming a stream of light through her blinds onto the hardwood floor.

Lying down beside her, he rhythmically stroked her hair and Carrie drifted off to sleep. But she was awakened by his hand creeping up her nightgown. His calloused skin snagged the polyester fabric as he made his way to her flat chest. She felt something against her leg. Lying still, she hoped whatever was happening would soon be over. Holding her breath, she acted like she was asleep. Carrie prayed he'd stop. Her hands lay by her side, flat against the sheet. When he reached down, it was then she pretended it was all a dream and made her mind float somewhere her father couldn't reach.

Waking up with him snoring next to her, she realized it hadn't been a dream. Some type of crust had hardened in between her legs and the arm swung on top of her chest felt heavy to the point she couldn't breathe. The pink nightgown she'd been wearing was crumpled beside her bed. His breath smelled of stale cigarettes and beer.

All her stuffed animals had fallen on the floor except one. She woke up sore and bleeding, not understanding what had happened.

That morning, as the sun peeked through her blinds, she heard her mother downstairs in the kitchen cooking breakfast. The smell of pancakes wafted up the stairs into the hallway and underneath her bedroom door. She heard the sound of cartoons coming from the living room. Rose was awake.

As her father woke from a deep sleep, she closed her eyes again, lying dead still. When she eventually opened them, he was gathering his clothes from the floor and casually walked out her bedroom door.

With blood on her sheets, she sat motionless on the bed. She hadn't had her first period. How would she explain the blood to her mother? She frantically gathered up her sheets and ran into the laundry room at the end of the hall. Without thinking, she ran down the hall naked. Shoving her sheets into the washing machine, she knew whatever had happened the night before was wrong. It was something dirty her father should never, ever do again.

As she stood in the cold air of the laundry room, she shivered and tried to plan how to prevent it from happening again. Maybe she could move her dresser in front of the door at night. Maybe she could put a chair underneath the door handle to stop him from entering. The pink chair in the corner of her room would not be tall enough. Maybe she could sleep in her closet.

Her mind raced for an answer. She panicked at the thought of another night with her father. She paced the room.

And then she remembered…Rose.

There was no way she could barricade her door now.

Listening at the laundry room door, she heard the shower running in her parents' bathroom and then heavy footsteps going down the stairs. She quietly tiptoed to the bathroom and slowly closed the door. She pressed the button to lock it.

Taking a washcloth from the cabinet, she wet it with warm water and sat on the side of the cold tub, wiping the dried blood from her inner thigh. The washcloth was stained. She threw it out.

Over the course of many years, her father raped her while she pretended to be asleep. When she heard the doorknob creak open, she turned on her stomach and buried her face in the sheets. She couldn't look at him and dared not lift her head to even breathe. Mouthing a scream each time he entered her, she didn't try to fight him. Instead, she lay like a dead animal—barely moving.

Only when she was alone did she cry out in utter frustration and torment. Lifting her hands into the air, she wept with inaudible groans. She wailed. And the sounds that came out of her mouth were from depths as dark as the deepest water.

Couldn't he see the pain he was causing her? Didn't he know she wasn't really asleep? How much evil fogged his vision? She wanted to take her nails and claw the scales from his eyes, ripping them all out.

Carrie often wondered if there was any good left in her, but dared not ask the question. She asked for forgiveness in prayer, although she wasn't sure if anyone was listening. But no matter what, no matter how high the price, she vowed to protect Rose from this unspeakable evil, even though she was being slowly suffocated by shame. Rose would grow up innocent and untouched.

Later, when Carrie found out about her father's cancer, she was happy he was dying. It was a welcome relief. The weight of abuse she'd been carrying with her was still there, but now it hovered slightly above her. Its shadow still loomed, but a little light was now peeking through underneath. She knew it would all soon be over and his body would be food for creatures that lived under the earth.

In all the years he'd raped her, she never once looked at his face, and he also never kissed her. At least some part of her body remained her own. For Carrie, it was something. She could save something for herself—something could still be given and not taken away.

Her first real kiss with a boy happened on her thirteenth birthday. It was strange for the kiss to come second, for the kiss to come after sex. Intimacy was meant to bloom in a particular order, and when it didn't, it felt confusing and wrong.

Drying her tears, Carrie blasted the vents at her face, trying to calm down the redness in her skin. She attempted to dry her t-shirt too, but it was soaked through. Taking her shirt off, she grabbed a tank top from her purse and put it on.

"Be strong," she shouted at herself.

"Be strong!" Carrie pounded her fists on her thighs, so hard she bruised them.

"Be strong! Damn it, be strong..."

Turning on the radio to help drown out her thoughts, she drove to a nearby gas station. Reaching down to the floor mats, she picked up the empty bottles of gin and crammed them in her pockets. She looked over at the pregnancy tests peeking out at the top of her purse.

Racing over to a trash bin, she threw the bottles away. Inside the station, she grabbed a half-gallon of milk.

"Want your regular pack, Carrie?" the girl from behind the counter asked.

"Not tonight, Molly. But, ah, do you have any ginger ale?"

"Check the back. If we do, it'll be there. That for Rose?"

"Yah, I need to ask her something. I'm hoping what I have to say goes down a little easier with it."

"Good luck with that."

Carrie picked up the paper bag and pushed open the door.

Will

Now that Danny was sober, Will mostly drank alone. He spent most of his paycheck at Falls Tavern. Will and a few other men from town kept it in business. For the most part, women didn't particularly like the bar, which was a good thing.

Falls was located on the outskirts of town, across the street from an abandoned rock quarry. It had an old Rock-Ola Jukebox in the back corner, high-backed dark pleather booths, and an old biker named Rusty behind the bar who sang Jimmy Buffett tunes underneath his breath. But even with his easygoing nature, Will knew there was a Remington 783 collecting dust somewhere behind the counter.

Rusty opened the doors early. His regulars were usually there waiting. Most of them stayed for last calls and stumbled home. And occasionally, on weekends, girls from out-of-town made their way inside.

Will leaned into the bar and glared at a group of women ordering a round of beers. They were laughing. *What the hell was so funny?*

He swirled his beer bottle then drank a shot of warm whiskey. He couldn't help but wonder if they were mocking him. Women's laughter made his skin crawl. And the way they looked at him out of the corner of their eye got his hackle up. It was probably some bach-elorette bullshit.

"You can never trust 'em, Will. You listenin' to me?"

Pat tried to get Will's attention by nudging his arm.

"You can never trust 'em." He slurred his words and leaned to the side like an old, unearthed electric pole.

Will pushed him in the other direction so he wouldn't fall off the stool.

"I once thought I was gonna marry a girl. I bought her a ring, flowers, everything. And when I got over to her house after work to pop the question, you know what she was doin'?"

Will didn't answer.

"She was doin' Steve in the driveway!" He slammed his fist down on the bar.

"I nearly beat the shit out of that guy. I opened the car door, pulled his ass out of the seat, and started hittin' him. She came around the other side screamin'."

Pat raised his hands up in the air, shaking them around, acting like a hysterical woman.

"You know what I did next?" He took another swig. "I dropped the ring and flowers on the ground and went to town on him. She called the cops, and I haven't seen her since. You can't trust 'em."

Pat put back another shot of whiskey and slapped Will hard on the back. Leaning forward, he put both arms on the bar, bowed his head, and stared into his lap. Will looked over at him. With Pat in a stupor beside him, Will sat quiet.

His life at Rusty's was simple and predictable. He liked uncomplicated. That's probably why he worked construction. When he left the job, he wanted to forget it, never worry about it. He needed each day to be over and not linger into the next. Early on, he'd decided that his freedom was more important than money.

For Will, the more life was black and white the better—no gray. Unfortunately, Carrie was all gray. He could never really penetrate her no matter how hard he tried. Even when they had sex, she looked straight past him, kind of like the gaze the girls in the magazines had that he'd stolen as a kid. The women in those magazines always had dull eyes, even though they were smiling. Carrie was like that too. Her eyes seemed vacant.

Sex was quick and unemotional with her, and she always left right after. She also liked keeping the lights on in the bedroom and the door wide open. It didn't really matter to him.

He'd met her at a bar on Court Street during the middle of July. She wore a bright orange sundress and faded jean jacket. He teased her because it was too hot outside for something like that. Her cheeks looked like they were stained with cherry juice.

At first, he tried with her, more than he had with any other girl he'd been with. He liked the look of her and how carefree she was all the time. Her glass was always half-full, and he found himself attracted to the energy that bounced off her. He wanted to plug into it. He also wanted more from her. He wanted them to really be together—be a couple—make it work.

But after a while, she wasn't good at returning his phone calls, and a lot of his texts went unanswered. As time went on, it made him feel desperate, like he was trying too hard. It was almost like they were opposite magnets. Every time he tried to get closer, she inched farther away. He repelled her somehow and he just couldn't figure out why.

Everything he tried got an opposite reaction. Like the time he surprised her when she was sleeping. He came home early from a night out and when he went to wake her, she freaked out, pushed him against the wall and then ran out to her car. She was so frickin' skittish.

A month ago, she'd asked to borrow some money and he gave it to her. This was the second time he'd loaned her some cash. He'd caught her going through his wallet too. And when he asked her when he'd see the money again, she made some excuse. He wanted to believe her but knew he'd never see the money again.

And this wasn't the first time this had happened to him. Carrie was just one in a long string of girls who used him—who just wanted something from him. They were always taking, taking, taking. The women he'd been with were never satisfied with what he had to offer, always wanting more.

"This is from the brunette at the other end of the bar."

Rusty passed him a fresh beer. It slid down the bar like a puck on ice. Will lifted the bottle in the air and nodded his head in her direction.

Walking with her hand grazing the mahogany countertop so she wouldn't fall over, she carefully made her way over to Will. Clearly, she was drunk but she was also sexy as hell. This wouldn't be a challenge.

The brunette introduced herself, and past that, he didn't bother listening to half of what she was saying. She could've been speaking another language for all he cared. Will was more interested in what he could do to her than with what she had to say. With a pause in the conversation, he got up to use the bathroom. She followed him in.

The Falls Tavern men's room was probably not the cleanest place to have sex with a woman, but clearly this girl didn't care and neither did he. He didn't even bother to lock the door. Hopping her up on the wet, soapy countertop, he barely kissed her before she lifted her skirt. *What was with women these days? Didn't they have an ounce of self-respect?*

Catching a glimpse of himself in the mirror, he'd already forgotten her name. It was over just as fast as it started. Will pulled up his jeans and tucked in his shirt. She barely cleaned herself up before he left the bathroom.

Unsteady on her heels, he saw her twist her ankle on a knot in the hardwood floor, but she was too inebriated to feel any pain. He was sure a lot of things would be a surprise to her in the morning.

"Well, aren't you going to buy me a drink?"

Will ignored the request and instead gave her a phony cell number.

"You can call me."

He walked past Pat who'd fallen asleep sitting up at the bar. Clearing his tab with Rusty, he got in his truck. Reaching into the glovebox, he grabbed his phone and checked his texts. There were three from Carrie.

"I need to talk to you."

"I have to tell you something."

"I'm pregnant."

The last two words quickly sobered him up.

Pregnant?

He thought she'd taken care of all that. Always disappearing into the bathroom after they were done, he assumed she had it under control.

He texted back: *"You sure it's mine?"*

His anger was slowly rising.

"Is this a joke or something? Why are you always lying to me? Do you need more money?"

That manipulative bitch!

He slammed his hand on the steering wheel.

He wasn't sure he was going to be able to control himself. Like a rocket waiting on a launch pad, he was moments from igniting. Slamming his door shut, he yelled into his truck cab and punched the dashboard.

And what about his other money! What had she done with that? He turned off his cell and threw it on the seat next to him, so hard it could've cracked the screen. He backed out of the parking space without looking.

Was she trying to trap him? If she thought he was going to pay for her bastard, she'd better think again. He wasn't paying for shit.

Skidding onto the road, he left a trail of dust as he drove off. Searching his pockets for some smokes, he was all out. Feeling like he was going to explode, he turned up the radio and tailgated the car in front of him.

"Where'd you learn to drive?" he yelled out his window and laid on the horn.

When he had the chance, he accelerated and swerved in front of the car, almost tipping his truck over. He sped down the highway dodging and weaving the other cars in front of him.

By the time he got home, his rage was at a simmer. He'd taken out most of his aggression on other drivers on the road, but it was an unstable calm. Still on edge, he was looking for anything to unleash himself on.

Pulling up to his house, his headlights shone on the neglected landscaping and Danny's car that was totaled in the O.U.I. When Danny swerved to avoid hitting the mom and baby in the crosswalk, he rammed the front of his car into an old sycamore tree that had a trunk as wide as a kiddie pool. Even though the car looked drivable, even repairable on the outside, the frame was cracked. It now permanently sat on a patch of unmown grass to the right of his garage.

Over the past year, the tires went missing and the driver's side window was smashed in. The radio was stolen, as well as the rear-view mirror, but the thieves were nice enough to rest it on four cinder blocks. Will had duct taped the hole in the window to keep the animals out, but still let the car sit and decay in his front yard with no plans to move it.

Walking past yellowed expired newspapers on the porch, he fumbled for his keys. His mail stuck out of a slot in the door. He wrenched the envelopes from the hole and walked in. Standing for a moment in the silence of the hallway, he winced and briefly regretted his decision to do the brunette.

Walking into the kitchen, he yanked the fridge open and light flooded the room. He grabbed a beer. Slamming the lip of the cap on the edge of the countertop, it flipped off and fell to the floor. Kicking the cap into the corner, he made the bottle vertical and finished half of it in one gulp. The red light was blinking on the answering machine.

"Will."

It was his father.

"Do me a favor. I got a phone call from your unhinged mother, and uh…she wants me to send her some money…surprise, surprise. But…uh…she also wants a glass punch bowl we got as a wedding gift. I think her stepson is graduating high school. For a party, uh…I dunno. But, uh, who knows where that thing is now? Look around and let me know. I think we put some boxes in Danny's old room. They might be in his closet. You can reach me at Debbie's. Thanks."

Will listened to the sound of his father's voice and felt numb. His words were like air moving around him. And the way he spoke about his ex-wife, Will's mother, didn't shock him. Will felt the same way. Hearing his father call her unhinged was probably the only thing they had in common. Their shared hatred of her was their membership in an exclusive club.

Even though they shared the same blood and last name, his father was still a stranger to him. Every time they spoke, it was as if they were meeting each other for the first time. The sterility of their conversations, their business-like transactions, reminded Will of the gaping hole between them that he was unwilling to fix.

Untying his laces, he stepped out of his work boots and walked down the hall to the bathroom. He stripped down and reached into the shower and turned on the faucet until it ran hot. Steam billowed from the top of the curtain. He stepped in and bowed his head before the water and let it run down his back. He leaned on the wall with both hands and stood there. He breathed in the heated, wet air and spit the water pooling in his mouth into the drain.

Stepping out of the shower, he dried off with a towel and put it around his waist, tucking it in at the side. He turned to the steamed-up mirror and rubbed a hole in the fog and stared at a hazy image of himself. Fog crept back in, and his face disappeared. He turned off the bathroom light and stood in the dark. A light came in through the crack at the bottom of the door. He looked down at it, momentarily unable to move, and willed himself to turn the doorknob.

As he walked down the hall to Danny's old bedroom, humid footprints on the hardwood floor trailed behind him. He flipped on the light and walked over to a small closet across from his bed. Opening the door, he pulled on a thin rope to turn on the light. It swung and the pink plastic tip hit his chest.

The closet was packed with boxes. He took two out and put them on the floor beside him. He flipped the lid off and thoughtlessly pulled out the contents of an old filing cabinet. Flipping the second lid off, he discovered it was much of the same but this one also contained class pictures in folders marked, "Willie" and "Danny." It was written in his mother's loopy cursive handwriting, not his father's chicken scratch.

Opening Danny's folder, he caught a glimpse of the blonde curls his brother had when he was younger. The bright yellow of his hair always shone like a gold crown in pictures. Will remembered Danny's curls attracted almost every blue-haired woman in town and was a magnet for teenage girls too. Just like a pregnant woman who got her belly rubbed by perfect strangers, Danny's hair was guaranteed to be tussled every time he left the house. There probably wasn't one palm left in Plymouth that hadn't touched his head, like a pastor's blessing.

But the pictures brought back painful memories too, ones that Will wasn't sure he wanted to remember. He recalled how his mother always lingered on Danny's picture a little longer than his and how she couldn't help pointing out the small details of his outfit. It stung his heart to know his mother was clearly smitten with his younger brother. And no matter how hard he tried to win her over, her heart was already set on Danny. Will could see why.

Danny had always been a cute kid and never gave her any trouble. He even let her hold him when he was mad, never trying to walk away. It was as if Danny was born without defenses. His damn stutter was even perforated armor out in the world.

Will had decided early on to develop a protective layer for them both, but it was complicated. Protecting Danny meant he had to care for someone whose mere existence was hurting him too. Torn, he felt he had to protect the very source of his deepest pain.

The shell Will constructed around himself formed slowly, almost imperceptibly. New scales emerged as he caught on to her subtle favoring of Danny. She stood when Danny entered the room. She served him his dinner first. There was an ease about her when Danny was near that was never present with him. And with each tip of the scale, a new piece of armor formed around his heart.

No matter how hard he tried, he could never get her to warm to him. He bent over backwards trying to reestablish the lost connection—reattach the desiccated umbilical cord. But nothing, absolutely nothing would revive it.

Will remained cold and distant on the outside of their intimate circle of two. The only way for him to keep warm was by stoking his inexhaustible resentment with an abundant supply of hate.

Even the smallest kindnesses toward Danny, like tucking him in first or running her fingers through his tangled hair, would result in an eruption of molten rage in his heart that he was never able to adequately clean up. A blackness settled into his chest and poisoned whatever was healthy around it. It ate at his goodness like a cancer. He wondered if there was any left.

Danny's room was virtually untouched since he'd left to live at the sober house. It was a time capsule. Balled up tissues were still on his nightstand and a coating of dust obscured the face of his alarm clock. Will sat on the bed, opened the nightstand drawer, and found a collection of souvenirs from past family vacations Danny had collected over the years—a key chain from Mt. Rushmore, a replica of the Willis Tower, and a shot glass from Bozeman, Montana. Hidden in the back of the drawer was an amber ashtray from a Best Western Hotel.

Will slammed the drawer shut, rocking all the contents inside, and leaned back on the bed. Staring up at the ceiling, he realized Danny had put up a poster of the moon, the one where the Earth was far off in the distance suspended in a sea of black. For a second, Will imagined himself on the lunar surface and closed his eyes.

Adjusting the pillow underneath his head, he felt some grooves on the wood headboard behind him. When he turned to see what they were, his finger followed along deep ridges that had been carved into the surface with a ball point pen. It read, *Danny & Willie. Friends 4-ever.* His muscles involuntarily tensed.

Walking down the hall to the kitchen, he picked up his cell and debated getting ahold of Danny, but then left the phone on the counter. He wasn't sure it was the right time to get in touch with him; so many things had turned to shit. Maybe it was best to leave the whole fucking mess alone. Maybe it was better to let whatever was left of the Goodman family just fade away and disappear into nothingness— erase the past two decades and pretend it never existed.

Will took out a cigarette and put it in his mouth. He sucked on the filter. Looking for matches, he opened the cupboard above the oven and laughed to himself. There was the damn punch bowl. He couldn't escape his shitty family even if he tried. The wasteland of what had been and never was or ever would be was all around him. He lived among fossils.

Daniel

"Would you like to join me owling tonight, son?"

Daniel was organizing merchandise on the shelves in the main garden store when Mr. Bailey popped his head around the corner.

"We'll leave when it's dark, in a couple hours. You can see them better in the dark, especially if there's a full moon. Their eyes shine and reflect in the moonlight. The weatherman said when the sun goes down it's going to be one of those rare cool evenings in the middle of July. Bring a sweatshirt or something."

"Sure thing, Mr. Bailey."

"Come to think of it, do you wanna borrow one of mine? I got this great one over at Bramhall's the other day. Boy, is it soft. I'll grab it before we go. You use it. I've got an old, paint-stained one in the storage area that'll do just fine for me."

"You sure?" Daniel asked, standing and stretching his back out.

"Of course. It'll look better on you anyways. See you at eight?"

Daniel smiled over to him and watched Mr. Bailey walk back toward the flower beds full of pink and purple impatiens.

Sometimes Daniel found it hard to believe that someone not related to him cared so much about him. With his father or his brother, even his mother, who shared his same body and blood, there was little connection. With Mr. Bailey, the only thing stringing them to each other was time and a bunch of words they'd exchanged over the past year. But Daniel felt those simple words held more glue than anything biological ever could.

No, he'd bonded with a complete stranger—actually two complete strangers. And they'd shown him more understanding, more love, more thoughtfulness than his whole damn family combined. It was Mr. Bailey and Paul. They were the two men leading him out of this wilderness alive and intact. They were filling in his gaps—helping to make him whole.

Taking a right on Watercourse Road, Daniel and Mr. Bailey listened to classical music on the radio as they drove to a thick grove of trees. He didn't recognize any of the music, but it always helped calm his nerves. Mr. Bailey was probably the only person he could sit in silence with and not feel awkward.

There probably weren't many people in the world that could handle silence. A lot of people hated it—like really hated it. They ended up thinking the other person was mad at them or that they were disappointed. But Daniel liked it that he and Mr. Bailey didn't always need to fill in the space between them. It made him feel closer to him when they didn't use any words to communicate.

But sometimes Mr. Bailey used their rides to talk about what was going on in the program or over at the sober house. He checked up on him, asking him questions that gently steered him in the right direction.

"I see the woods. It's just a little past there."

Mr. Bailey pointed over to a cranberry bog where two gentlemen were dressed in white from head to toe, carrying a beehive. Daniel could just make out the netting around their heads. He cracked open the window and let in some cool air.

"Hey, I was thinking about your dad the other day." Mr. Bailey said, as he pulled down the sun visor.

"Really?" Daniel hadn't expected those words to come out of his mouth.

"Well, I didn't tell you last week because it looked like you were having a rough day, but I saw him wandering around the greenhouses while you were out on a delivery. He looked kinda lost."

"I had no idea he'd come to the nursery. What do you think he wanted?" Daniel furrowed his brow.

"He said he wanted some potting soil, but he eventually left empty-handed."

"Potting soil?"

"Potting soil and a bag of bird seed for his feeder." He tried to remember the order.

"That doesn't make any sense. He doesn't even know how to garden." Daniel stared straight ahead.

"Well…what I think he wanted was you, son. I think he was looking for you."

"But why now?"

"I'm not really sure, but it got me thinking. It occurred to me that you might not be doing so well after your O.U.I. if it wasn't for him?"

"I-I really find that hard to believe, Mr. Bailey. You sure you're talking about my dad?"

"I take it you're still pretty mad at him?" Mr. Bailey asked as though he was ignorant of some of the things his father had done to him and Will when they were young. He asked even though he knew perfectly well what type of man his father really was.

"Yah, I'm still m-mad. Wouldn't you be?"

It suddenly got under Daniel's skin that Mr. Bailey was treating his dad like such a nice guy. He respected Mr. Bailey, but had it been any other person, he might've hopped out of the truck and walked home. He wasn't ready to talk nice about a man who'd been emotionally absent most of his life. And, if truth be told, was the main reason why his mom left. Jacob Goodman, Jr.—a nice guy? What was Mr. Bailey smoking? His father was just a bitter, middle-aged man who treated women and his children like second-class citizens, more like property than people.

"I was just curious, have you two spoken lately? Maybe that's what prompted the visit?"

"Not recently, no... Potting soil?" Daniel shook his head.

"I'm not sure that's the point, Daniel. I think it was more of an excuse to visit."

"I know, Mr. Bailey. I just find it weird. He's made no other attempts to come s-see me. Anyways, all this talk about my father—it's not easy for me."

"I hear you, son, but have you ever told him how you feel? Shared your anger and disappointment with him?"

"Yah, I've done all that. I've told him everything, but he just doesn't understand why I'm so angry. He blames it all on my mother. He takes z-zero responsibility."

Just speaking about the relationship with his father made his skin heat up and his blood pressure rise. His cheeks flushed.

Mr. Bailey turned to him, but Daniel peered out the window, unable to look in his direction.

"Let me tell you something that's taken me years to learn myself." Mr. Bailey turned off the radio. "I've learned that even if I tell people the truth about how I feel, there's no guarantee they're going to hear me. People are only willing to hear what they're willing to hear and are pretty much tone deaf to everything else."

Daniel shifted his weight in the seat.

"So, where does that leave m-me?"

The last thing in the world he wanted or needed right now was a lecture about his father.

"We need to seek out safe people who will listen to us and then figure out a way to grieve the loss of the ones who won't."

"But I don't know any safe people. I don't have a long list of people who will l-listen to me, ones that really care. I can count them on one hand, two fingers."

"That sounds about right."

"But why can't they hear, Mr. Bailey? What's the m-matter with them?" Daniel's voice pleaded for an answer he knew may never come.

"The plain truth is, it doesn't really matter if they can't hear you. You need to ask yourself, are you brave enough to move forward even if they never hear you?"

"I don't know yet…maybe."

"It took me years to figure that one out too." Mr. Bailey patted his shoulder.

Pulling over, he parked the truck on the side of the bog and turned off the ignition. The only light coming in through the windows was from the moon halfway up in the sky.

"People are complicated, as you well know. They can hurt you to the point you're not sure you want to go on living and then make you feel so good as if you'd won the Boston Marathon. They're not all one thing. Most of us are somewhere in the middle, but it's not our job to judge them. Our only job is to judge how we want to be treated by them. People operate out of their own woundedness and some woundedness is worse than others. Whether or not they can hear you is not about you, son, it's about them."

Daniel looked at Mr. Bailey who was now staring straight at him.

"If you treat people with dignity and respect and they don't repay in kind, then they're the ones with the problem—not you. Stop blaming yourself, stop beating yourself up over their bad behavior. You didn't do anything wrong."

"It's about them, not me?" Daniel sat further back in his seat.

"You got it."

Mr. Bailey grabbed his cell and turned to get out of the truck. Daniel unbuckled his seatbelt and moved slowly. Sometimes a conversation with Mr. Bailey left him feeling like he'd stood up too quickly off the couch—a little woozy.

They unloaded the gear in the back of the truck and Daniel handed Mr. Bailey the scope. His head was still swimming.

"What types of o-owls are we listening for?"

"Screech and barn owls. When we get out in the field, we need to be as silent as possible. They can hear us a mile out. Just follow me. Walk in my tracks, it'll make less noise and be easier for you."

Daniel lifted the binocular strap over his head and quietly walked behind Mr. Bailey through a thick grove of scrub pines. Small tree branches and twigs cracked underneath their boots. Branches snagged the arm of his sweatshirt. He heard little feet scurrying under the brush of the bushes. When they reached a clearing in the trees, Mr. Bailey stopped on the edge of the wood.

"Listen. You hear that?" He crouched down and pulled Daniel along with him.

And like a steamship blowing its horn in the fog, Daniel heard a hoot coming from high up in the branches. They stood still and waited patiently for it to call again. Daniel found himself forgetting to breathe. When it came again, Mr. Bailey called back to it.

"It's over this way." Mr. Bailey pulled him along.

Finding the tree branch where the owl was perched, they were transfixed by it. Daniel didn't bother getting out the scope. He watched as the owl rotated its head without moving its body. It briefly examined them as if they were prey, and, with a single flap of its wings, jounced the limb and silently flew away. Its wings barely moved as it effortlessly glided through the air.

Mr. Bailey whispered, "Majestic," and Daniel knew exactly what he meant.

He and Mr. Bailey waited a half an hour longer listening for more owls, but that was the only one they heard all night. Daniel looked at his watch and noticed it was getting close to curfew at the house.

"I think we'd better head out, Mr. Bailey. I've gotta get back."

"Wish you could stay longer." He smiled.

They walked back down the same path they'd come in. Daniel followed behind Mr. Bailey around the perimeter of the bog.

Dried-out, withered cranberries from past harvests littered their path. A small house to the right of the bog had a single candlelight on in the front window.

It was so quiet, it felt as if they were walking in a soundproof box. Not a single car passed on the road and Daniel thought that was one of the best parts about living in Plymouth. The town and the country were not too far apart. Plymouth felt pretty rural in certain areas of the county. There was enough space for both people and pastures.

"Daniel?"

"Yah, Mr. Bailey?"

"You know she didn't have to leave. She could've stayed."

Mr. Bailey picked up the conversation as though no time had passed. Twigs snapped under their boots as they continued to walk.

"But there's someone who did stay. He did an awful job of it, but he hung around. He didn't leave."

Daniel stared at the ground and kicked some dirt out from underneath his feet.

Why was Mr. Bailey hell bent on ruining a perfectly good moment? What he was saying was true, but the words tore at his heart. He'd managed to keep his mother on a pedestal all this time, even though she'd walked out. Daniel wasn't sure he was ready to dethrone her just yet.

"I hear what you're telling me, Mr. Bailey, but can you be g-gentle."

He was finally getting what Paul was talking about all this time.

"The truth tears me up inside sometimes. I dunno, but it feels like drinking battery acid. It strips everything raw."

"Sorry, son." Mr. Bailey turned to check on him. "I'll go slow. Do you want to keep on talking or should I just shut up now?"

"You seem like you need to get some things off your chest. If you go slow, I think I can manage."

Daniel took the scope from around his neck and held it in his hand, then pulled off his sweatshirt and handed them back to Mr. Bailey.

"Do you want to know why I gave you a job at the nursery?"

Daniel reluctantly nodded his head.

"The truth is, I was helping your dad out after he'd helped me. I won't go into too much detail, but I'll just say that Mrs. Bailey was caught stealing some money back when she was drinking—a lot of money. It was your father who helped us sort out paying back the debt. When he reached out to me to give you a job, I couldn't refuse. And now, son, I'm glad I didn't."

Daniel wasn't sure what to do with all this information. This new perspective of his dad would have to steep awhile—settle in.

"Are you sayin' I should reach out to him?"

"Think about it. There's no rush. And only do it if you want to."

"But won't that be like condoning his behavior—what he's done? Mr. Bailey, I'm not a machine who can forget some of the things my f-father has said and done to me. I'm not a machine that can pretend it never happened."

"Nor should you, Dan."

"He hurt me. He hurt my mother. He hurt our family."

"I know." Mr. Bailey nodded his head.

"This will sound kinda funny, but I feel like a deer when the hunter has poor aim. I live with my dad's arrows sticking out of me.

They haven't killed me, but they've come close. And they're w-wedged in so tight, they never want to fall off. I'm strugglin' to forgive him. It's like, even if I remove the arrows, the scars will still be there underneath. There's no way to erase what's he's done."

Mr. Bailey reached out to touch his arm.

"Dan, I didn't mean to upset you tonight. I just wanted to talk. It's never a good time to talk about the hard stuff." He squeezed his arm. "I bet I've scared you off from going owling with me again. I won't be such a downer the next time, I promise."

Daniel gave him a quick nod and dug his hands deep into his pockets. Emerging from the scrub pines, he stared at the gravel in the road as he walked back to the truck. He slumped in and rolled down the window.

They drove home in silence along Long Pond Road and Mr. Bailey dropped him off at the top of the driveway at the house.

"See you tomorrow, Dan?"

"Yah, see yah."

He shut the door and took a deep breath. Mr. Bailey's headlights disappeared, and he stayed at the top of the hill, staring up at the moon.

He'd only been alive nineteen years, so how did his life get so complicated? How was it possible that so many things had already turned to shit?

The night wasn't at all what he expected it would be. Everything felt upside down and backwards. He rubbed his head. It would take a while to process all what Mr. Bailey had said to him—if he was able to process it at all.

Walking up to the front door of the residential facility, an older two-story Cape with three gabled dormers, he tried to take a few deep breaths. *In…out…in…out.* He dropped his shoulders.

The house was a voluntary living arrangement for recovering alcoholics and addicts who were looking for support and accountability before living independently. Many had been kicked out of apartments or their parents' home and needed a safe place to start again.

Nestled in the backwoods of south Plymouth, the two-story home housed five men who were committed to sobriety but not much else. Ironically, most of the men kept up with all their other vices like gambling, swearing, smoking, and women, but just didn't drink or use while they did it.

Some, but not many, were there to make a complete change—do a one-eighty like Daniel was hoping to do. He knew he stuck out. And let's just say improving yourself in areas that didn't necessarily need improving didn't go over too well with some of the other residents. When he first entered the house, he expected to find more men like himself, but that never happened.

Daniel walked by one of his housemates smoking outside. He'd been there awhile. Cigarette butts were piled on the ground near his feet. Daniel smelled him from a foot away, the smoke had permeated his clothes and hair.

"Want one?"

"N-No, thanks."

Daniel was tired and wanted to get inside.

"Where've you been, G-Goodman?"

"Out o-owling with my boss. It was fun, but not very many owls tonight."

Daniel couldn't tell if he was mocking him or not, but he sensed something was off with the guy and tried to ignore it. It wasn't worth decoding his tone.

"Owling, what's that?"

"Just what it sounds like, looking at and l-listening for owls."

"L-Looking and l-listening for owls. And you find that interesting?"

The man blew his inhaled cigarette smoke directly into Daniel's face. Daniel turned his head to breathe in fresh air.

"Yah, I guess I do."

Daniel moved closer to the front door.

"Don't you want to hang out with me, Goodman? We could listen for some owls out here in the woods. It's pretty quiet and no one's around. What'd ya say?"

The man got up from the metal chair he was sitting in and stood a half-a-foot taller than Daniel.

"I've been sittin' on this porch smoking all night. I'm bored as shit. O-Owling sounds like a good time." He grinned.

"Sure, but it's been a l-long day. I gotta be up early for work."

Daniel tried to remain calm, but also scanned for an escape route. His heart beat faster and a buzzing sound got louder in his ears. His stomach muscles clenched.

"Are you slow or something? And what's with the fuckin' stutter?"

He flicked his butt into the night air and pulled another one out from the carton. The lighter wouldn't start right away, and he ground the flint under his thumb until it sparked.

"What's your p-problem?" Daniel raised his voice a little.

"Nothin'. It's just irritating as shit. Has anyone tried to knock that stutter out of you? Would a right hook solve the problem? A concussion? A crowbar?"

The man dropped his cigarette and it fell in between the floorboards of the porch.

"I don't have a problem." Daniel stood his ground.

"Come on, Goodman, let me give it a shot and see if I can c-cure you."

The man cocked his arm back and brought his full weight forward. Before Daniel could register what was happening, a fist hit his chin, knocking him to the ground. The taste of iron pooled in his mouth. He spat red onto the rotted wood floorboards.

Stumbling to his feet, he moved his jaw back and forth with his hand, making sure it wasn't broken. He couldn't believe the argument had escalated so quickly. Daniel could tell the man wasn't satisfied with a single blow and looked ready to go at him again. Although he had every excuse to fight, he kept both hands down at his sides. He buried his hands deep in his front pockets.

"Come on, Goodman. I think it's working." The man prodded him.

Daniel spat out crimson again. Without hesitating, the man cocked his arm back and landed the next swing in the socket of his eye. He stumbled back and then held out both hands to block his face.

"I can't. D-Don't. I'm not gonna fight you." He took another step back, off-balance. "I need to be here. I can't get kicked out."

He kept his hands up, blocking his face.

"I've—I've got nowhere else to go."

And with those few words, the man stood down. Daniel managed to make his way inside.

Taking two stairs at a time, he charged into the bathroom and grabbed a washcloth from the cupboard. Getting it cold under the faucet, he held it to his eye and sat on the side of the tub. There was a small gash in his lip. It was oozing blood, but no teeth were loose. He looked in the mirror and touched the bruised areas around his eye. Blood soaked the washcloth.

He looked like a prize fighter after a match. How did that happen? And how was he going to explain this to Mr. Bailey? A recovering alcoholic with a black eye and busted lip didn't scream trustworthiness.

Sitting on the tub, he leaned forward and hit the side of it with his fist. *Damn it*. He felt like a coward for not fighting back. If he'd wanted to, he could've taken him—crushed his nose and driven a fist through his cheekbone. He worked hard for a living and didn't sit around smoking all day at the house.

If that punk came at him again, he wouldn't stand down, even if it meant getting kicked out of the house.

Carrie

She sat patiently in the waiting room thumbing through old magazines, feeling like a fish out of water. Three women sat with their husbands in chairs placed around the walls of the room. One was getting her belly rubbed and the other two were holding hands. Carrie was alone and barely showing. Although just this week, she'd graduated to a rubber-band fastener for her jeans. A woman at work showed her the trick to keep her pants up. It was handy because now she was in between sizes, too big for her old clothes and too small for maternity ones. A rubber band was low tech and the perfect price point.

Digging in her purse, she searched for a pen and found one at the bottom of her bag, along with a bobby pin, two cough drops, and an old Trident gum wrapper. Not seeing a trash can nearby, she threw the trash back inside.

Georgia O'Keeffe posters hung all over the walls, along with various scenes of the Southwest. The waiting room was uninspiring shades of mauve and lavender. If she hadn't been so nervous, the colors were bland enough to lull her to sleep.

The questionnaire she'd been handed at the check-in desk was specific, detailed, and very personal, which made her squirm a little in her seat. The blue ink was slowly running out in her pen and the clipboard refused to stay on her lap. It was too slippery. She uncrossed her legs to better balance it and stop it from slipping. Although these were only minor inconveniences, she was having trouble keeping her irritation in proportion to the actual problem.

Shaking the ink down into the nib, she carefully read the questionnaire. How much of the truth was she willing to tell?

When did you begin menstruating? (*I think 12*)

Have you ever been treated for a Sexually Transmitted Disease? (*No*)

Do you drink (*Yes*) If so, how much (*Too much*). Have you ever used drugs? (*Yes*)

If so, list: ( )

At what age did you first have intercourse? ( )

Is this your first pregnancy? (*No*)

If no, was it a live birth? (*No*)

How many miscarriages have you had? ( )

Have you had an abortion? (*Yes*) How many? (*1*)

How old were you? ( )

As she reached the end of the questionnaire, she realized her heart was pounding out of her chest and a headache began to thump at her temples as pressure radiated to the back of her head.

Writing down answers, very personal answers, was overwhelming. Suppressing the urge to burst into tears, she was almost desperate enough to stand up and unabashedly weep in front of perfect strangers in the waiting room, looking for some comfort.

"Carrie, Carrie Dorset," the nurse called from the door and waited for a response.

She reached for her purse and stood up holding the clipboard close to her chest.

"Hello, Carrie." The nurse smiled warmly. "What I want you to do is go down to the end of the hall. The women's bathroom is on your right."

The nurse pointed in the same direction.

"I want you to get a specimen cup and fill it about this high if you can."

She gestured to an invisible line on a cup.

"There's a Sharpie in the bathroom to write your name on the cup as well."

She looked at Carrie to see if she understood her directions. Carrie kept a steady gaze.

"Then, meet me in room three on the left-hand side. Take everything off from the waist down and get in a gown. Then have a seat on the table."

The nurse finally paused to take a breath.

"But go ahead and keep your socks on. Those stirrups are so chilly. Are you here with anyone else?"

Carrie shook her head.

"Have I given you too much to remember?" She tilted her head and lifted her eyebrows.

Carrie shook her head again and feared that if she spoke, tears would come and not stop.

"And that questionnaire, you can finish it in the exam room."

Carrie walked down the hall to the bathroom. It was cramped inside with specimen cups stacked at the back of the toilet on a plain white paper towel. A large Dixie cup with Sharpies was balancing on the sink countertop. Carrie made the rookie mistake of trying to write her name on the cup after she'd finished filling it up.

It was a strange sensation to write her name on a warm cup of urine and try to do it without spilling. When she was through, it looked like she'd spelled "Cami" and not Carrie, like a careless barista at Starbucks.

Twisting the lid on tight, she wiped off the container and left her cup inside a wall cubby labeled "Specimens," then washed her hands.

The examination room was cold and white, without a speck of color except for some yarn characters someone had knitted to cover the stirrups. Both yarn people were smiling.

The Georgia O'Keeffe posters in the waiting room were now replaced with motivational posters saying, "Teamwork" and "Success." Although Carrie thought a more appropriate poster, at least for her, would have read "Scared" and "Fearful." She was fairly certain manufacturers didn't make those kinds of posters.

Unhooking her rubber-band fastener, she took off her jeans. She rolled up her underwear and stuffed it in one of the pockets and kept on her socks like the nurse had instructed. Sitting on the exam table's crinkly paper, she straightened a paper sheet over her lap and waited in silence. A plastic model of a birth canal sat on the exam-room counter. It wasn't long before she heard papers shuffling outside her door and then a single knock.

"Carrie? Hi, I'm Dr. Robertson. It's nice to meet you."

Dr. Robertson was a tall woman with short gray hair and glasses that took up most of her face. When she smiled, two dimples surfaced.

The doctor held out her hand. Carrie shook it and smiled as best she could and tried to act as natural as possible.

"I just want to let you know what we're planning on doing today."

Carrie sat quietly listening and nodded her head every now and then.

"First, I'm going to give you an external exam and then you're going to have an ultrasound so we can take a look at the baby." She smiled warmly. "Is that all right?"

"That's great," were the first words out of Carrie's mouth since she'd walked in the door.

"Would you mind lying back and scooting your butt to the very end of the table as far as you can go without falling off? Okay... closer...okay, a little closer...perfect!"

The doctor turned her swivel seat and grabbed some blue non-latex gloves out of a box fastened to the wall. She put them on with a snap and adjusted the lamp so it shone directly on Carrie underneath the white paper sheet. Unconsciously, Carrie tried to move her knees together just as the doctor asked her to spread them further apart.

During the short period of time it took the doctor to set up and put on her gloves, Carrie's anxiety started building. She attempted to keep a smile on her face and pressed the back of her head against the pillow. As the doctor reached to touch her down below, a hot flushing feeling started to flood Carrie's chest and cheeks. They felt as if they were on fire, like she was suffering from a high fever.

Lying back on the exam table with her feet up in the air, she felt exposed, as if the entire world could see her shame. It was a small relief that Dr. Robertson seemed unaware of how uncomfortable she really was. But as the doctor talked her way through each step of the exam, it was becoming increasingly impossible for Carrie to hear her. Her anxiety caused a buzzing sound in her ears that drowned out the doctor's voice.

The lamp light was warm on her inner thigh. Concentrating on the heat, to steady herself, her mind began to race with questions.

Could the doctor see what had been done to her? Could she see she'd been raped or how broken she felt?

Carrie chewed a fingernail down to the nib.

Looking down to the end of the table at her legs hidden underneath the paper sheet, she felt detached from the lower half of her body. In slow motion, she watched the doctor pull out a long rod from the side of the ultrasound machine and place what looked like a condom on top of it. Slathering it with warm jelly, the doctor slowly inserted it. Carrie winced, which was ironic. She was experienced now. She was no longer a girl, and she lamented all the things that had been taken through that hole. The exit was wide.

The doctor turned the ultrasound screen to face Carrie, and for a moment, it looked like white mountains, black oceans, and tiny bubbles dancing back and forth. Tears began to well up in her eyes, pooling in her ears and on the paper pillowcase beneath her head. Salty tears burned her cheeks. Ignoring the steady stream down her face, she fixated her eyes on the screen and didn't avert her gaze.

The last time she was in this position, she was preparing to have an abortion. On a cold-autumn morning, Carrie's father brought her to a clinic outside of town and handed her cash for the procedure. He signed the paperwork in the waiting room but didn't go back with her when they called her name. A few hours later, she was brought out of the recovery room in a wheelchair and was taken out to his car. The engine was running. It was parked outside the automatic doors of the lobby. She and her father didn't speak on the way home.

"It has a strong heartbeat. Can you see it on the screen?"

Dr. Robertson helped Carrie get a better view and pointed to a small, white object.

"You see here? It has a good and steady beat. Everything looks fine for now, Carrie," she said reassuringly.

"I'll just need to see you back in my office in a month for a check-up and get some blood drawn at the lab. I have a feeling we'll be seeing a lot more of each other."

The doctor looked down to jot some notes in Carrie's chart.

"It's a miracle," Carrie whispered to herself, mesmerized by the bean with a flicker in its chest.

"Would you like me to print out some pictures? How many copies would you like?"

"One is fine. Thanks."

Once the doctor left the room, Carrie took a deep breath exhaling completely. She involuntarily shivered. Pressing her hands on her forehead, she massaged her temples.

Grabbing a tissue from the counter, she wiped her eyes. She couldn't stop staring at the black and white ultrasound picture in her hand. It didn't seem real. Taking the paper sheet off her lap, she wiped the jelly from in between her legs and got dressed.

Leaving the obstetrician's office, she headed west down Deer Road toward the pond. She was about twelve weeks along. The baby was due in March.

Parking her car in the gravel lot, she took a short walk through some scrub pines and hiked down a small embankment. The pond was empty except for a few ducks making their way to the other side. She unbuttoned her blouse and folded it, then slipped off her jeans and placed them on top of her shoes. She took off her socks. Unclasping her bra with both hands, she laid it on the pile and slipped out of her underwear. Undoing her hair from a braid, she let it fall to her shoulders.

The water at Deer Pond was warm on top, but cool just a few inches down. She and Rose would swim there during the summer when they were kids.

Floating on her back, she saw a small rise at the bottom of her stomach. It wasn't much, but she stared at it as if it was something alien, not quite a part of her. It was different having someone else with her all the time, kind of like a secret friend. Although this friend wouldn't remain a secret for very long.

Taking stock of herself, her loneliness felt lighter. And she wondered how something the size of a bean could make her feel less alone, maybe even a little stronger inside. She'd been in the company of people a thousand times its size and had often felt all alone. She grasped somehow, although she couldn't put it into words, that the merging of two bodies into one felt holy. Sacred.

She whispered aloud to the small bump, "Hello, down there."

Closing her eyes, she floated on top of the water, feeling the warm sun on her skin. She was sleepy. Opening one eye to stare up at the sun, she closed it again. She spread her legs and arms out wide and let the water touch every inch of her. Taking a deep breath at the surface, she let her legs fall. She sunk to the bottom of the pond letting the air out slowly, air bubbles rising to the top.

Looking at the surface of the water, it almost looked like another world. She bent her legs and propelled herself upward. Breaking through the water, she caught her breath again.

Daniel

He was wide awake before the sun came up and lay in bed staring at a tree branch through his bedroom window as it dipped back and forth from the wind. He wasn't sure how long he'd been staring at it. Reaching his hand up to his eye and then to his chin, he delicately touched his bruises. They were still sore. His pillowcase was stained pink in patches.

Hesitant to leave his room, he listened at the door. Going into the bathroom, he filled up a sample cup and left it in a lock box on the floor. Drug tests were collected at noon each day, and if you were found using, you were asked to leave.

A few months ago, one of his housemates took off and ditched the test. They eventually found his body in a car down a dead-end street on the outskirts of town. Some kid walking his dog discovered him. He'd overdosed.

Daniel wanted to pay his respects and attended the funeral. During the service, the guy's mom cried hard. She cried so hard that sometimes the cry wouldn't come out of her mouth. It stopped in her throat. The guy's dad, on the other hand, sat dry-eyed staring into space. The kid who died had two younger sisters. Daniel thought they probably didn't really understand what had happened to their older brother. He heard around town the kid's parents separated a few months later.

Maybe the dad didn't cry because he expected it to happen. Daniel assumed all parents of addicts somewhere in the back of their minds expect it to happen. They're all waiting for "the call," and it was a miracle if it didn't happen. But it would've comforted Daniel knowing the dad was sad and missed his son. He would've felt better if he'd seen the kid's father cry. But for whatever reason, that never happened.

Since he was up early and couldn't go back to sleep, he decided to go to a meeting. He caught a ride from one of his housemates who was headed that way.

They pulled into the parking lot of the Methodist church just as it was filling up. Daniel walked in a few minutes before it started. Some people were talking to each other, while others just wandered around with coffee in their hand. A few chain-smoked up until the very last minute and then stubbed out their cigarettes in a pail full of sand at the front doors.

Daniel tried not to sit by any heavy smokers. The smoke reminded him of his dad and Will. It also reminded him of the guy last night who pummeled his face. The smell made his stomach churn.

Paul advised him to sit near an open window, if possible, and to take some deep breaths to calm down. But windows were sometimes hard to come by. If he couldn't sit by a window, he tried to sit by a fan—anything that moved some air around. He found any breeze touching his face to be soothing. The intermittent gust of air reminded him to breathe.

When he first got sober, he attended AA meetings every day. Sometimes he attended twice a day, one before school and one after.

He didn't have a choice. There was a deep need to be with people who understood him, who were going through the same things he was. He felt he couldn't breathe without those meetings, as though the rooms contained a special type of oxygen just for drunks.

After the O.U.I., he used to hyperventilate a lot. His stomach was clenched all the time. He only breathed at the top of his chest and didn't even realize he was doing it until he started to feel dizzy.

He even hyperventilated in his sleep and woke up gasping for air in the middle of the night. Paul told him it was anxiety and recommended some breathing exercises to help him calm down. For emergencies, he now carried a brown paper lunch bag in his back pocket.

At school and sometimes at the nursery, he would sit in a bathroom stall and breathe in and out with the bag covering his nose and mouth. Inflating and deflating it with each breath, his anxiety gradually subsided.

Meetings had also helped release the pressure that built up inside him all day. He had probably replaced his drinking habit with a meeting habit, but at least he couldn't get into trouble that way. Now two years sober, he went to meetings seven times a week and sometimes more if he felt he needed some extra support. And when he was there, there was always someone he knew.

There were pros and cons to living in a small town and being an alcoholic. There wasn't much anonymity at meetings; practically half the town went. Jack, who pumped gas over on Shady Nook was there. The guy who owned the convenience store on Samoset came too. Even Mr. Bailey's wife, Eleanor, attended. It was all private and confidential, so naturally they didn't speak about it outside of the church. Daniel was comforted knowing that a lot of people were broken and struggling like he'd been. He felt less alone.

Today a lot of people showed up on edge, as though they needed the meeting to start right away. He'd been there before and it was rough. He'd white-knuckled it through some refreshment lines too. A few people were obviously hung over. He smelled the alcohol seeping out of their pores. They sucked on breath mints, but they weren't really fooling anyone—at least not here.

He saw a gentleman outside in the parking lot he didn't recognize, which was unusual. When the man opened his car door, there were at least a dozen crushed up beer cans on the floor mats. The old man parked slanted, taking up two spaces.

He drove a beat-up sandalwood Chevy Malibu with an out-of-state Georgia license plate. Daniel examined his face. It was covered in small broken red veins, and his nose was a dark shade of purple. Before the meeting, Daniel found him standing in line for coffee directly in front of him.

Keeping his head slightly down, Daniel didn't want to make eye contact. But out of the corner of his eye, he saw the man pour something into his coffee cup that he'd hidden in the front pocket of his dirty, red flannel shirt. The name on his tag read "Bert."

As Daniel reached over for the sugar at the back of the table, he heard a small bottle fall to the ground. The old man next to him was too inebriated to notice and didn't hear the racket it made when it hit the tile floor. But instinctually, Daniel quickly went to pick it up. Handing it back to him, the man only nodded.

"Daniel!" Eleanor stiffened up, and by her body language he knew she'd seen the bottle.

"Eleanor. How are y-you?"

"I was a lot better before I saw what I just saw. And where'd you get that shiner?" She looked genuinely concerned.

"Are you here with this man? What's this all about? Have you been drinking too?"

She leaned in to smell Daniel's breath. He backed away, which made it look even more suspicious.

"I-I was—"

His stutter, combined with his nervousness, made it virtually impossible to respond without sounding as if he'd done something wrong. He already sounded naturally guilty.

"It fell and I was j-just handing it back to him."

Daniel wasn't sure how strongly he should plead his case.

"You had me worried for a second. I'm sorry for coming on so strong. I didn't mean to go on the attack. That wasn't fair of me."

She looked down and then back up again.

"Your eye, it just looks terrible. Come sit next to me, and after the meeting, we'll do something about those bruises." She reached up and gently touched his cheek.

"They are k-kinda sore."

"I think I have just the thing to soothe them at home."

Eleanor patted his hand.

Taking a sip from the Styrofoam cup now filled with lukewarm coffee, Daniel noticed the faint smell of gin on the tips of his fingers. Most likely it was from the small bottle he'd picked up for the man a few minutes ago. They were dry now, but the aroma was still strong. He put his cup down and wanted to go wash his hands.

Down a narrow flight of stairs lined with preschool posters, he found the church's daycare bathroom and opened the door. The loud fan and lights came on suddenly by motion detector. The lime green walls were smudged with dirty handprints and a swath of rainbow paintings. The white sink basin was in technicolor. Red plastic paint brushes had been left on the side of the porcelain sink to dry.

He pushed open a stall door and saw toilets half the size of what he was used to. The rusty faucet squeaked on, and he rinsed and washed his hands while humming, "Mary Had a Little Lamb" two times like the sign on the wall instructed him to.

Cupping water in his hands, he wet his face. Soggy brown paper towels were provided on the other side of the sink. He tried to pick up a fresh one from the middle of the pack, a move that only made all the other paper towels wet too.

Drying his hands and face, he looked into the mirror and caught a glimpse of a mural behind him. It was a forest scene with a baby amidst wildflowers and surrounded by all different types of animals— an owl, a horse, some rabbits and squirrels.

Reaching into the front pocket of his jeans, he pulled out three bottles. The first one was empty, as well as the second. He lined them up on the edge of the sink. He reached in for the third and gripped it tightly in the palm of his hand, so tight he thought he might break the glass. Untwisting the lid, he drained the last bottle and rinsed out the sink. He threw them away and used half of the paper towel pile to cover them up.

Walking up the staircase to find Eleanor, he had second thoughts about leaving the drunk man standing in line at the refreshment table. He shouldn't be driving. It was stupid of him to give him back his bottle. He did it without thinking, turning away from him to try to soothe

Eleanor's anxiety. The man was obviously intoxicated and had driven himself to the meeting. Daniel knew he had to do something.

Frantically searching the hall even though the meeting had already started, he approached Eleanor in her chair. Tapping her shoulder, he crouched down beside her.

"Have you seen the man that was ahead of me in line for coffee?" he whispered.

"No, I haven't." She patted the seat next to her. "Come sit with me. They've already begun."

"I need to find him. It's dangerous for him to be on the roads."

"You're right, Daniel. Try the kitchen or the bathrooms. Maybe he's smoking in the back. Keep me posted." She looked concerned. "I'll be praying you find him."

Daniel gave her a half-hug and jogged to the back of the room.

He searched the narthex and stuck his head in the church library to see if he was there. No luck. Opening the sanctuary doors, he looked to see if anyone was sitting in the pews. They were empty. He searched the kitchen and prayer room—empty again. He ran down to the bathrooms and opened the door. No one. In a last-ditch effort, he ran out to the parking lot and searched for his car.

Scanning the lot, he looked for a beige Malibu with Georgia plates.

It was gone.

Carrie

January

"We're so glad you called, dear, but there's no need to worry. Those are called Braxton-Hicks contractions," the nurse at the obstetrician's office reassured Carrie.

"I thought I was going into pre-term labor," Carrie said as she sat in her car in front of her apartment building.

"I was in the grocery store, and I suddenly got this tight feeling on the right side of my stomach." She rubbed her hand over the location where it happened. "It felt like my muscles were clamping down."

"Yes—Yes," the nurse interrupted. "I understand, dear. Now, what I want you to do is go home and put your feet up for a while. Forget about any excess stressors in your life if you can. Relax a little, okay? I see on the calendar you have an appointment with Dr. Robertson next week. Is that correct?"

"That's right."

"Good. You must take care of yourself, dear. It's hard work cooking a little human being, isn't it?" She laughed at her own joke.

"Get a nice cool glass of water, and if you're able, take a little nap. Call us if it continues and we'll see you next week if we don't hear from you first."

Carrie ended the call and felt cautiously reassured. Wanting to believe the nurse, she still had her reservations. Reluctantly, Carrie knew there was nothing to do but take her advice.

Turning off the engine, she grabbed her purse and the shopping bags from the passenger's seat and opened the car door. A blast of frigid air hit her face, fogging up her glasses making it virtually impossible to see. She waited until they adjusted before moving any further.

She tried to button up her winter coat, but her protruding belly wasn't cooperating. Maternity winter coats were out of the question—a luxury she couldn't afford. She made do with her old one, bundling up with layers underneath. Besides, the baby was its own heater, keeping her toasty from the inside.

Even though the temperature outside was raw and bone-chilling now, thankfully the winter had been mild with very little snow on the ground. A storm would come on a Monday and dump six inches, but by Friday it had melted on account of the sun.

As a New Englander, Carrie knew better than to trust a mild winter. Mother Nature always had her way and sometimes with a vengeance. She'd seen it snow as late as St. Patrick's Day and as early as Thanksgiving. She'd even known it to be hot and humid on Christmas Eve. There was really no way of knowing what the day would bring weather-wise, and because of that, she kept three coats of varying thickness on her coat rack throughout the year. She was prepared for anything.

Before getting out of the car, she placed the plastic grocery bags on the ground near her black and tan snow boots and reached for the cell phone in her purse one more time.

Scrolling down, she pulled up Will's last text which was sent over seven months ago. *Was it really that long since they'd broken up?* His last text ended with the word *whore* which still stung when she read it.

She absentmindedly chewed on a fingernail trying to decide if she should text him for help. The doctor's bills were piling up and she'd already received a call from a collection agency. They worked out a payment plan, but money was still as tight as a noose.

She and Rose were in dire straits and had virtually no one to turn to but themselves. But asking Will for money, she wasn't sure. He was so angry in his last text, and she'd made no attempt to return the other money she'd borrowed—no, stolen—from him. But she was desperate. She tentatively touched the reply space on the screen and started to type:

"Hi, Will. I know this is out of the blue, but can you help me out with some of the medical bills for the baby? Please respond when you have a second. Thanks."

She watched the blue line pulse on the screen and stared at the blue send-arrow sign for what felt like an eternity. With her heart pounding in her chest, she practiced her Lamaze breathing to calm down. Impulsively, she stopped thinking about it and pressed send. She quickly shut off her phone and shoved it in the bottom of her purse.

Getting out of the car, she walked to the stairs leading up to her apartment. She held the rail on the way up. Her legs were unsteady.

The apartment she shared with Rose was in a two-story building with twenty apartment units, eleven on the first floor and nine on the second. Every apartment looked out over a battered and cratered parking lot with weeds growing up through the asphalt in the summer. The front of the building faced Searchlight Drive. The windows facing the street contained pretty flower boxes attached to them, and the shutters and trim were painted a deep navy blue. To passersby, the outside of the building looked well taken care of, however, the parking lot had been left to the elements.

When they first toured the apartment building, the manager informed them of a secret rooftop garden accessible from a staircase around the corner from the vacant unit. It wasn't much. In fact, it looked a little dilapidated and wasn't very much of a secret. It was accessible to all residents of the apartment building, although the manager admitted it didn't get much attention.

Carrie wasn't sure the garden was much of a selling point. The manager was a tad too overzealous about a few tattered beach chairs and some dried-out flowerpots haphazardly arranged on the rooftop. However, once Rose stood up there and saw a very distant view of the ocean and heard the harbor bell toll in the distance, she was sold on the apartment. She begged Carrie to put down a deposit.

Luckily, it was only a mile walk to the store where Rose worked and was on the same bus route as her school—Plymouth North. It was also not too far from Carrie's job, so she could check in on Rose during her lunch hour.

The unit contained second-hand furniture and a dated kitchen and bathroom. Although the carpets were worn, it was relatively clean. Most of the furnishings were brown and drab, but it had "possibility" according to Rose. The manager that day also introduced them to their potential neighbor.

Next door to the vacant unit lived a woman from Brazil who knew very little English. However, she'd been blessed with a precocious, bilingual daughter named Luzia who was happy to help with introductions. Luzia translated for her mother, although it wasn't always necessary.

Her mother pointed to herself and said, "Marissa." She spoke softly and deliberately. Luzia repeated her mother's name to Rose and Carrie, "Marissa."

They both smiled and tried to suppress their laughter. Rose promptly stuck out her hand and pointed to herself, saying, "Rose," and pantomimed smelling a flower.

Carrie and Rose moved into the apartment soon after their mother left for Florida.

For the most part, Rose was a good roommate. She never remembered to take out the trash, which made Carrie wonder if she had the memory of a goldfish. However, Rose skillfully loaded the dishwasher and was meticulous about the laundry.

She wasn't a bathroom hog either. Carrie wondered if Rose spent more than twenty minutes getting ready in the morning. It was always vacant. Her sister wore very little makeup, just a touch of mascara and some lip gloss. And she always tied her beautiful copper hair up in a ponytail for work, even though Carrie begged her to wear it down sometimes. Rose never listened, as little sisters rarely do.

Rose's milky skin was flawless, but it was her long legs and naturally pink lips that Carrie envied most. She was a natural beauty both inside and out. Carrie was pretty, but she required a little more elbow-grease to make herself presentable in the morning. But she'd been told on a few occasions that she and Rose shared the same face shape and brow line. They also had the same smile and golden flecks in the irises of their eyes. Everyone could undoubtedly tell they were sisters.

But the most beautiful thing about Rose was that she didn't realize she was so pretty, or she didn't care. She possessed a peacefulness about her that felt otherworldly at times. It was as though she knew answers to questions no one ever bothered to ask. There was a stillness to her that Carrie wished she possessed as well.

In high school, Rose was popular but didn't have many close friends. Carrie knew Rose didn't have the time or energy to invest in friendships. She wanted to, but there never seemed enough hours in the day. Her friends at school still had their parents around and only worked for spending money. For Rose, it was more complicated. And Carrie felt guilty Rose had had to grow up so soon.

Rose was also religious, something Carrie had constantly struggled with her entire life. She could never quite suspend her disbelief long enough to cross the threshold of a church on a Sunday morning. She felt like an outsider, as if she didn't belong. Although she probably wouldn't admit it to anyone else, she judged churchgoers and thought they were phony hypocrites. But what Rose always tried to tell her was that church was more of a hospital than a country club. If anyone was going to change her mind about the place, it would be her.

Occasionally when Carrie was getting ready for bed, she heard Rose's muffled whispers behind her closed bedroom door. Oftentimes, she was tempted to knock but felt like she'd be disturbing something important. She tried to respect Rose's privacy as best as a big sister could.

Rose kept a black, leather Bible by her bed, and although Carrie never saw her open it, the bookmark was never in the same place twice. Curious about it, she picked it up a time or two. But whenever her fingers touched the tissue-like paper, she got an uneasy feeling every time. The words it contained, the places and people it talked about, were from a different world—another time. How could it possibly relate to her now or here in this place? That was then and this was now, and she wasn't sure how the two lined up or if they should. She'd leave the believing to Rose.

Carrie unlocked the apartment door and found Rose cooking dinner while listening to the radio.

"What's for dinner?" Carrie dropped the grocery bags on the counter and started to unload them.

"I had a hankering for some chicken pot pie."

Carrie plugged her phone into the charger on the wall and slipped off her shoes.

"What's in your hand?" Rose looked over at what Carrie was holding.

"It's a cracked eggshell. I just picked it up. I found it under the staircase. I think it's a starling's egg. It's probably been there since last spring. I could barely see the old nest hidden between the cracks in the wood."

Rose stirred a bubbling pot on the stove.

"Have you ever seen this color blue before?" Carrie played with the two shells in her hand. "I brought the egg up for you to see it. In all this gloomy weather, the bright color caught my attention. I'll put it by the sink if you want to take a look later."

Carrie left it by the faucet and walked down the hall to her bedroom.

Although it wasn't much, she hoped her small gestures were making a dent in any unspoken resentments Rose may still have. Rose had always had a fascination with birds, and she hoped this cracked egg, however small, would be seen as one of many humble peace offerings she was willing to make.

Rose

Putting the pie in the oven, she rinsed her hands off and picked up the pieces of shell and brought them to the desk in her bedroom. She wanted to try to glue it back together. Rummaging around her desk drawer, she found the glue and poured some out on a scrap piece of paper. With a Q-tip, she gently applied glue to one of the shell's cracked surfaces—a white line formed. She picked up the other half of the shell and attempted to fit them together. It was like a puzzle. After a few tries, it slipped together. As she waited for the glue to dry, she admired the stunning shade of turquoise. It was brighter and bigger than a robin's egg, maybe a little prettier too.

Hearing a faint and low knock at the front door, Rose went to answer it, bringing the mended egg with her.

"Hi, Luzia."

Luzia stood in front of her with wet hair, the back of her nightgown soaked. She'd left her apartment without a coat on and was shivering.

"Miss Rose, what are you holding?" Luzia reached into her hand to see what was there.

"I just glued this starling egg back together because it was broken. I wanted to see what it would look like whole. Pretty, huh?"

They quietly admired it in the half-light of the evening.

"Can I hold it?" Luzia's curiosity took hold of her, but Rose blocked her hand from grabbing it too hard.

"It's still wet. Here, be gentle with it."

Rose rolled it into the center of Luzia's palm and cupped her hands underneath hers so it wouldn't fall out.

"My mother was wondering if you and Carrie wanted to join us for dinner tonight," Luzia spoke but didn't take her eyes off the egg. It had obviously entranced her.

"Did you see the nest? Were there any other eggs?"

"Yes, we'd love to, and no and no." Rose dutifully answered in quick succession. "I made a chicken pot pie. I'll bring it along."

"Yes, I'll go and tell my mother. When you come over to my house, I will give you a little stand to put your egg on so you can look at it on your nightstand. Okay? So it won't fall over."

"You have a display for a little egg?" Rose's curiosity was piqued.

"Yes!" Luzia smiled broadly. "It's a little toilet from my Barbie playhouse. I think the egg will fit inside it. It's pink. I think it will look pretty with the blue egg sitting in it." She looked up at Rose, and since she was very serious about the suggestion, Rose didn't dare tease her about it.

"Thanks, Luzia. Carrie and I will be over in a bit."

Luzia carefully handed Rose back the egg and closed the door. Rose walked the tiny egg back to her desk to dry some more and then felt a small clench in her heart.

Seeing Luzia was always bittersweet. Rose was about the same age when she cut herself, but she didn't like to think back to that time.

It was all so silly of her, and she preferred to act as though it had never happened. She put it out of her mind. But when the thought did come to her, she quickly tucked it away like a forgotten tissue buried up a sleeve. She knew it was there but couldn't see it.

Rose knew the origin of her sadness. It came from the aching loneliness she felt as a child. She had few friends, but she felt most alone at home with the people who were meant to love her. And somehow, silently—slowly over time—a hatred for herself crept in and grew like ivy in the darkest corners of her heart. There was no way to stop it. With two parents barely around to take care of her, and Carrie often out of the house, she remembered sitting alone on Christmas Eve watching *It's a Wonderful Life* in the dark all by herself.

Rose could never figure out what was so detestable about her, what turned everyone away, when all she wanted was to be held and loved. The only person she ever felt close to—really close to—was her grandmother.

Eight years ago, she opened a kitchen drawer after school looking for a pencil to do her homework and found a knife that had been misplaced. Without really thinking, almost on autopilot, she picked it up and brought it to her wrist and pressed down. Nothing happened. Her wrist wasn't cut, but the action was so abrupt she terrified herself. What had she done? But then, almost immediately, she tried it again. She was detached from herself in a way she didn't realize until that very moment. It was as if someone else was doing it, not her. She didn't even cry.

With the second attempt, she sliced her small wrist and red blood seeped from the line and pooled into her hand. The blood was bright. It felt warm. The last thing she remembered was falling to the floor.

Waking up in the emergency room, Rose came home a few days later with a white bandage covering her left wrist. That night Carrie snuck into her bedroom. Taking her arm, she drew with pink and green marker, blotted flowers on her bandage. Carrie tried to cover it with a garden, attempting to make the ugly somehow beautiful.

The timer on the oven beeped.

Rose called down the hall to Carrie about their new dinner plans. With oven mitts on, she carefully removed the pie and set it on the counter to cool.

She was agitated thinking back to her zombie-like state when her own thoughts were a surprise to her. How could that be? How could her own thoughts, her own feelings, catch her off guard? She knew she was blind to certain parts of her own pain, and in a way, harming herself was an attempt to bring all the parts of herself back together again. But the pain she ignored back then was screaming out to her, so much so it was willing to drain the blood from her body in order to get her attention.

Rose sat in silence at the kitchen table, staring blankly at the wall. She concentrated on her breathing.

"Ready to go, Rose?"

"I'm not that hungry anymore. Would you mind going without me? Give my apologizes to Marissa and Luzia."

"Of course, but why?"

Carrie grabbed the keys from the counter.

"I just feel like going to bed. I got tired all of a sudden. It just kinda came over me."

"Do you have a fever? Are you sick?" Carrie lifted a hand to her forehead.

"No, it's not that…" Rose pushed it away.

"Can I bring you back some dessert?"

Rose nodded her head, as Carrie closed the front door behind her.

After a moment, Rose stood up and wearily walked down the hallway to her bedroom. In front of her dresser mirror, she stared at her reflection. Tears welled up in her eyes. She barely had the energy to wipe them away. Bringing her hand up, she hit her image, almost breaking the mirror. Unable to change her clothes, she turned off the light. Crawling into bed with her shoes on, she sobbed.

☾

"Yoo hoo, Rosie!" Dottie waved and fast-walked over to her in the store parking lot. Pumping her arms back and forth, she covered a long distance in a short amount of time.

"Let me catch my breath, doll." Dottie put her hand on her heart and bent over a little. She was breathing hard and fanned herself down by flapping her hand in front of her face. Tiny beads of sweat appeared on the bridge of her nose despite how cold it was outside.

"Did you hear the awful news this morning?"

Rose hadn't watched the news in ages, totally clueless about current events.

"Was it the Russians again?" She attempted to sound informed, so Dottie wouldn't consider her a complete idiot.

"On no. Nothing like that. Oh, I'm not sure I can say it without tearin' up. You know Fran who works in the stockroom? She was hit by a drunk driver last night."

Rose froze.

"Is she okay?"

"She was crossing Water Street when a car came around the corner, the police say, at over forty miles an hour. The doctors informed her parents that she's most likely going to live, but right now she's in serious condition over at the hospital. It was touch and go for a while. I hear they're going to med-flight her to one of the bigger hospitals in town, one that's more equipped to help with that type of trauma."

"That's awful, Dottie. I can't believe it. Do they know who did it?"

Rose had just seen Fran the other day scurrying across the street to catch the bus home.

"Yes, doll. It was some older man with a Georgia license plate. He died in the crash when he lost control of his car and it hit an electric pole. He was too sauced to hit the brakes. Firemen had to pry him out of his Chevy with the jaws of life. Can you say, 'jaws of life' when someone is dead when they rescue them?" Dottie paused. "It doesn't matter. Forget I even asked the question."

"Will she be able to walk?"

Rose shuddered at the thought of Fran being paralyzed and in a wheelchair the rest of her life.

"I honestly don't know, the poor little lamb. She's already had two surgeries, and when she's stable enough they'll move her."

Dottie took out a hanky from her coat pocket and blotted under her eyes.

"Oh, I'm going to smear my mascara."

She tried to clean her running makeup without the aid of a mirror.

"Maybe someone from the store should visit?" Rose asked.

"I'm planning to. I just want to see where she gets sent, which hospital in Boston."

"Maybe I'll try to go with you."

Rose crossed her arms in front of her chest to keep warm.

"I'll let you know when she can have some company. You're such a sweetheart, Rosie. I promise to keep you posted." Dottie rubbed Rose's shoulder.

"But now, how do I look, pumpkin?" Dottie put the crumpled tissue she'd used back up her coat sleeve. "I need to be presentable, especially today with all this hubbub going on. There will be so many questions and I need to be strong for the other employees. I don't want them to see that I've been bawlin'."

Dottie fixed a hair out of place and tightened her scarf.

Rose's head spun with the news about Fran. She couldn't help feeling the world always wanted to swallow the most vulnerable whole. It fed on the weakest, the smallest ones with the least defenses.

Dottie lifted Rose's chin.

"Goodness. I'm glad we're working the same shift today. I've missed seeing your pretty face."

Despite what had happened to Fran, Rose appreciated the compliment. She was feeling tired and run-down this morning. It took more effort to get out of bed these days.

Practically every hour of her day was filled and there was very little time to rest anymore or just be a teenager. It was as if she was on a fast-moving treadmill where the stop button had broken off. There was no end in sight. It was a never-ending marathon of responsibility and chores.

Rose had also picked up a second job cleaning dishes in the basement of the hospital in the evenings.

"Rosie, I've been meaning to bend your ear all week. Every time I got a free minute to myself at the store, can you believe it, I got interrupted? First, it was Charlotte getting locked in the freezer, and then Bill at the deli counter went and got his finger sliced in the meat cutter."

She raised her eyebrows in disbelief.

"He didn't so much as bleed, but a little piece of his index finger did get thinly sliced." She couldn't help hiding an impish grin.

"We had to go ahead and throw out a whole pound of smoked turkey meat! Then disinfect all the equipment. Can you believe it?" She stuck her tongue out in disgust and added a, "Y-U-C-K" for good measure.

"There's never a dull moment in this store, but never mind all that. I should've asked, how's Carrie doing?" She looked eagerly at Rose. "A little birdy told me they saw you two together at the hospital the other day. Can it really be that time already?"

"Well, she's getting ready to p—"

"Before I forget, what's this I hear about you getting another job over at the hospital? Doll, you're going to wear yourself out!"

Dottie reached out and pulled down Rose's wool cap, then brushed some small snowflakes off her shoulder and hat.

"I worry about you!"

"I know, Dott."

"I'm sorry, I didn't let you finish. I'm being such a scatterbrain today, Rose. You'll have to forgive me. I feel like I'm juggling five balls and a feather in the air. I'm off my game. I would blame it on the menopause, but that can't be my excuse for everything. I just feel so flustered this morning. If you don't mind, I'd better get in there. See you in the locker room?"

"Sure, see ya in there."

She watched as Dottie ran on ahead.

Rose wished she could do more for her, but she was also stretched thin. Rose and Carrie were gradually being worn down like a stone with a single drop of water. The nonstop pace was boring a hole through them both. When would she ever be able to come up for air?

Preparation for the birth and nursery required Rose to take on a second job. Carrie couldn't be expected to help more, especially with her growing belly. Watching her waddle around these past few weeks was painful enough. And besides, no one would be willing to hire an extremely pregnant employee knowing full well she'd soon head out on maternity leave.

Thankfully at the store, Rose was able to buy baby items on discount. Each week she brought home a few new things to add to the growing pile. But how much stuff did one baby need? The amount of equipment for a small human being was staggering.

With just a month before the birth, Carrie's bedroom was practically packed with baby gear mostly still in their boxes. Just last week they'd borrowed a truck from a friend to bring home a crib and some other bulky items they found at Savers.

Dottie was kind enough to give Rose a super-special employee discount on one of the rocking-chair display models. She made it an early Christmas/birthday/everything gift for Carrie, as she planned to breastfeed. The chair had a little smudge on one of the armrests, but other than that, it was in perfect shape. It was nothing a little bleach and elbow grease couldn't take care of.

Rose found packing all the items into the truck required a Ph.D. in puzzle-solving. It resembled a massive Jenga tower—one wrong move and it would all topple over. And because Carrie wasn't allowed to lift heavy furniture, Rose had to ask for help—more like plead for help—from a man in the store's loading department. She promised to pay for his lunch, and she hoped he wouldn't ask her to eat with him. She suspected he was married, although he never wore a ring. However, the pale line on his left finger was enough of a clue that he was.

As Rose walked to the store entrance, her mind wandered back to the day of the move and her conversation with Carrie which still disturbed her. She was still debating whether she should contact the police or make some sort of report.

"Have you heard anything from Will?"

"No."

"Does he know it will be here any day now?" She tried to push Carrie a little further.

Carrie only shook her head.

"He doesn't want to know. He's made it clear he's not interested in the baby." She looked Rose directly in the eyes.

"I didn't tell you earlier because I didn't want to worry you, but there was an incident after Christmas with Will that shook me up. Even thinking about it now gives me goosebumps."

Carrie lifted her sleeve and showed Rose her arm. The little hairs were sticking up straight.

"At the restaurant, we did a late Secret Santa gift exchange. It wasn't much, just five dollars or so. But when I headed home that night, I stood in the carport of the hotel looking for my keys in my purse. David, the nice valet guy, came up and gave me a big hug. He told me he was my Secret Santa. I should've known because he broke the rules and spent more money on me than he should. It was something for the baby."

"Then what?" Rose interrupted. Her voice had an edge to it.

"Well…as I was thanking David, Will happened to drive by and saw us together—hugging. That's all. It was strange because I recognized the rattle of Will's truck exhaust and broke free from David, on instinct. It was my first time seeing Will since last summer."

"And…"

"And…through the window of his truck he started yelling at me, calling me names—awful names. He was furious." Carrie shivered and rubbed her arms.

"Why was he so angry? You two were broken up."

"I don't know." Carrie shook her head. "He started honking his horn, hitting the steering wheel, and threatening to get out of his truck. I thought he was going to attack David and me, but he eventually drove off screeching his tires. I think he'd been drinking. I-I don't know."

"You and David are just friends. It doesn't make any sense."

Rose tried to pry Carrie for more clues, but Carrie wasn't willing to discuss what happened any further.

"It's just you, me, and this little fellow." Carrie rubbed her protruding belly.

"But wait…"

"Rose, I really can't talk about it more." There was a coldness in her voice. "Really, it's over. I've moved on. I know this is hard for you to understand, but there are certain things in my life I can't dwell on—won't dwell on. I choose to shut the door and move forward. I'm not one of these girls that can talk things to death. It's easier for me to contain certain areas of my life and that confrontation with Will is one of them. If I thought too much about it, well, I don't think that would be very good for me or the baby."

"But Carrie…"

"I know it's going to be difficult for us at first, but I just want to say thank you in advance for all your help. I couldn't have done it without you. I can't do it without you."

She leaned in to give Rose a quick side-hug, as her belly was getting far too big for a proper one.

"You're such a good sister."

Rose slowly unfurled her frown.

"But you know what's not so good?" Carrie shook her head. "It looks like you and I are complete failures at packing a truck. We can't even fit the stroller in!"

They both laughed and looked over at the stroller sitting outside all by itself.

"Can I ask a huge favor? Please don't kill me." Carrie looked sheepishly over at Rose. "Would you mind walking it home?"

"With it empty?"

"Y-Yes." Carrie's reply resembled more of a question than a statement.

How could she refuse? Rose was mortified, as any teenager would be, but agreed to walk the mile home with an empty baby stroller.

She dramatically threw her purse in the stroller and grabbed a baby blanket from the truck and placed it over the purse. She fluffed it up a little, hoping people would think the lump was an actual baby. Rose started walking as Carrie drove by.

"You're the best, Rosie! I love you!" she yelled out the window and blew Rose a kiss.

"Just you wait, Carrie. After the baby's born, you owe me big time!" Rose yelled back as Carrie turned the corner.

☾

Heading upstairs from the hospital cafeteria where she now worked washing dishes in the evenings, Rose needed to turn in another copy of Carrie's MassHealth card to the birthing center for her pre-registration paperwork.

Taking two steps at a time, Rose surprisingly ran into the priest whom she'd helped in the store parking lot last summer. He was bent over collecting some papers that had fallen out of his Bible. Rose wondered which direction he was going.

Reaching down, she helped him collect the scattered scraps of paper on the ground. She handed him a laminated card with a picture of the Virgin Mary on one side and a copy of the Lord's Prayer on the other, which had fallen on the step in front of her.

"Help me out here."

The priest snapped his fingers in the air trying to remember where they'd first met.

"I was the one who helped you in the parking lot last summer."

Rose handed him another paper.

"That's right!" He wagged his finger in her direction. She could see the lightbulb going off above his head.

"I meant to thank you that day." He smiled. "I'm sorry I left without saying anything, but I think I was in shock. The dog came out of nowhere and it was so hot. I couldn't think straight. I'd just come from a funeral."

Rose sensed the incident still bothered him.

"But just so you know, the dog survived. Patches and I are good buddies now. I get to take him on walks when his owner's out of town. It was touch and go for a while, but the little guy made a full recovery."

"I'm happy to hear he pulled through."

"Me too." He playfully wiped his brow.

"I also wanted to tell you that I did go back and fill out one of those 'above-and-beyond employee-appreciation cards.' I left it with the store manager the next day. I think her name was Dottie. I had to make it out to 'the girl with ginger hair' because I didn't know your name. I hope you don't mind."

"Of course not."

"Where are you headed now?"

"My sister's having a baby, a little boy. He'll be here soon. The birthing center wants a copy of her insurance card, and I told her I'd take care of it for her since I work here part-time now."

Rose sneezed unexpectedly in the dusty stairwell.

"God bless you." He winked without skipping a beat. "A little boy, goodness. Is she telling anyone the name?"

"She's planning on naming him Duncan. His full name will be Duncan Henry Dorset."

Pride swelled in her chest just saying his name aloud.

"I like it. Names are important." He nodded his head. "I think people live up to their names, don't you agree?"

Rose nodded too, although she hadn't really given much thought to the idea.

"I once had a doctor named, Dr. Shot. I kid you not! And I also worked for a landscaper named William Oak during the summer when I was a teenager." He smiled broadly.

"Maybe Duncan will end up working in the drive-thru at the local donut shop," Rose added.

"Names often set an unconscious expectation for the child. I read that once in a Reader's Digest magazine somewhere."

He continued to sort out his papers while he talked to her, looking up every now and then.

"My own dear mother had eight children, and before each of us was born, she'd say the name she'd picked out for us with the title, Supreme Court Justice in front of it. She wanted to make sure it sounded dignified enough. I think Supreme Court Justice Duncan Henry Dorset sounds like a fine name."

"Thanks, Father." Rose stumbled for his name, as she reached out to shake his hand. "I don't think we've formally met. I'm Justice Rose Evangeline Dorset. It's nice to meet you."

He chuckled. "Hi, Rose. I'm Walter. Father Walter Isaiah Callahan."

When he smiled, the wrinkles around his eyes became much deeper.

"Hopefully, I'll be seeing you around the hospital sometime soon. I like getting to know all the faces around here. But now, don't let me keep you any longer. I know you have some important business to take care of."

He patted her hand a few times before breaking his grip, like a grandfather would do.

"I look forward to it."

They parted and Rose bounded up the stairs again. She needed to make a beeline for the birthing center so she wouldn't be late for the GATRA bus getting home. If she missed it now, there wasn't one for at least another hour.

Before opening the door to her floor, she paused in the stairwell and turned her ear toward the steps. The stairwell had an echo and she faintly heard Father Callahan hum a tune she didn't recognize as he headed down the stairs. The shuffle of his shoes on the gritty steps made it impossible to identify. She wondered when they'd meet again. They seemed to have a strange way of bumping into each other in the oddest places.

Will

"How's it going?"

The cashier nodded at Will as he entered the store. He'd been standing all day and his legs were heavy. He dragged them along. Covered in drywall dust, his irritated lungs spasmed. Letting out sporadic, shallow coughs, he wiped white powder from his forehead and rubbed it on the back of his jeans. A mask hung around his neck. His biceps were sore from reaching up all day.

"What aisle's the detergent?" he yelled over to the man standing with his back to a wall of lottery tickets and chewing tobacco.

"Straight in back of you to the left."

Will held his hand up and turned. Stopping at the endcap, he grabbed a bag of Utz and walked down the aisle and searched for something cheap.

"Where've you been?"

Will dropped his head. He recognized the familiar voice and saw a man standing in a navy-blue golf shirt and white Callaway hat further down the aisle. His shoes clicked on the linoleum floor as he walked toward him. The last time they'd seen each other was at their graduation from North.

"What's up, dude?" The guy reached out his hand, smiling broadly.

Will tried to wipe the remaining powder off onto the back of his pants and shook his hand.

"Nothin'. What's up with you?"

Will half-smiled and gritted his teeth. They were on the football team together the Thanksgiving they beat South.

"Just visiting the parents. There was a golf expo at The Pinehills and I wanted to show my fiancé our old high school and where I came after school for the best fried chicken."

He laughed and crossed his arms in front of him.

"You doin' some reno to your place? You still livin' in town?"

Will paused for a second, put his hand through his hair, and wondered how many questions this clown was going to ask before he got bored and walked away.

"Nope, working construction. Doin' drywall over at East. They had a leak. Yah, I'm still in the same place."

He ripped off the mask hanging from his neck and shoved it in his front pocket and took a wider stance.

"It's strange being back. Nothin' ever changes. It's like a time capsule. At least the food's getting better and the golf." He stuck his hand in his pocket and pulled out a tee. "They've got a wicked good course over there, it's a Nicklaus."

"I bet. I'll, uh, have to take your word for it. But I've gotta run."

Will pointed to the exit.

"Oh, yah…good seeing you." He slapped Will hard on the back. "I'd better go too. She's waiting in the car. We're, ah, expecting and she has a little craving."

He shook a pint of Ben & Jerry's Cherry Garcia ice cream in his hand.

"After the wedding, when I'm back in town, let's go for a drink." He turned and walked toward the counter. Will heard his shoes click past the automatic doors.

Rolling his shoulder, Will cracked his neck and reached for the detergent, accidentally dropping the bag of Utz on the ground.

"Is this yours?" A store clerk tapped him on the back and handed him the chips.

"Thanks."

"No problem, sir. Can I help you find anything? I see you're in the baby care aisle, are you looking for any particular formula or diapers? Any pacifiers? My mom swears by Huggies. They keep the baby dry and comfortable. They don't fall apart when they get wet. There's all different sizes—small, extra small, whatever you need."

She pointed to the boxes on the shelves below.

"But if you have a girl, maybe you want Pampers. I don't really know, but they're all here in this area."

She waved her hand around the section and smiled.

"No, ah, just getting some detergent."

Will held up the bottle.

"Oh, sorry, my bad." She hit her forehead with her palm. "Jumping to conclusions again. Don't tell my boss."

She headed toward the door at the back of the store as Will looked at the baby formulas on the shelf in front of him. He tentatively picked up a can and read the label, not really sure what he was looking for.

Staring at the baby on the logo, he thought of Carrie. And for a moment, he wondered if he would have been the type of man to get her ice cream. Would he have stopped and done something like that? Would he have gone out of his way for her?

But then he remembered, he had been that way. At one point, he'd bent over backwards trying to make her happy. Shit, he'd let her steal money from him and didn't go after it when she never paid it back. She'd drained his wallet dry, and she wasn't getting any more.

He shoved the formula back on the shelf.

Hell, he didn't want kids anyways. He'd have been fine if his stuff only consisted of mutated swimmers with four tails or it was empty down there. There was no way he wanted to populate the planet with more Goodmans. Another version of himself, walking around— one was enough. He clenched his jaw.

Heading to the counter, the cashier rang up the chips and detergent. Will handed him a twenty.

"Give me a Powerball too."

In the parking lot, Will stepped on the side bar of his truck and got in the cab. Looking in the rearview mirror, he looked like a ghost—his hair and forehead, his eyes and cheeks, were covered in white powder.

He hit the steering wheel with his hand.

What the hell was a Nicklaus?

Daniel

Pulling on a flannel shirt this morning, he noticed his arms were bigger. The sleeves tighter. The top button pulled open a little more. During the winter months at the nursery, Daniel mainly stacked bags of salt and gravel. He also stacked wood pellets for indoor heating and large heavy bags of black sunflower seeds for the birds. Every Monday and Friday afternoons, he also made a delivery of hay out to two horse farms. His body was feeling stronger, leaner, healthier. His mind was clearer.

He'd been without a car since his O.U.I., so he usually borrowed the nursery's truck nicknamed Sugar. Sugar was an eighteen-year-old red Ford pickup truck that tended to veer toward the left. Sugar was also the truck Mr. Bailey drove his bride home in after their wedding at the Presbyterian church, which was located on a hill overlooking the harbor. The church stood only a few blocks from Daniel's old house and loomed like a great white lady over the entire town.

He knew Mr. Bailey would never sell Sugar. He'd loved her back to life so many times that the repair parts were now worth more than the actual car itself. And Mr. Bailey kept a picture of himself and Eleanor tucked in the driver's side sun visor. Daniel caught him looking at it a time or two. Some edges were torn and it was a little sun-faded, but it was the kind of worn when you knew someone had stared at it long and hard. Mr. Bailey cherished that picture.

If Daniel didn't know better, he'd have thought the edges were worn out because of Mr. Bailey's great love for his wife, which they were, but Mr. Bailey sat him down the other day and told him a different story. A part of the story he'd never heard before.

A few afternoons ago, when he went to grab his paycheck from the back office, Mr. Bailey was there filing a large stack of paperwork that had been accumulating on his desk. They got to talking about some small stuff, but then the topic got more serious. Mr. Bailey spoke about his youngest son, Ian, who was killed in a mountain bike accident about eight years ago on a path near Hatchet Pass. Ian was with his older brother, Ben, at the time.

"It happened on one of those warm and sunny days at the very end of fall, a day you don't expect to be warm. It was one of those days when you've been cooped up for a while and you can't wait to go outside, so you have to go because you know that's pretty much it until spring starts." He leaned forward in his chair and brought a hand to his mouth. "Ian was, ah, riding a path he'd taken a thousand times before with his brother. It was the last run of the night and he hit a rock. He, ah, flipped his bike and hit his head the wrong way. He died instantly. He was fifteen…"

From what Mr. and Mrs. Bailey had said of him, he seemed like a really nice kid.

Mr. Bailey told Daniel, "You two would've been good friends."

He liked hearing that. It made him feel good knowing he would've been a good friend to his son.

Mr. Bailey also told him that Eleanor's drinking problem began a little while after Ian's death. What was at first an evening glass of wine, turned into an afternoon glass of wine, which turned into a mid-morning drink. She eventually got to the point where she had to drink just to get out of bed in the morning. She simply couldn't cope. When she began to hide a flask in her morning-coat pocket, he had the courage to tell her she wasn't fooling anyone. That's when she got some help.

Daniel asked him if he ever thought about leaving Mrs. Bailey because of her drinking problem.

"No, son, when God brings two people together, you can't fight it. He's got a plan for you both and he wants you to see it through. In my book, you just don't mess with that kind of authority."

But Daniel also understood if someone didn't want to stay married. Living with an alcoholic was tough, and it probably wasn't worth staying if the other person wasn't interested in getting any help. It'd be like choosing to abuse yourself every day—to treat yourself less than every day. He respected Mr. Bailey's opinion, but he didn't necessarily share it. He didn't think God worked that way, but what did he know, he wasn't a preacher.

But when he listened in his AA meetings to some women talk about the rough treatment they'd endured from their alcoholic husbands, that was proof enough to him that staying in a marriage wasn't always the best thing to do. It could be pretty dangerous for spouses and their children, if not physically, then emotionally.

Daniel had heard Mrs. Bailey tell her side of the story at meetings, so it was good to hear Mr. Bailey's side of things too. It was important to hear how drinking affected other people. After hearing Mr. Bailey's story, Daniel could just imagine him sitting in Sugar wearing out the sides of his wedding picture.

It was clear Mr. Bailey wasn't a quitter. He didn't quit on folks or on just about anything. He thought people threw out too much stuff in this world. They got so used to throwing stuff away, that if it was broken, they just tossed it. But Mr. Bailey said people were different. When they were broken, they were worth fixing. Daniel held on to that thought like a kid would his teddy bear.

He liked spending time with Mr. Bailey because he was a good man to talk to. He was simple. What he said wasn't simple, just the way he lived his life was and that's the way Daniel wanted to live his life too.

Back when he drank, his life felt complicated—too complicated. He couldn't keep up with his schoolwork. He was constantly lying, trying to keep his story straight. He stole. He disappointed friends who were genuinely trying to help him. Sadly, they didn't talk to him now. He really screwed up and he guessed there were only so many times a friend could forgive him.

Mr. Bailey had also been encouraging him to build bridges with people too, no matter how bad the building materials.

"You don't always have to cross those bridges, but it's wise to start pouring a good foundation just in case—something strong to build on over time."

Since Daniel wasn't sure about his dad, Mr. Bailey thought it might be a good idea to build a small bridge with Will, even though they hadn't spoken in quite a while.

Driving back to the nursery with the window half-down, the heater blasting warm air at his feet and the sun brightly shining in his face, Daniel's shoulders dropped and he felt a wave of peace come over him. These moments didn't happen to him very often, so he savored it.

It was hard to explain, but he felt like he was headed in the right direction, doing what he was meant to be doing. In that moment, he wasn't trying to be someone he wasn't. He wasn't beating himself up for the things he'd done in the past. He wasn't worried about what his life was going to look like in the future. He was just sitting in Sugar enjoying life—this one moment in time. It felt like some of the pieces were finally fitting together.

Not wanting to let go of the moment, he pulled over and sat on the side of the road and parked just before the red-roofed barn. He watched the horses as they huddled close together. It felt good to slow down and take it all in.

A few years back when he was still drinking, he'd had a similar feeling. It was also another reason why he decided to stop drinking and get sober. He was driving home from school and came across an accident at a four-way stop. A car was overturned in the intersection and a fire was building in the engine. He felt the intense heat about a foot away as he approached the car. A man was slumped over the steering wheel. The car was getting so hot that he had to use his shirttail to open the car door and was able to drag him to the side of the road. As he waited for the ambulance, he tried to comfort him. That's when the same feeling came over him—just then.

At that moment in time, he'd reached a point in his life when he'd done so much wrong that he was willing to do anything right, even if it killed him. He was willing to die for a guy he didn't even know. Honestly, he couldn't stand disappointing himself one more time. He would've tried to save him even if the car was engulfed in flames. He needed to redeem himself somehow.

Mr. Bailey told him once, "Life is full of choices that lead you either up or down like a sideways V. And the more wrong choices you make, the further you are from making the right ones. At a certain point on the downward slope, you don't even recognize what good choices are anymore. You're too far gone."

But Daniel had to believe that one good choice could skyrocket you back up. Not so far up where you'd be considered a good person, but far enough up so you could recognize bad choices again. Daniel believed a really good choice recalibrated you. He believed that's what happened to him at the intersection that day. He gave himself a good boost in the right direction.

Almost back at the nursery, he pulled into the Shell station to fill up the tank and get a car wash. It'd been a while since he'd cleaned the salt off Sugar's undercarriage, and he wanted to make sure she wouldn't rust over the winter.

Getting out of the truck, he headed inside to get the code from the cashier. She looked familiar, but he couldn't place her. He tried to recall her jet-black hair and light blue eyes. She smiled at him as if she recognized him, but he still didn't know who she was. He pulled his cap further down on his head.

"How's it going?" She closed the register and looked straight at him.

"G-Good, thanks. Can I get a carwash, please?"

He stared at the counter, not wanting to look up. Something about her made him feel uncomfortable.

"You don't remember me?" She punched in the code for the carwash.

No, he didn't remember her, and he felt her eyes boring into the top of his head. A sudden wave of shame swept over him, but he wasn't sure why.

"Your brother comes in here all the time, but I never see you two together."

"Oh, yah."

"Where've you been?"

"Just working. N-Nothing special." He quickly glanced up, but then stared down at the counter again.

She passed him his change and receipt.

On her left hand, in the rounded corner between her thumb and her forefinger, there was a small tattoo of a black skull.

He remembered who she was.

"Maybe we can party again with Will? Do you still have my number?"

Daniel felt sick to his stomach. Grabbing the change and receipt, all he could manage was a nod before he pushed open the doors.

Getting in the truck, he had sudden flashes of the night he'd spent with her. Hazy and incomplete memories of drinking and drugs, and of doing and saying things he wished he could take back—things he couldn't imagine doing now. There were also large blocks of time he couldn't account for.

He had memories of Will undressing her and giving her pills, and making her drink more than she should. He had memories of her passed out in Will's bed and then waking up to find her naked in his bed with the sheets soaking wet.

At the time, Will reassured him that nothing had happened between him and the girl. He told him that he'd put her in bed with him to have some fun if Daniel ever woke up. But he didn't trust what

Will said, and he couldn't exactly remember what had happened. The only thing he could remember was in the morning, seeing her tattoo, and feeling as though some part of him had died that night.

Carrie

T here was a single knock at the apartment door.

"Carrie, can you get that?" Rose called from the bathroom.

She was lying on her bed looking through the book, *What to Expect When You're Expecting*. She'd picked up an old copy from the library when she visited last week. An avid reader, Carrie devoured books and was surprised she'd never heard of this one before. The librarian recommended it.

It was hard for Carrie to believe how big the baby was getting from month to month. All the information felt a little overwhelming, but thank goodness, it took almost ten months to prepare for the birth. At least she wasn't an opossum with a thirteen-day gestation period.

She put the book on her nightstand and went to answer the door.

Opening the front door, she noticed a large box on the welcome mat. It'd been left at the door. She poked her head outside and looked down the walkway only to catch a glimpse of a brown baseball cap bobbing down the apartment steps.

She wasn't expecting anything to be delivered. She and Rose hadn't ordered anything online. Maybe it was something for the baby, possibly an early baby gift, but from whom?

Carrie kicked and nudged the box into the kitchen and grabbed a pair of scissors from the junk drawer. She pushed the box over to their small kitchen table and took a seat in one of the chairs. Although the box was labeled "fragile," it had clearly taken a beating. In fact, it looked like an old moving box, one that had been used too many times. Words and labels were crossed out by black Sharpie pens and old yellowed tape was still stuck on the corners.

Turning the box over, she looked at the return address. The postmark was from Florida. The only person she knew living in Florida was her mother. She didn't recognize the address and there was no name in the top left corner, but the town looked familiar. Carrie was surprised, but happy her mother had sent a gift for the baby. It was unexpected.

When Carrie first told her mother she was pregnant over the phone, she was met with complete silence. It was so quiet on the line that Carrie worried if the phone had disconnected. Her mother was still there but remained quiet. Carrie awkwardly fumbled for words to say in order to fill in the gap, but still not a word from her mother.

She spoke rapidly, stringing words together, hoping they were all making sense. But after a few minutes of nervous chatter, she gave up and stopped talking. She waited for her mother's response which was a long time coming.

"Well, I hope you're not expecting anything from me. I'm not going to take care of it," her mother spat over the phone.

Carrie was speechless. The volume of words she'd spoken only moments earlier seemed to all dry up. There were a thousand, no, a million responses her mother could've said about the news. But all she had to say was, "I hope you're not expecting me to take care of it."

Carrie wasn't expecting her approval or even a shred of happiness. She had just hoped for some civility and maybe even a little kindness.

The baby was Carrie's responsibility. She knew that and hoped her mother knew that too. But how hypocritical! She said that knowing full well she'd basically relinquished her own duties as a mother long ago. It was Carrie who'd taken care of Rose for most of her life.

Looking down at the box, her heart felt heavy and she grieved the relationship she wished she could've had with her mother. But it was not to be, nor would it ever be. But really, what did she expect?

Considering the phone conversation with her mother, the package on the doorstep took her by surprise. She got her hopes up a little. Carrie was just happy her mother had made even the smallest gesture of kindness. No matter what her mother's misgivings were, she was grateful for even a little recognition that her grandson was on the way.

She used the scissors to cut a line in the tape at the seams. Opening the flaps, Carrie removed wadded-up newspaper and some dingy bubble wrap. She noted, on the inside of one of the flaps, it read, "Girl's Stuff."

She looked for a note, a card, but couldn't find one. She reached in and pulled out two plastic bags closed with string at the top. She cut the string and opened the first bag. It smelled musty, as if it had been in an attic for years.

Reaching into the bag, she pulled out an old worn-out teddy bear. It was clearly loved to death. One of its eyes was missing and the stuffing was coming out in places. Looking in the bag again, Carrie immediately recognized one of Rose's favorite stuffed animals. It was a green dinosaur named Rexi.

Inside the plastic bag were some old cassette tapes, seashells, a disheveled Barbie, and a beaded-plastic bracelet. There was also a folded-up poster that Carrie hung on her bedroom wall as a girl. It was a picture of a beautiful black stallion.

The last item she pulled from the bag was Rose's old pair of pink-ballet shoes. When she turned them over, she saw a hole in the white leather at the bottom, and small parts of the stitching was coming loose. The pink ribbons were now tea stained.

Carrie searched again at the bottom of the box for a card but still found nothing. Maybe the last bag was intended for the baby. She pulled out the second plastic bag. It was lighter and less bulky than the first. If it was something for the baby, it was definitely something small.

Carrie cut the string and opened it up. The same musty odor wafted up and irritated her eyes and nose. She sat staring at its contents almost in disbelief. But suddenly closed the bag when she heard Rose coming out of the bathroom, walking down the hall.

"Ready to go?"

Rose started to collect her things in the kitchen. Carrie watched her grab her purse and car keys.

"Come on, slowpoke! You're moving slower than molasses in January. Dottie says that all the time at the store." Rose smiled and shook her head.

Carrie sat silently.

"I see you got the box from mom with all the old stuff from our rooms. She accidentally packed it when she left for Florida and called me the other day to tell me it was in the mail. She wanted to return it to us because I guess her new place doesn't have much storage. She didn't really have a place for our old things anymore. She said something about starting fresh."

Carrie stared straight ahead.

"You all right?" Rose knelt in front of her, waiting for a response.

"Fine. Let me get on my shoes. I'll j-just be a second."

Carrie hastily stood up from the table and took the plastic bag with her. She closed her bedroom door and stood there. Opening the bag again, she slowly pulled out a child's size pink polyester nightgown.

She wadded it in her hands and silently screamed into the fabric. In a silent rage, she pulled at it, but it wouldn't tear. She whipped it furiously against her closet and bed. She tried to rip it apart, tear it, but then crumpled on the floor in tears when it stayed intact.

"Carrie? We gotta go," Rose called her from the kitchen.

Quickly stuffing the nightgown into her front-sweatshirt pocket, she furiously wiped her tears away. Trying to compose herself, she put on her shoes and took a deep breath. She walked slowly into the kitchen.

"Are you driving, or am I?" Rose asked cheerfully.

Carrie nodded in her direction.

"Are you sure? You know you're taking your life into your own hands!"

She excitedly jumped up and down and didn't seem to notice the pain written all over her face.

"I picked this up for Dad." Rose held up the plant she'd bought to place at their father's grave. It was a small, red geranium.

They walked to the car.

Carrie was silent for most of the drive over to the cemetery. She looked out the window at the tall, bare scrub oak. It started to mist, and pin-prick raindrops appeared on the windshield. Rose hummed along to the radio.

His grave was at the back of the cemetery toward the far-end border. A cinderblock wall stood two feet from his headstone. His grave was in an area that looked as if it was rarely mowed. The flowers they left the last time were still there, but now desiccated and deteriorating.

Rose dusted off the headstone, clearing away some dirt and twigs and placed the plant on top. A slight wind could've easily knocked it over, but Carrie didn't say anything. She let it be.

Looking over at Rose, she saw her head was bowed. Carrie instead looked straight ahead, feeling the full weight of the thing she carried in her front pocket. It felt like a thousand pounds.

"Do you mind if I take a minute by myself?" Carrie asked.

Rose nodded and picked up the old, rotted flowers and slowly made her way back to the car. Carrie made sure she was back in the car with the door closed before she knelt in front of his grave.

She choked on hot tears.

"You son-of-a-bitch. You son-of-a-bitch," Carrie mumbled underneath her breath as she began to claw the dirt in front of her. "I hate you." She quietly seethed.

Her rage was so powerful, she felt as if she had enough strength to knock down the headstone with her bare hands.

She dug a shallow hole in front of his grave and slipped the night-gown out from her front pocket and put it in the hole. She covered it with clumps of dirt and dried grass and pounded the top with her fists. She made small movements so she wouldn't raise any suspicion from Rose, who was most likely watching her from the car window.

"Now YOU live with this shame!" She sobbed. "This-This is your shame, not mine anymore."

Carrie wiped off the dirt from her hands on her jeans and pulled the sweatshirt hood over her head. With difficulty, she got up.

Standing on the mound, she put the full weight of her body on top of it and stamped her rage into the ground. She wiped her tears on her sleeve and turned to go back to the car where Rose was waiting.

Arriving in the parking lot of their apartment, Carrie quickly got out of the car and swiftly walked up the stairs as fast as she could.

"Carrie?"

Rose followed behind her.

Carrie left the front door open, rushed into the bathroom, and locked the door behind her. She faintly heard Rose call her name but ignored it.

With adrenaline pumping through her system, she felt like she may pass out. She closed the lid of the toilet and sat down to catch her breath, leaning her head in her hands. She couldn't stop shaking. But instead of calming down, she was becoming more and more agitated. Her heartbeat began to rise, and she bounced her right leg rapidly up and down, trying to distract herself from the massive panic attack overcoming her.

Slapping her face, she tried to snap out of it with no relief. With her head in her hands, she looked through the strands of hair to the left at the cabinet underneath the sink.

And she remembered what was there.

Hidden behind her brushes and hair products was a hair dryer box pushed to the back of the cabinet wall. Ripping open the cabinet door, she frantically pushed the bottles to the side and reached for the black box.

With her hands shaking, she opened the lid. She practically tore the box apart trying to get at what was inside. Reaching in, she slowly pulled out a small red bag and unzipped it. It was still there. In the bag was a single pill, as well as her old spoon, lighter, and rubber tourniquet. For the first time all afternoon, she was overcome with a wave of relief.

Taking the spoon, she melted the powder and water with the lighter and drew the warm liquid into her old syringe. Wrapping the tourniquet around her upper arm, she used her teeth to tighten the slack and waited for a vein to bulge from underneath her skin. She kept the tourniquet in her mouth in case she needed to pull tighter and stared at her arm. While holding the syringe a few inches from her skin, her breathing was shallow. Anticipating the release, for the panic to dissolve in an instant, her vein popped and a small smile crept up the corner of her mouth. She lowered the syringe to her vein.

But just before inserting the tip, she felt a strong kick come from her belly. She dropped the needle into the sink and released the tourniquet from her mouth.

"Damn it!"

Unutterable groans fell from her mouth. Her heart felt as if it might break, and her sobs were so loud it brought Rose to the door, frantically knocking.

"Carrie! Carrie! Are you all right in there? What's going on? Let me in right now!" She pounded on the hollow door. "Please!"

Unaware if she had the strength, Carrie reached for the knob. Rushing in, Rose looked startled at what she saw on the countertop.

Taking the needle from the sink, she pushed the liquid from the syringe down the drain and broke the needle in two. Carrie was unable to speak and sat there motionless with tears streaming down her face.

Gently unthreading the tourniquet from her arm, Rose knelt in front of her and held her in her arms.

"What were you thinking? What's going on? What-What is all of this?"

Carrie shook uncontrollably as Rose held onto her shoulders. She found it hard to speak with a lump in her throat. She heaved with sobs.

"Ro..." Carrie whispered.

"Yes?"

"Ro..."

"I'm here."

"I-I have something to tell you."

She couldn't hide it any longer. What spewed forth was the rancid truth of what their father had done to her. Vomiting out the poison she'd swallowed for so long, it heaved out of her like black tar. She watched as Rose resisted the temptation to put her hands over her ears.

In the course of a few hours that afternoon, the space—the valley—that had always stood between her and Rose was slowly closing.

☾

Carrie sat in the Episcopal church parking lot. It was an old stone building at the far end of town. She sat writing in her journal that was now thick with scraps of paper, doodles, and little notes she'd compiled over the year. She collected them in a black and white composition notebook she always kept nearby. It was the place she wrote down her thoughts and feelings, where she vented and tried to sort things out. It was getting so full that she'd need a new notebook soon. But for now, she kept her secret thoughts bound tightly with a thick rubber band.

Flipping through the notebook toward the front, it gave her butterflies in her stomach remembering her bumpy road to sobriety. The beginning pages of her journal reminded her of a dark basement with a lightbulb swinging from the ceiling. Sometimes it was still frightening to go down there and take a look. But it was her pregnancy, it was Duncan, that gave her the strength to finally quit. If it weren't for him, she'd probably still be using or drinking. He gave her strength she didn't know she had.

Only a week had passed since her breakdown with Rose in the bathroom. She wrote about it and forced herself to remember, even when she'd rather forget. She wasn't used to shining a light in certain areas of her life, but the only way to get past the pain was through it—never around it.

For her, the notebook was written in indelible ink and couldn't be erased or denied, only read and remembered.

Carrie gathered her things from the car and locked the door. She planned to speak at tonight's NA meeting where before she'd only really listened. Most of the time, she felt too raw and exposed to share anything.

Sobriety made her tender, more porous. Without the armor of drugs and alcohol, even benign interactions with others went straight through her. She felt more, which was a good thing, but it also left her resonating with emotions she didn't always know what to do with. She was more in the habit of numbing everything out—keeping it all at a distance. The drugs and alcohol deflected the pain, but now she had no other choice than to confront it head-on.

Feeling heavy with Duncan and a few days past her due date, she knew it was now or never. Before Duncan was born, she was determined to be the author of her own story. By speaking tonight, she wanted to rewrite the pages written by her father or by Will or by any other man she'd been with out of desperation or by force. She would begin to repair old story lines and start to write new chapters. There was no better place to start than here, and no better people to start with than with people who were willing to do the same. She wanted to shed the old skin and begin to grow the new.

Taking a seat in the back of the church, Carrie scanned the room looking for new faces she didn't recognize. Placing her bag beside her feet, she silenced her cell phone and spit out a piece of gum in a tissue and put it in her purse. It was mostly quiet in the sanctuary, so Carrie took the opportunity to pray. She was new to it and still not sure if anyone was listening. It almost felt as if she was just talking to herself. But she tried to let the words come out of her heart and float away, hoping someone was there to catch them.

When it was her turn to speak, Carrie felt her body exhaling. Walking to the front, she turned to face the audience.

"Hello. I'm Carrie and I'm an alcoholic and a user. I was raped at a very young age by my father and have recently gotten out of a verbally and physically abusive relationship with my baby's father. As I get ready to bring this baby into the world, I'm scared. Honestly, I'm scared, but I'm hopeful of the new path my life is taking. I'm two-hundred and seventy days sober."

She rubbed her belly without thinking.

Carrie sat down and trembled a little, realizing the number would've been drastically less if she'd gone through with using last week.

The woman sitting next to her leaned over.

"Hi," she whispered and held out her hand. "I'm Sarah."

"Hi, Sarah. Carrie. Nice to meet you."

They were both careful not to draw any attention to themselves while others were speaking.

"I'm glad you spoke tonight. I've seen you here a lot lately."

"Thanks, I thought it was time I shared. I needed to. I mean, I wanted to."

"When are you due?"

"Any day now." The thought brought a smile to Carrie's face. "When I'm here next, let's exchange numbers," she told Sarah. Carrie sadly had to cut the conversation short. "Right now, I actually need to go."

She collected her things from off the floor.

"Tomorrow's my little sister's confirmation and I have a lot to do before then. I'll see you next week?" With her purse in her lap, Carrie stood up.

"See you next week." Sarah waved.

Walking toward the wood and stained-glass doors of the church, Carrie noticed a janitor tidying up at the back. He was organizing the back table in the small annex loaded full of hymnals and devotionals. He neatly stacked a pile of Bibles in the side corner and took out his duster.

"Excuse me, sir, do you have a place I can throw this away?" Carrie lifted a small plastic bag.

"Yes, miss. There's a public restroom just around the corner to your right. There should be a trash receptacle in there."

Carrie turned in the direction his hand was pointing. She opened the door, and it took her eyes a moment to adjust to the light. The trash bin was under the sink. The room smelled of disinfectant and cinnamon sticks, an overpowering Plug-In was to blame.

Opening the plastic bag, she took one last look at the red purse at the bottom.

"Never again," she said loudly, as the door unexpectedly opened and a woman walked in.

"I'm sorry, dear, were you talking to me?" the woman asked as she approached the sink.

"No, sorry. I was just saying goodbye to something."

She threw the bag in the trash.

Walking through the annex, she took a deep breath and felt giddy. What seemed impossible to get rid of before was no longer an unsurmountable obstacle. She nodded to the gentleman cleaning up on her way out.

"Thanks for your help."

With her heart bursting, she remembered Rose. A cool breeze blew through her strawberry blonde hair. Tomorrow was an important day, and she was happy to share it with her sister. Rose's confirmation had been put on hold for a few years because of her parents and the baby, but now it was her time.

As a present, Carrie had splurged on a full beauty treatment for Rose with Dottie's help—hair, makeup, nails, a new dress—the works. Carrie was determined to make Rose feel special, if for only one day.

Looking down at her cell, there was a text from Dottie:

"Hiya! I wanted to let you know the eagle has landed. Rose arrived at the beauty salon and she's tickled pink about her gift! See you soon...xoxo."

Rose

She'd never felt so special. Looking in the mirror, Rose barely recognized herself. The reflection was quite different than the one she'd seen earlier this morning. She rarely let her long, copper hair down from a ponytail. And she was far more used to seeing herself in an apron than a lovely ivory lace dress. Turning, she admired herself in the mirror.

The hairdresser at the salon had kept her hair length and color the same but added a few layers and highlights to frame her face.

"People would just die for that hair color," she said.

Examining her eyes and lips in the mirror, she'd never worn that much makeup. Her nails were done too. Now that she worked as a dishwasher, she didn't see the point of doing them on a regular basis. They'd most likely chip from the water and dish soap.

The dress was elegant, and she ran her hands up and down the sides, admiring it. It was an ivory crepe cocktail-length dress with pretty little lace-cap sleeves. She couldn't deny she looked pretty in it. Around her neck was a delicate gold cross—a present from Dottie. She also bought the perfect pair of nude peep-toe kitten heels for Rose to wear. Since she'd never worn heels before, they seemed like the perfect height for a beginner.

Rose had been waiting to be confirmed since she was thirteen, but so many things got in the way that she always ended up postponing—her grandmother's death, her father's, her mother leaving, and then Carrie and the baby. It was always put on the back burner. But being confirmed in the church, making a commitment to God, was what she wanted to do. Her relationship with God was important to her, even if not many people around her completely understood it. But today she felt happy—really happy. It was something that she hadn't felt in a long time. And nothing, absolutely nothing, could ruin this day—too many things were going right.

Not wanting to keep Dottie and Carrie waiting any longer, she peeked her head out the door.

"What a vision! Don't you think, Carrie?" Dottie beamed. "I don't think I've seen someone so pretty. Well, maybe not since seven this morning." She winked and fluffed her hair on one side.

"Rose, do you like it?" Carrie asked.

"I love it!" Rose thought she might cry. "I've never felt so beautiful."

She obliged them with a twirl.

Dottie handed Rose a crumpled tissue she kept hidden up her cardigan sleeve. Blotting the tears from under her eyes, she was careful not to mess up her newly applied makeup. She fanned her face to stem any more tears from falling.

"When I spotted that dress, I knew it had your name written all over it. I said to myself, 'Dottie, that dress is almost as beautiful as Rose is.' And Carrie came right on over to the store and bought it for you. It was the perfect color too. Your complexion just shines in ivory."

She leaned in for a hug.

"I want you to know how much I appreciate your help. And I also want you to know how much I love you. When the baby comes, we may not have the opportunity to go all out on your eighteenth birthday, so I wanted to highlight this special day for you instead."

Carrie repositioned the cross hanging around Rose's neck and tucked a piece of hair behind her ear.

"Thanks, Carrie, for going to all this trouble. I know this last week hasn't been the easiest with everything we talked about."

Rose took her hand and swung it a little. An unexpected chill ran down her spine when she flashed back to the scene in the bathroom. A lump formed in her throat.

"You're, ah, you're the bravest person I know. Even though I don't say it often, I really look up to you. I-I love you."

Rose leaned in to hug her.

"I appreciate that, sis. I love you too."

Carrie kissed her on the cheek.

"You two ready to go out to dinner and not let this look go to waste?" Dottie chirped.

Rose smiled and turned to grab her purse off the chair.

"I'm so hungry. I know what I'm ordering at Mamma Mia's."

Rose checked her reflection in the mirror one more time.

"Ugh…Rose, Dott? I think we may have a change of plans," Carrie said, looking down at a pool of water forming at her feet and making a small pond in her red shoes.

"I think Duncan has other plans," Dottie said, lifting her eyebrows and smiling.

Quickly gathering her work clothes from the dressing room, Rose carefully escorted Carrie to the car. Borrowing a few towels from the hairdresser, she placed them on the seat for Carrie to sit on. Rose shut the passenger side door and looked over at Dottie at the far end of the parking lot. The lamppost above Rose's head flickered.

"I'll meet you over there," Dottie hollered and waved.

Rose got in and sat down with a thud.

"I can't believe this is happening!"

Rose looked over at Carrie and shook her head.

"You and me both."

Adjusting the towels beneath her, Carrie sat back in the seat.

White knuckling the steering wheel, Rose put the car into reverse and stopped.

"Carrie, you're going to be a mom!" Rose couldn't help sounding astonished. "And-And I'm going to be an aunt! How is that possible?" She beamed.

Rose was tempted to run every red light from the hairdressers to the hospital. She supposed that's what nervous husbands felt like too.

"Do you mind if I say a prayer on the way to the hospital? I promise I'll keep my eyes open."

"Of course, Rose, please."

"Dear God, please watch over Carrie and Duncan tonight. Keep them safe and in your care. And please be with Dr. Robertson too. Thank you for your many blessings. Amen."

Carrie added a quick addendum to the prayer.

"And God, if Duncan is born tomorrow, please help Auntie Rose forgive me for spoiling her big day again."

They held hands as Rose drove to the hospital.

☾

Rose sat motionless, unable to move. The air had been sucked out of the room. She was trembling. Her hands were blocks of ice. The blood had drained out of them.

Ever since they'd rushed Carrie back to one of the operating rooms, which was a little less than an hour ago, she'd been sitting quietly in a chair next to Carrie's bed, staring at a battlefield of blood-stained cloth and sheets. She faintly heard nurses in the hallway outside. It was all muffled voices and machine beeps. They began to rotate through her room, asking if she needed anything. "A drink? Something to eat?" Rose refused and stared at a blank wall.

Shock had catapulted Rose into another dimension where everything seemed strange and unreal. The sadness welling up in her chest was suffocating. She wondered if she'd been taken to another planet. The people, her surroundings—even the air she breathed—was unfamiliar.

Newly born to this strange planet, Rose was desperate to get back to her own, but she knew it no longer existed. She was here to stay. She sat without thinking.

Just a short while ago, she'd been bargaining with God. She'd begged him for Carrie's life, but he'd ignored her pleas. He was deaf to her cries.

How did all this make any sense? How could this be what God wanted? Rose moaned to herself and occasionally some of the moans became audible.

And her thoughts quickly turned from sadness to anger boiling just beneath the surface of her skin. What could possibly be the purpose for taking Carrie away from her new baby? *Why God? Why her?* Rose silently argued with the air and wept.

One minute she was holding her newborn nephew, stroking his red cheeks and kissing his little fingers, and the next minute, Carrie was being rushed out of the room. Rose remembered how Carrie held him on her chest before she lost consciousness—her arms falling to her sides.

"Code blue!" Dr. Robertson yelled to a waiting team of nurses in the hall. Duncan was also taken for observation. She stood alone.

When it was over, the doctor told Rose it was postpartum hemorrhage. They told her Carrie's uterus was enlarged due to too much amniotic fluid. Her blood pressure had suddenly dropped, and she went into shock.

"We were unable to save her," echoed in Rose's ears.

A night that started out like a dream had descended quickly into a nightmare. Rose heaved. She wept for Carrie. She wept for Duncan and herself. She wept for the new life they planned to make together. Now the hole of loneliness in her heart suddenly felt permanent and unfixable.

As she sat in the room trying to process the information the doctors had given her, she had a sudden need to hold Duncan in her arms.

"I need Duncan—now! Please, please bring him to me!" she begged one of the nurses.

Rose needed to hold him, smell him, and feel his small body next to hers. She needed to rock him to soothe herself. An anxious wave crashed over her.

"Where is he?" she demanded, wiping tears from her eyes.

She needed him almost as if he were air for her to breathe. She paced the room.

"Rose, he's on his way from the nursery now." The nurse quietly tried to calm her.

Rose waited, bent over, and hung her head in her hands. It was almost two in the morning when they handed him to her. He was peacefully sleeping, blissfully unaware of what had just shattered both their lives. As she held him, her tears were absorbed into his blue and pink flannel baby blanket.

A little before dawn, Rose fed him a bottle and gently placed him in his portable bassinette. She walked over to an oversized chair in the corner of the room and tried to get some sleep. Any evidence of his birth and Carrie's death had been cleared away. She was exhausted and could barely keep her eyes open.

Still wearing the ivory dress from the night before, she pulled a blanket out of the closet and lay back in the chair, falling into a deep sleep. She didn't wake until a bright-orange sun flooded the room. Soon after sunrise, Father Callahan peeked his head inside.

"Rose," he whispered, knocking quietly at the door as he entered.

"Rose. It's Walter. Father Callahan." He waited until they caught each other's eyes before he came in any further. "They've told me what happened and that you wanted to speak with me."

"Father," Rose whispered. "She's dead."

As she said the words, tears flooded her face. Her eyes were red and puffy, and her cheeks were stained with dried, white rivers of salt.

"She's gone." Rose gulped and took two shallow breaths in quick succession.

He slowly approached her in the chair.

"I know, Rose." He spoke softly. "I've come to talk with you and pray with you, if that's okay?" He patted her hand. "I know you're scared. I know you feel alone right now, but I promise we'll get through this together."

He took a seat.

"F-Father." She stopped mid-sentence. There weren't any words for her feelings. There was nothing to say.

As he leaned in to hug her, Rose saw Duncan sleeping in the bassinette just over his right shoulder. And for a moment, a silent peace washed over her. She felt temporarily calm.

"I know you won't remember everything I'm going to tell you now, but before I leave the hospital today, I'm going to give you the phone number of a woman I want you to call when you get home. Her name is Eleanor Bailey. She handles the baby care and services programs for the town. I'll reach out to her for you, but I want you to get in touch with her as soon as you're able. She's going to be a big help going forward."

He continued to pat the top of her hand.

"I've also arranged with social services for you to take Duncan home. They see no need for him to go into foster care, seeing that you're so near to your eighteenth birthday. With help, they'll allow you to care for him. I'll stop by later today and check in on you and Duncan. You can call me anytime. I mean it. But now, I want you to get some sleep."

He stood to go.

"Thanks, Father."

"I'm here for you Rose. We're all here for you. You're not alone."

She watched him walk away. The door quietly clicked closed behind him. Unable to sleep, Rose stood up and walked over to the bassinette and picked up Duncan. She rested him in her arms and smoothed down what little hair he had on his head. Looking out of the window, she saw an unplowed field bathed in golden light. Tall grass mixed with wildflowers danced in the morning sun and ocean wind.

The responsibility of taking care of another human being felt crushing. Pacing the room, she searched Duncan's face for answers she knew he couldn't possibly provide. What was she going to do? Only a girl herself, she couldn't take care of him alone. She could barely take care of herself. But now Duncan was the only family she really had. And his little body was half Carrie. How could she let go of that? If she kept Duncan, she'd always have a piece of Carrie with her.

"I promise I'll do my best, Duncan," she whispered in his ear. "I'm so sorry. I didn't expect for this to happen. I wish it'd never happened. I just want you to know, I love you."

She kissed him gently on the forehead.

☾

2:11 PM

"Hand me that little lump of sugar, Rose."

Dottie held out her arms. She'd arrived at the hospital after going home to get some rest and change her clothes.

"You sit down, doll, and put your feet up awhile."

Rose took a deep breath and nodded as she walked over to the chair.

"Rosie," Dottie whispered, trying not to wake Duncan up. "What do you need to do now? Can I take you home and help get you settled? It's all been so much. I feel so weary. I can't imagine how exhausted you are." Dottie's hair was undone, and Rose noticed her socks didn't match.

Rose was taking everything one minute at a time. If she thought too far in the future, she felt overwhelmed. She needed Dottie's help to stay focused, but what she really wanted to say to her was—*what do I do? I feel like I'm drowning.*

"I know I have to sign some paperwork for the funeral home to come get Carrie."

She paused, fearing tears welling up. Rose had reached a point where her tears and words wanted to pour out of her simultaneously.

"The doctors have signed Duncan's release forms, so we can go home anytime."

She bit her bottom lip. Duncan began to fuss, and Dottie handed him back to her.

"I need help gathering Carrie's things and putting them in that plastic bag over there to take home." She pointed toward the closet.

"Sure thing, pumpkin."

Dottie got straight to work as Rose silently swayed Duncan back and forth, not realizing she was moving.

"Darlin', did you ever get through to your mother?"

"I did but had to leave a message."

"What'd you end up saying?"

Dottie picked up Carrie's blouse and began to fold it.

"I asked her to call me back. I didn't have the heart to tell her in a message. I told her it was urgent, but she hasn't tried to reach me."

Rose looked down at Duncan. "If she doesn't call me back, I'll try again later."

Under her tears, Rose's heart burned with anger. Every time she tried to reach out, her mother was always absent. She was tired of running after her, trying to make her care. It felt as if she was constantly chasing her, but her mother never wanted to slow down. What type of person played hide n' seek with their own flesh and blood?

Rose watched as Dottie picked up one of Carrie's shoes and placed it gently into a plastic bag, as though it was a priceless item. She moved slowly, with reverence. Although Carrie's clothes were only made of cloth, it looked like Dottie folded each item carefully as if they were made of glass.

"Are you going to call Will and tell him about the baby?"

Rose and Will had never met and she planned on keeping it that way. She'd seen a picture of him once on Carrie's phone. He had common features, nothing that stood out. The only thing Rose remembered about the picture was her mental note of him—*dirt bag*.

"No, not yet." *And maybe not ever.*

The room was clear now. All of Carrie's belongings were now packed away. She stood, looking around the room. There was nothing else for her to do but go home.

Rose buckled Duncan carefully into his new car seat. He looked so tiny, and his head flopped over to the side. She put on her seatbelt and adjusted the rearview mirror.

Dottie dropped the plastic bag with Carrie's things in the front seat and leaned in for a quick hug goodbye.

"Doll, I'm here if you need me. I promise. I'll call you tonight."

She shut the door and gave it a pat. Knocking one more time, Rose opened the window.

"If you have any questions, just call day or night. And Sugar, anytime—really."

Worry was etched all over Dottie's face.

Rose had refused Dottie's offer to follow her home, mainly because she needed some time to think. She needed time to catch her breath, focus on Duncan, and try to process the events of the past few days. It would be easier for her to do it alone in silence.

Driving home, Rose thought about Dottie's generous offer. At the hospital, Dottie told her that all her co-workers had pitched in and set up a special fund to help her pay for her living expenses while she was on maternity leave with Duncan. Even Trish threw in a few bucks. Dottie insisted she take at least two months off to get Duncan situated. The store had also set up a GoFundMe page and donation jars at every register. They were already full.

Dottie gave her some motherly advice too. "Sweetie, my mama always said, 'sleep when the baby sleeps.' You're going to be exhausted getting up at all hours of the night feeding your little guy. Both you and he need a chance to recover and get to know each other. I don't want to see your face in the store before your leave is over. You hear!"

Dottie wagged her finger in the air.

Rose hadn't taken a single baby-care class with Carrie. She didn't think she needed to, and now she didn't have the slightest clue about what to do with a baby. She was meant to be an aunt, not a mother. Duncan had been an easy baby so far, the entire twenty-three hours she'd known him. But what if he fussed and she couldn't calm him?

What if he got sick? What if she couldn't do it all? She'd have to reach out and ask for help, neither of which she was very good at.

When they arrived home, Father Callahan had called and left a voice message on her answering machine. He'd organized a group of women in the parish to babysit Duncan once she had to go back to work. Although it wasn't a permanent solution, it would tide her over until she could make other arrangements. There was so much to do, but she felt so tired. Feeling like she was in a constant state of slow motion, everything took so much more effort.

Next to the answering machine was a pile of mail that included a stack of unpaid bills. Rose nervously looked at the pile. Under her grief, she felt a large swell of panic.

Breathe, Rose. Breathe.

It didn't make any sense, but she was also angry at Carrie that she was now all alone. How could Carrie have done this to her? How could she have left her?

Close to the bottom of the pile were two folded pieces of paper stapled together. She didn't recognize them and opened them up. On top of one form, it read, "Living Will." It had been filled out by Carrie. Scanning the sheet, Carrie noted her wishes for long-term care, specific physician instructions, and organ donation.

On the second sheet it read, "Last Will and Testament." This paper was very brief and had a lot of legal terms Rose didn't understand. It said, "I give guardianship of my children to Rose Evangeline Dorset in case of death or incapacitation." It was signed Carrie Madeleine Dorset and was dated February 2016.

Rose dropped them both on the counter and wept.

Will

9 hours earlier – 5:24 AM

Face down on the bed, Will searched for his cell on the night-stand and knocked over a small lamp. It dropped onto the hard-wood floor.

"What?" he answered, his voice was scratchy and hoarse.

"Will. It's me, Michelle," she whispered on the other end of the line.

"Give me a sec."

He pushed himself up and sat on the edge of the bed. Shivering, he wrapped the comforter around his shoulders. Out of the window, he saw the black night giving way to blue sky.

"What's so important it couldn't wait?" He rubbed the sleep from his eyes.

"I really shouldn't be calling you. I mean, I could get fired for this, but I thought you should know."

"Know what?" He coughed and rubbed his chest.

"Your ex, Carrie. She's dead."

"What the fuck are you talking about, Michelle?"

He wasn't sure he heard her correctly.

"I was working the nightshift at the hospital and heard some staff talking in the break room that there was a death on the maternity ward. One of the nurses mentioned Carrie's name. I don't know the details, just that she died."

Over the line, Will heard the beep from her car fob and the buzz from her car door when she opened it. He sat silent.

"You were going to find out anyways, and I really thought you should know."

He heard her start her ignition.

"I'm sorry for calling you so early, but I wanted you to hear it from a friend. Sorry. Will...you still there?"

"Yah, t-thanks."

He was trying to sort out the information in his head, still confused as to what she was saying.

"Let me get this straight. You're saying tonight, Carrie died. She's dead."

The fog started to clear from his head. The hardwood floors were cold underneath his feet.

"I'm sorry, I really am. I know you two were broken up n' all. I should probably let you go. I dunno. Sorry for calling so early. I just didn't want you to be caught off guard in the morning when the news broke."

"Okay, yah. Thanks." He leaned forward and bent his head down and stared at the floor.

"Let me know if you need anything, 'kay?"

For a moment, he felt irritated by her pity.

"Yah…later," Will said flatly.

"Night, Will."

"Goodn—" He went to end the call.

"W-Wait, Michelle." He sat up straighter. The comforter fell from his shoulders.

"Yah?"

"What, uh, what happened to the baby?"

"It's a boy."

"He's alive?"

"Yah, DCF gave him to a relative. I don't know much more than that."

Will hung up and put his hand on top of his head. He looked around the room. An orange speck of light appeared near the bottom sill of the window and crept slowly across the floor. The room was quiet except for the swirl of fan blades spinning above his head.

Grabbing a cigarette and his lighter from the nightstand, he drew a deep breath of smoke into his lungs. The warm air soothed the back of his throat and he coughed. Exhaling, he watched the white cloud get pushed down by gusts of air above his head. Biting the filter, he inhaled again and let the cigarette hang from his lips. He coughed again.

Reaching for his jeans at the end of the bed, he pulled out his black worn wallet from his front pocket. Inside the billfold, he took out a folded picture. It was of Carrie and him at the movies after they'd seen The Martian. He was sticking up his middle finger to the camera, smirking, while Carrie made bunny ears above his head. The bottom image was blurry. It caught them leaving the booth too early.

He inhaled again and blew smoke out of the side of his mouth.

Outlining her hair with his finger, he then ground the lighter with his thumb. He stubbed out his cigarette in an ashtray on the nightstand and coughed.

Getting up from the bed, he walked over to the window and looked out. The moon hung in the sky, hiding behind white billowy clouds that quickly drifted east.

Glancing at the picture again, he leaned against the windowpane and dropped his head.

Shit.

Daniel

While feeding the fish in the koi pond and filling it up with water, he saw her walk by. He temporarily lost his grip on the hose and soaked the lower half of his jeans and boots. She was pushing a stroller and leaning over every now and then to check on her baby. Her hair fell to the middle of her back and was the color of orange honey. She was the most beautiful girl he'd ever laid eyes on.

From the first moment he saw her, he felt drawn to her. He got a flutter in his heart right dead in the center and stopped what he was doing when it happened because he'd never felt something like that before. Shaking his head, he tried to brush it off but couldn't stop himself from thinking about it. Then it happened again. This time it was more difficult to ignore.

But there was something different about her—foreign. If he had to put it into words, she reminded him of a snowy owl that'd flown too far south of the Arctic. She looked out of place. In his head, he called her S.O.

For a second, he thought about calling Paul and telling him about the flutter in his chest, but then decided not to. The thought of her was tender to him and he worried talking about it with someone else would somehow take the sweetness out of it.

"Hey, Mr. Bailey, do you have a minute?"

He caught Mr. Bailey jogging to the greenhouses.

"Sure do," he said, brushing off encrusted dirt from his pant leg.

Mr. Bailey blew his nose in a handkerchief, took off his glasses, and started to clean them with his shirt.

"Do you know that girl over there pushing the stroller?" He pointed in her direction. "She looks pretty young to have a baby."

He couldn't help staring at her.

"There's something different about her, but I just can't put my finger on it."

Mr. Bailey cleared his throat and squinted. He shaded his eyes with his hand.

"Well, son, that there is Rose Dorset and her nephew Duncan. I'd say he's a little over a month old now."

Mr. Bailey picked up the hose and continued filling the koi pond.

"What you're looking at is grace, son, that's when love and duty meet. I read that in a book somewhere."

Mr. Bailey shook his finger in the air, trying to remember the book title.

"I have to say that girl is something special. I don't know her too well, but I do know she's been through a horrific tragedy, and she's doing her best to take care of her sister's son. She's about as good as you get."

Daniel shoved his bandana in his back pocket and took the hose from him.

"I'm sorry but I've got to help another customer. Find me later, okay, and we'll talk some more."

Mr. Bailey gave him a quick pat on the back.

The sun shone in his eyes, and he squinted, watching her walk down the sidewalk. His heart ached for her a little and it felt as if a tether was connected from his head to his heart. Every time he thought of her, it would pull, but he didn't even know her! What was he thinking?

Feeling a little ridiculous, he gave himself a slap on the face and told himself to get a grip. He was tempted to pour the hose on top of himself to cool down.

"Daniel, have you seen Mr. Bailey anywhere?"

Eleanor interrupted his daydreaming. She was wearing a large straw sunhat and carrying a pair of pruning shears.

"I think he's near the greenhouses."

"Can you do me a favor and ask him if he's preaching this week-end? I haven't had a chance to copy his sermon notes and I just need to know when to do it."

Daniel knew Mr. Bailey was an assistant pastor at the Presbyterian church, so it was no wonder he was always quick to tell an anecdote or two.

"Of course, Mrs. Bailey. No problem."

"Are you singing in the choir this weekend? You know how I love hearing your beautiful voice."

"You know I can't h-hold a tune. You're just bein' nice. I'm there to fill in the holes when someone doesn't show up."

"I am not!"

She grinned.

"You're a fine singer and you know we always need more men in the choir."

Eleanor swatted a bee flying near her face.

"And don't forget to let me know what Mr. Bailey says, all right?"

"Will do."

He watched as Mrs. Bailey headed back to the shop and his heart hurt for her knowing that her son was no longer alive. How did parents survive that—having to go on living and breathing when all they probably wanted to do was crawl into the ground beside them and hold them?

"And Daniel?" she called to him again. "Would you mind doing me one more favor after work? I need someone to deliver this basket of baby supplies to a friend, but I have an appointment I need to get to. I can't do it myself. Would you mind taking it over for me?"

"Sure thing."

"Come and see me after work and I'll give you her address and all the supplies. The gift basket is going to a real sweet girl named Rose Dorset. She has a new baby, her nephew, actually. All you need to do is put it on her doorstep. She's expecting it."

Mrs. Bailey thanked him with a broad smile, and at that exact moment, had she wanted to, she could've knocked him over with a feather.

He didn't get anything done the rest of the afternoon at work. Chores that were usually pretty quick were done painstakingly slow. He moved like ditchwater. He was also getting a little panicked about what he was going to say to her. How would he get the words out with his stutter?

He glanced at his watch about a thousand times and accidentally overwatered the geraniums again. Gathering the garden hose, he wound it up. His hands filled with wet dirt as he coiled it.

He really wanted to see her again but was also frightened of wanting something or someone too much. Repeated disappointments made taking a leap of faith seem like skydiving without a parachute.

As the sun got ready to set over the greenhouses, he made his way back to the perennial flower beds and clipped one pink rose. Scooping up the basket full of items for the baby, he waved goodbye to Mrs. Bailey. She was on the phone and waved back at him. He stuck the rose on top of the basket and made a beeline for Sugar. Starting the engine, he put her in reverse.

Climbing two stairs at a time at her apartment complex, his heart was virtually pounding out of his chest. He'd been nervous with girls before, but this time it was different. He was nervous and determined. He had this gut feeling he was meant to know her. They were meant to meet.

Tucking in his shirt, he tried to smooth down his wavy hair and quickly did up the buttons on his shirt sleeves. Placing the basket in front of her door, he knocked and took a deep breath—something he needed to remember to do more often.

Looking down the line of doors in the corridor, all the wall paint was chipped, and her door light flickered like a butterfly's wing. The tiles on the ceiling were stained from past leaks, and a bike leaned against an exterior brick wall.

"Who is it?"

He heard her on the other side of the door.

"Hi, uh, h-hello?"

He cleared his throat.

"I'm here to drop off something for the baby. Mrs. Bailey s-sent me."

She opened the door and he winced, wondering if the fluttering would start again. Drawing air into his lungs, he found it difficult to breathe. He put his hand to the right of the door frame to keep upright.

"Ah, Mrs. Bailey asked me to drop this off for you and the b-baby."

He handed her the basket.

She took out the rose and smelled it.

"Thank you." She smiled warmly. "I'm Rose."

She reached out her hand and then opened the door a little wider.

"And this is Duncan."

She pointed into the living room where a baby was sitting in a bouncy seat.

"I appreciate you bringing this by."

He felt her words go straight through him.

"It's my pleasure. I'm Daniel, by the way. I work at the nursery with the Baileys."

"Would you like to come in? Meet Duncan?"

"A-Another time. I need to get back to work. But, uh, Rose, if you want to, come by the nursery sometime. Duncan can feed the fish in the koi pond. I mean, you can f-feed the fish."

He laughed, hoping she was used to adults who babbled too.

"It was nice meeting you, Daniel." She smiled.

He loved hearing her say his name.

"And thanks again. Maybe I'll take you up on your offer some-time soon."

She broke eye contact with him and looked down at her feet.

"I'm, uh, headed back to work soon and I only have a few more days to spend with Duncan. I'll try to come by."

They caught eyes again.

"See you soon then, Rose. It was nice to meet you as well."

After she closed the door, he ran to the truck and just stood there for a second. He gave Sugar a slap on the roof.

Hopping in the truck, he drove to the nursery. His heart felt like it was on fire. Mr. Bailey might need to hose him down after all.

Rose

As soon as she shut the door, she smiled. That was unexpected. Rose assumed it would be Mrs. Bailey coming by with the basket and not some blue-eyed, sandy-haired boy she'd never seen before. She liked the waviness of his hair and his sweet nervous stutter. Still taken aback, she leaned against the door and took a deep breath.

Getting on her tiptoes, she reached for a vase in the cabinet above the refrigerator and grabbed her grandmother's old hobnail milk glass. Filling it with cool water, she placed the pink rose from the basket inside.

"Duncan, isn't it pretty?"

Rose smelled the bloom again and admired it. And suddenly a fond memory of her grandmother bubbled up to the surface and filled her heart. She touched the bumps on the vase and smiled. For a moment, she found herself lost in the warmth of her grandmother's love.

Glancing over at Duncan, she saw he'd fallen asleep in his bouncy. Walking over to him, she held a finger under his nose to see if he was still breathing. Adjusting his blue gingham cotton blanket so it covered him to his waist, she gently kissed him on the forehead.

Since he was her only source of conversation day in and day out, lately Rose had gotten into the habit of putting on silly English accents just to make him smile.

"Would you care for some tea, sir?" He looked at her quizzically. And by tea she meant a bottle and a burp.

"Let's keep it dignified, please!" she'd say if he really let out a big one.

And she saved, "Yes, your majesty," for the middle of the night when she was dead-on-her-feet tired.

Mrs. Bailey and Dottie were still giving her tips on mothering. However, both had commented separately on how well she was getting the hang of it. She was a natural nurturer.

But Rose was still struggling with loneliness, especially in the middle of the night when she was feeding Duncan alone. The hours crawled by. The apartment at nighttime was too quiet. It left her with her own thoughts for a dangerously long time, thoughts of hopelessness and desperation that often lingered into the morning.

Most nights, Duncan slept in a white crib beside her bed. When he got hungry, she'd pick him up and feed him. Turning on the nightstand light, which was dim enough not to wake him, she'd sit in the twilight listening to the sounds of his rhythmic gulping.

It was at this time, when the world was fast asleep, she acutely felt an emptiness in her chest. In the day, she shook it off by calling up Dottie or taking Duncan for a walk in the stroller. It was comforting to be around other people, even if she didn't know them. The light of day evaporated her sadness for a little while, but the nighttime was a different story. There was nothing she could do to distract herself then. She just had to bear it.

The only thing Rose found that helped the ache in her heart was when she concentrated on the little pleasures of the moment, like the heaviness of Duncan in her arms or the sweet way his head smelled. She loved listening to the little cooing noises he made and his attempts to smile out of the corner of his mouth.

Holding on to the insignificant but precious things soothed her most in the middle of the night. Finding a way to be thankful provided a respite from her sorrow.

As a little girl, she'd had to do much of the same. With her parent's volatile relationship, Rose often felt alone. There had even been a distance between her and Carrie that only recently she understood.

Back then, she tried so hard to make their relationship stronger, but there'd always been an invisible barrier between them. Carrie never got too close to her, and her father paid her very little attention. Her mother was often too preoccupied to notice. In a house full of people, she always felt isolated—ignored. But it was also in that house that she learned to think and focus on the little blessings in life.

After this afternoon, after her chance meeting with Daniel, there was now another thing to be thankful for.

As she sat in the dim light of her room feeding Duncan, she thought of him. She tried to remember the exact color of his hair and the pitch of his voice. She tried to remember his smile and what shirt he was wearing. It brought a smile to her face remembering the way he stumbled through some of his words and the way his warm hand felt when she shook it. And now, when she thought of him, it tugged at her heart. That was strange.

The blessing of the memory of Daniel would be enough to get her through the night tonight.

Duncan was usually first to wake her, but this morning, as the sun peeked through a crack in her drapes, Rose felt wide awake. She hopped out and made her bed. Today, she was determined to get Duncan on a proper schedule as best she could. She was headed back to work in a few days and wanted the women in the parish to have a solid routine to follow. She knew Duncan wouldn't be a fan, but it still had to be done.

She made a checklist for the day.

SCHEDULE	TO DO
6 AM feed Duncan	Daily devotional
10 AM feed & nap	Laundry
2 PM feed & nap	Run dishwasher
5 PM bath	Take out trash
6 PM feed	Visit Bailey's
10 PM feed & bedtime	

Writing the to-do list filled her with a quiet anticipation, especially when she wrote, "visit Bailey's." But she'd learned not to get her hopes up. Remaining level-headed felt safer, but always less exciting. Hope was something she was careful not to feel without good reason, and she only liked to have it in small doses. But when her cautious nature and boundless optimism crashed into each other, the battlefield was always her heart. She had a difficult time deciphering whether her caution was just fear in disguise. She longed to rip off the armor of fear she wore each day. With all her heart, she desired to live freely— hopefully, whole-fully.

Not getting her hopes up or running from her fears was a bad habit she wanted to break, so she decided to pencil in "break bad habit" on her to-do list. She laughed at her methodology, a to-do list to conquer fear. It was a start. Even though she'd scheduled it, it wasn't so far-fetched a plan to phase it out of her life. She'd been holding her breath too long and needed to exhale. Sick of playing it safe all the time, when would she ever learn to throw caution to the wind?

The only time she'd allowed herself to feel reckless was in high school, when she drank a beer a senior offered her at a party. It was the only party she went to her entire time at North. In the backwoods, over near the horse farms, she sat on a wood log by a campfire and felt normal for once in her life. Feeling the fire warm her skin, she didn't even like the taste of alcohol. That didn't matter. Talking to people she'd only smiled at in the halls, she laughed and drank the entire bottle.

Unsnapping Duncan's onesie, Rose flashed back to a conversation she'd had with her mother at Carrie's funeral, one she was still troubled by.

Per Father Callahan's suggestion, Rose had made arrangements with Donaldson's Funeral Home on Court Street, a beautiful two-story white house with black shutters. They'd offered their services for free. And the hotel Carrie worked at paid for the coffin and burial plot. If it wasn't for the support of the community, Rose wasn't sure how she could've afforded it all.

Her mother swallowed a gulp of wine from a plastic cup.

"Carrie always had the worst luck. Ever since she was a little girl, a black cloud followed her. I always told your father she was born into the world on a pile of spilled salt."

"It wasn't bad luck, Mom. What happened to Carrie was a tragedy—a horrible accident."

Her mother sat further back in the seat.

"Some people seem to attract a boatload of negative energy, you know, dark forces in the universe. They have bad chi. They're born under stars that are misaligned or something like that."

Her mother searched her purse for something.

"I'm not sure what negative forces you're talking about, or that some people attract more than others."

She regretted getting cornered by her mother.

"I don't think Carrie's life was like that. I think you're attributing things to her that she had no control over. Obviously, she was troubled, but I'm not sure how much of that was directly her fault."

Rose attempted to hold a mirror up to her mother's face, although it went unnoticed.

"Some people are just a magnet for disaster. They attract the scum and lowlifes of the earth and chronically make the worst decisions. Your sister was one of them," her mother said offhandedly, without an ounce of pity for her dead daughter.

"I'm not sure I'd categorize all of Carrie's actions as decisions. Some of them were coping mechanisms—a means of survival. Not everything was her choice, Mom."

Rose glared at her.

"Honestly, there's a fine line between choice and circumstance. As adults we make choices, but as children we are sometimes set on paths we don't want to go down and have a hard time veering from when we're older. If you've always lived in a desert, Mom, how do you know to look for rain?"

Her mother sat silently and refused to look in her direction. She then took another large gulp of wine and placed the cup on the table beside an empty coaster.

"She was a junkie, Rose, a plain and simple junkie. How can you be so naïve? Her whole lifestyle eventually caught up with her, all the druggin' and boozin'—all the men. How do we know she wasn't using again?"

Her mother tilted her head and stared at Rose.

Her response was so callous, Rose stopped talking. She knew her arguments would go unheard. They were a waste of breath. But in a last-ditch effort to change the subject and find some means of connection in what little time they had left together, Rose asked, "Do you have anything to say about today? Did you like the service? The minister?"

"Do I have anything to say? Did the minister even know Carrie? By his description of her, he made her sound like a saint. Total hogwash. And I'm seriously thinking of suing the hospital and that Dr. Robertson for malpractice. Is that saying enough, Rose?"

Rose choked on a cookie she was eating.

"Malpractice? Dr. Robertson tried to save Carrie's life. How can you blame her or the hospital when you weren't even there to see how they tried to help her—what lengths they went to?"

Rose sat on the edge of her seat.

"Can you not see their utter negligence? I'm surprised the doctor showed her face here at the funeral. She has a nerve."

"A nerve. She's here to mourn her patient's death. I'm touched she came and paid her respects."

"Oh, innocent Rosie." Her mother said her name sickeningly sweet as she adjusted her tight-fitting black dress. Finding a cigarette in her small purse, she pulled one out. Rose noticed the wrinkles on her leathery hands didn't match the smoothness of her face.

"I suppose we won't see eye to eye on this or anything today, so let's stop talking about it. We'll let the past be the past. Let's just enjoy these stale crackers and cheese instead, or will you find fault in the way I chew my food?"

Her mother put her paper plate on the table and stood to leave.

When the funeral reception was over, Rose's mother flew back to Florida. Only a year ago she was weak and fragile, now she'd grown mean and unforgiving. She was hard, as if a heavy brick had replaced her heart.

In the time she'd been away, Rose no longer recognized her. She was a stranger. There was no longer a cord or even a string connecting them together. Their blood ties were as thin as water, diluted by the ice running through her mother's veins.

Daniel

He picked some dirt out from underneath his fingernails and swallowed hard. He caught a glimpse of her copper hair from down the street. Something shined in the corner of his eye. Even though he'd waited for her all morning, hoping she'd come, when he finally saw her, his confidence plummeted. His palms were sweaty, and he couldn't help adjusting his baseball cap back and forth. Trying to catch his reflection in the koi pond to see if he had any dirt on his face, the lily pads were in the way. He tamed his hair under his cap and paced back and forth.

Dan, you gotta calm down. Pull yourself together.

Dusting off his t-shirt and jeans, he cleaned out pieces of hay from his pockets. He wiped off the back of his neck with his blue bandana and shoved it in his back pocket.

He looked around for something to keep him busy, occupied, anything to distract him from all his nervous energy. He didn't find anything except his untied bootlace. Bending over to tie it, it took him a second to remember how because of all the adrenaline pumping through his system.

"Daniel?"

He saw her shadow before him and her painted toenails a shade of bright pink. He looked at her slim ankles. She was wearing brown-leather sandals and had a dark-brown freckle on top of one of her toes. He started to sweat.

He looked up her legs slowly. The sun was at her back, and he couldn't see clearly right away. Standing up, he squinted. It took him a second to see her come into clear view.

"Rose?"

"I thought that was you," she said, lifting Duncan out of the stroller.

She held him over one shoulder. Wearing a white, floppy hat, his chubby thighs pressed against her forearm. Rose rubbed his back.

"We, ah, thought we'd take you up on your offer to feed the fish."

She didn't make direct eye contact with him, but instead looked down at his shirt and then back up at his baseball cap.

"I'm so g-glad you came." The words fell out of his mouth in staccato. "I was just about to feed them. Do you mind waiting here while I go get the food? It'll only take a s-sec."

She nodded and he ran to the storage room tripping on a hose along the way. He looked back to see if she saw him, but she was tending to Duncan.

When he reached the storeroom, his hands and eyes weren't working together. In his frenzied search for the fish food, he managed to tip over a terracotta pot, knock over a sad looking cactus, and some wire cages for tomatoes. He was making such a racket, a customer looked in to see if everything was all right. He smiled at her and grabbed the bag of food.

Taking a deep breath, he stood in the door frame of the storage room for a moment before jogging back to her.

Breathe, Daniel, breathe.

He ran over to the pond.

"Was it a good day to come?"

She moved her sunglasses to the top of her head.

"Yah, great. I'm glad you're here. It was a slow morning. I could use the company."

He bowed his head, a little worried he may start blushing for being so overeager.

"How long have you worked at Bailey's?"

"'Bout a year now."

"Do you know them well?"

He wasn't sure how to answer. He wanted to be truthful, but it didn't seem like the right time or place to tell Rose his full story.

"Ah, they're like a second f-family to me," he offered.

"Mrs. Bailey's been very helpful with Duncan."

Rose played with the blue trim on his onesie.

"I've never met such kind people," she said, swatting a bee away.

"I hear that a lot. I couldn't agree with you more."

He smiled at her. She smiled back.

"Do you live around here?"

"No, um, I live over near Great Herring Pond. I share a place with a few o-other guys."

They walked over to the koi pond near the front of the store, and she gently placed Duncan back in the stroller. He'd fallen asleep. She repositioned the stroller to be in the shade, out of the sun.

Daniel handed her some fish food.

"Just sprinkle it in. They come up pretty close to the surface of the water when they see food coming their way," he instructed. "Don't be scared if they try and suck your fingers off."

He winked at Rose, waiting to see her reaction.

"I'm not scared," she replied confidently, and then laughed when the mouths in the water opened and closed rapidly in between the lily pads.

"They're pretty aggressive when it comes to their food."

Standing beside her, he couldn't help studying her—the gold flecks in her eyes and the curve of her shoulders.

She was totally entranced by the hungry mouths and let out a little laugh when the fish made her drop the food. The sunglasses perched on top of her head also came perilously close to falling in the water. He was content just holding the bag for her.

"Dan, you got a minute?" Pete yelled from over near the loading dock.

"Sure, be right there."

Daniel handed her the bag. "You mind?"

He ran over.

"Sorry to interrupt you, man—really."

Pete smiled and gave him a punch in the arm.

"Ed's on break and this truck needs to go. We just need to unload a few fruit trees, a couple bushes, and that pot of honeysuckle."

Pete jumped up on the truck and disappeared into the back. He reemerged and handed Daniel a hydrangea.

"Where do you want me to put them?"

He reached up to grab the plant.

"Line them up against the fence near the back, to the left of the greenhouses."

They unloaded the bushes and honeysuckle and worked together to off-load the fruit trees.

"Is she a friend of yours?" Pete grunted his question as they moved the heavy trees.

A few times he almost lost his grip. The grit on the pots made his fingers slip as he held onto the lip of the bucket.

"Mmhmm." Daniel grunted back, as he caught a glimpse of Rose through the tree limbs. She was looking over at him as well, smiling.

"To be honest, I just recently met her through Mrs. Bailey. She needed me to run an errand for her."

They dropped the tree and it thudded into the dirt.

"I'm j-just getting to know her."

He batted the grit and dirt from his hands.

"Have you asked her out?"

He didn't know what to say, but before he could answer, Pete hit the brim of his cap down over his eyes.

"You better, boy, or I will!"

Daniel lifted his cap and rubbed his eyes. He jokingly pushed Pete away.

"Thanks for the help."

Pete left to lock the truck gate.

Rose was adjusting the sun visor on the stroller when he returned.

"Sorry about that."

He was still breathing hard from the effort.

"You're working. I think I'd better get Duncan home. I still have a few things to do around the apartment."

She handed him back the bag of fish food. Adjusting Duncan's hat, she stored the diaper bag underneath the stroller.

"Ah, R-Rose." He summoned what little courage he had. "Would you mind if I walked you home?"

He anticipated she'd decline his offer.

"Sure." She bit her lip and smiled.

"Great! Let me get permission from the boss, but it shouldn't be a problem. I'll be right back."

He hightailed it over to Mr. Bailey who was taking stock of the storeroom.

"Can I walk her home, Mr. Bailey?"

"Walk who home?"

"Rose Dorset."

"I don't see why not." He playfully nudged Daniel's arm. "Tell her I said hello."

"Most definitely." Daniel turned to leave.

"Hey, Dan, before I forget... Did you get a chance to text Will back?" He looked up from his reading glasses.

"Oh, uh, I completely forgot! I'm gonna do it now. Thanks for the reminder."

Daniel pulled out his cell phone from his back pocket and hollered over to Rose, "I'll meet you in the front!"

She waved back.

Daniel read Will's text again:

"Hey, Danny. Long time no talk. I was at Falls the other day and thought you might like to get together. Put a few ones back. Call me."

He was disappointed that his brother took his sobriety so lightly. Maybe Will didn't know what to say, but Daniel was tired of making excuses for him.

"Hey, Will. Let's meet at Deer Pond for some fishing tomorrow night instead."

He took a breath and pressed send, then hurriedly handed Mr. Bailey the fish food.

"Good luck, son." Mr. Bailey winked at him.

☾

At Deer Pond there was a chill in the air. When Daniel arrived, Will's black truck was already there. He waved over to him and grabbed the fishing poles and tackle box in the back of the truck.

All day at the nursery, Daniel's anxiety had been building, anticipating this moment. He feared Will and for good reason. Will was reckless and brash in every area of his life. He was all sharp edges.

Daniel knocked the tackle box against his leg to distract himself.

From what he'd heard around town, Will wasn't sober, and, in certain circles, he had a notorious reputation for getting drunk and picking up women. Daniel wasn't really worried he'd want to drink with him again. He was more worried that he'd want to drink to calm himself down after fishing with Will.

Paul told him he could text him any time. He also reminded Daniel that it would be a very different relationship than the one they'd had before. They would have to get to know each other again as men and not boys. They'd also have to find things to do together that didn't involve drinking, which would be tough. Will managed to make drinking a part of every waking activity.

After all this time, Daniel still wasn't sure why he was so intimidated by Will—why he felt so weak when he was around him. Daniel was different now. He didn't need to fear him. He could make his own choices and was free to live his own life—chart his own course. He wasn't Will's puppet anymore.

Taking a few deep breaths, he concentrated on the creak of the tackle box as it hit against his thigh. He was here to fish and get to know his brother again. He was here to build a bridge, as Mr. Bailey would say.

"Sorry, I'm late."

Will was smoking and dug the butt of his cigarette into the dirt. Wearing a worn flannel shirt and jeans, Daniel noticed his baseball hat. It was the same one Will wore when he helped coach his high school's baseball team a few years ago.

"What's that old hunk of junk you're driving?"

Will looked over at Sugar.

"That's Mr. Bailey's truck. He let me b-borrow it."

Daniel bent over and placed the tackle box down.

"How've you been? How's life at the house?"

Will walked over and gave him a hug.

"It's been g-good for me, but I'm thinking I may try to get a place on my own sometime soon. I'll probably look somewhere closer to work."

Did he really mean what he was saying to Will? The words came out of nowhere.

"Well, good for you," Will said as he took out some bait. "I'll have to come over and help you move out of that shit hole."

He patted Daniel hard on the back.

He let the comment pass.

"By the way, I got a call from Dad the other day. He asked how you were doing. He was curious how the sober house was going and seemed real interested in what you were up to. I told him I didn't know much. He was wondering if we both wanted to come over to his new girlfriend's house for dinner. I told him you probably weren't interested."

Daniel was uncomfortable with the fact that Will had spoken for him, especially when his feelings on the subject may have changed.

"Thanks for passing on the message. I'll try and reach out. W-What's going on with you, Will?"

He untangled his line.

"Nothing much. Work, Falls, home, and an occasional girl here and there."

Will cast his line into the dark water and made a rude gesture with his hands.

"What about you? Got a girl or do they not let you have girls at that place?"

"T-There might be someone."

He let it slip out and then kicked himself for saying something. It probably wasn't the best idea letting Will into his personal life just yet.

"Well, well, well, little brother's gettin' some." Will chuckled to himself. "Little brother's got a piece on the side."

"N-No—it's not like that."

Daniel quickly tried to shut down the conversation.

He was getting the distinct feeling building a bridge with Will would take some time. It wouldn't happen overnight. They were almost on two separate levels and didn't have much in common anymore. And if he wasn't going to talk about drinking with Will, and Rose was off-limits, what would they talk about?

The whole thing felt impossible. If he wasn't willing to stoop as low as Will and Will wasn't willing to get his mind out of the gutter, there probably wasn't any use in continuing the connection.

But just as Daniel was about to give up hope, an idea popped into his head. And, at this point, he'd do anything to find a way to reconnect. It was really now or never. He was either willing to build a bridge or he wasn't.

Taking a leap of faith, he gave it his best shot. Against his better judgment, he opened himself up wide.

"Will? Do you ever remember your dreams when you wake up?"

"Not really. I usually pass out and don't remember shit."

Will broke out another cigarette from a pack he kept in his shirt pocket. He swatted some gnats away from his face. The cigarette hung from his mouth.

Daniel threw his line into the water again.

"I usually don't either. I sleep p-pretty soundly, but for the past three nights in a row I've had the same dream—the exact same dream. The people, the place, the feelings are all the same. It's kinda weird, but it's also r-really clear."

He was rattled by it. All the details were the same, and he woke up each time with a feeling of warmth permeating his body.

"And…" Will said, taking another drag of his cigarette. "This is some fascinating shit, Danny."

"A-And, uh." He swallowed hard. "I have this dream where I'm on a train with a little boy sitting next to me and we're headed into an orange sunset. Across the aisle is a beautiful woman looking out the window. The cabin is filled with a warm, orange glow. All I can do is stare at her hands, which are folded in her lap."

He reeled in his line.

"I'm looking over at her hands and I-I notice she's wearing a gold ring. The next thing I know, the sun hits the ring in just the right spot and the glare b-blinds me for a second. That's when I wake up."

He finished his story and hoped Will wouldn't make another sarcastic remark, making him regret ever telling him something so personal.

"That's pretty strange. Three nights, you say?" Will was frowning, as if he was actually considering the dream and taking what Daniel said seriously.

"Yah, three nights in a row."

He threw his line back in the water.

"Do you think someone's trying to tell you something? Like a ghost or something?"

Will undulated his voice to make his question sound spooky.

But for some reason, what Will said struck a chord. It hadn't really occurred to him until that very moment, but yes, maybe someone was trying to tell him something. But who? And what?

Will quieted down and Daniel sensed he was probably anxious to move on to other topics. Thankfully, it wasn't long before the gnats really got going and they had to pack up their gear.

"Let's do this again, little brother. I've missed all the shit we used to do together. I know you had to go to the sober house, but damn, it hasn't been the same without you. Our house is way too quiet. Maybe we could shoot some hoops together. The net's still up."

The bugs started to swarm the pond, flying like a moveable carpet. Will grabbed Daniel's fishing poles and put them in the back of the truck for him.

"I'd like that," Daniel said, wondering if he really meant it or was he just saying it to make Will feel better.

"Hey, Danny." Will opened his truck bed. "I'm serious. If you ever do get a girl, I wanna meet her."

He slammed the truck bed closed. Daniel winced.

"Thanks, W-Will. Let's keep in touch."

He waved goodbye and got in the truck.

He sat there, and for the life of him, he couldn't understand why he'd told Will about his dream. Of all people, he told Will! It didn't make any sense.

Maybe he'd told Will because it was haunting him, and he couldn't let it go. To be honest, he couldn't find a good reason why he'd told him. But he may have given him something to think about.

As he watched Will's truck drive away and the sun melt like butter into the pond, he thought about the laughs he shared with Will growing up, when they used to drink together. He remembered being happy with him, but somehow the happiness he felt with him always faded away to an empty feeling. Having fun with Will usually translated to regret later on.

And it got Daniel thinking about how happiness can feel different with certain people. With Will it felt hollow. But when he thought about Rose at the koi pond, feeding the fish and the warm smile they shared, the happiness that filled his heart seemed to get bigger. It even expanded. It filled his heart so much, he could feel it even now.

He shut his eyes and found himself saying a quiet prayer to himself. Ever since he'd started AA, it was becoming more of a natural habit. He liked talking to God. Bowing his head, he let a wordless prayer form in his heart.

And suddenly, he sat straight up.

Alarm bells went off inside of his head. It was almost as if he'd put his finger in a live socket. He felt jolted awake.

"The woman in my dream, the woman in my dream is Rose!" he said aloud.

It was Rose, and that little boy was Duncan! Why hadn't he thought of that before? He couldn't believe it hadn't dawned on him sooner. He felt something lift off him. It was almost as if a fog cleared in his head. Was this what some people called a moment of clarity? It sure as hell felt like one. One moment his head was full of thoughts and feelings he didn't completely understand, and the next moment, he felt clear, steady—certain.

He'd never experienced anything like it before. And the fear he'd carried with him his entire life was gone now too. The dog that never left his side had suddenly vanished. He'd never felt this certain about anything in his whole entire life. He couldn't believe it, but right then and there, he made a decision that would change his life forever. But was it really clarity or was he just plain crazy?

Daniel needed to get back to the nursery and talk to Mr. Bailey. He looked at his watch. He backed out of the lot. It was hard to contain himself. He knew Mr. Bailey would be expecting him because he'd borrowed Sugar and the fishing poles. But making a right onto Searchlight Drive, he started to worry about how Mr. Bailey would take his sudden news.

He didn't have a great track record for making the best decisions in the past, and he didn't want to disappoint him or have him think he was relapsing. Even though their discussion would be difficult, Daniel was willing to take a chance and share with him what he planned on doing. He deserved to know the truth, no matter how absurd.

Daniel knew his motives would be suspect on account of his alcoholism. He knew his behaviors and actions were constantly being dissected and analyzed, not only by him, but by others as well. Since he hadn't been very trustworthy in the past, it was only natural they would be suspicious. But this feeling of clarity wouldn't, no, couldn't be ignored. It was coming from a place deep inside him that was good—that was pure. He couldn't betray it.

He pulled into the nursery and slammed on the breaks. He flew out of Sugar, forgetting to shut the door behind him. Scanning the nursery, he caught a glimpse of Mr. Bailey over by the hydrangeas. He was bent over moving some plants. Daniel started running, and his legs couldn't get him there fast enough.

Rose

Rose's 18th Birthday

"And you're listening to WFCC, 107.5, your Cape Cod classical station." Rose adjusted the volume on her grandmother's old radio, the one she'd inherited after her passing. The 40's station they used to listen to wasn't airing anymore, but Plymouth was close enough to the Upper Cape to pick up the classical station.

Lately, she was in the habit of going up to the rooftop garden after she'd put Duncan to bed in his crib. She would grab the baby monitor and stop by Marissa's apartment to let her know where she was going as an extra precaution. Sometimes Luzia would come and sit in front of Rose's door playing with her Barbie collection until she came back down.

The rooftop garden consisted of an old beach chair, discarded plastic flowerpots, a withered tomato vine, and some twinkle lights. It wasn't much, but it was enough of a space and a view to help her mind wander, allowing her to find some peace of mind and reclaim a small portion of her youth. However, since this morning, she was now officially considered an adult. She didn't feel like much of one though on the inside, the place where it mattered the most.

Taking a mug of hot tea with her and a cupcake with a single candle in it, she repositioned her beach chair to get a better view of the harbor. She also brought a blanket with her to keep warm. Tonight, the boats were all specks and the gull's cries were muted. But on certain nights when the wind blew just right, she could smell the ocean. For an hour or so on the rooftop, she daydreamed.

Rose was aware her old plans would take more time to come to fruition and she was resolved not to give up. Her dreams for her life remained the same, but with Duncan they would need to be altered a bit—okay, a lot.

College was still on the table, but she'd require family housing now. She may even go to night school if she could afford a babysitter. And ever since Carrie's death, she'd been thinking about becoming a nurse. The kindness they showed her, the gentleness, how sweet they were to her, made her want to do the same for someone else.

Everything would just take more time. Time was both an enemy and a friend. It was abundant and felt as if it was running out all at the same time. Her thoughts turned to Carrie and then to Duncan and finally to herself.

Before Carrie's death, she'd worked hard to prepare for college. Now it felt like the brakes had been slammed on.

A few nights ago, Rose realized she needed to make time her friend. Time was not being stolen from her, instead, it was being given to her. It was a gift. Gratitude was becoming a recurrent theme in her life.

However, for all her efforts to be thankful she was not immune to tears, especially when she was alone. The rooftop was now becoming the place she came to cry and surrender her sorrows. She took a sip from her mug.

Rose knew she'd made a choice to do something hard, maybe something even insurmountable. And since her mother had informed her at the funeral that she wanted nothing to do with baby, she knew she was on her own.

Her mother had encouraged Rose to give Duncan up for adoption to a good home, but Rose had refused. She knew blessings would come, just in different ways. And just because something was hard, didn't mean there wasn't any goodness in it. It didn't mean there wasn't any joy to be found. Duncan was worth the effort. He was her family now and families stick together, or at least she thought they should.

She also understood her mistakes would need to be smaller now because they were mistakes that would affect Duncan as well. There was a threshold of how far she could fall and at eighteen there were still so many things she didn't know. There were so many hidden pitfalls and trapdoors. But there was one mistake she knew she'd never make and that was letting go of Duncan. She'd never, ever do that.

Picking up her vanilla-sprinkled cupcake, she lit the candle and cupped her hands around the dancing flame.

"Make a wish, Rose," she whispered to herself.

She closed her eyes and blew out the candle.

As she sat back listening to the harbor bell toll in the distance, Rose let her thoughts wander to Daniel. She wondered where he was and what he was doing. Was he thinking of her too? She smiled when she thought about feeding the fish and a warmth filled her heart when she remembered the walk home. Feeling half asleep from the busy day and sea air, she shut her eyes.

But she suddenly woke to the red light flashing wildly on the baby monitor beside her.

Picking it up, there was loud knocking at her front door. She faintly heard her name being called. The voice didn't sound familiar. She immediately tensed up and stopped breathing so she could listen. The hairs rose on her arms and the back of her neck. Who could it be?

Quietly getting up from the beach chair, she tiptoed down the side stairs barely breathing, and slowly craned her head around the corner.

The forceful knocking made the monitor streak red in her hand. It took her a second to recognize who was standing there.

Daniel

He'd never asked a woman to marry him before. He wasn't sure of the right words to say. He'd never had a steady girlfriend, or truthfully, any girlfriend at all for that matter. Only kissing a girl about a handful of times in his life, he was beyond inexperienced with women.

When he told Mr. Bailey at the nursery of his intentions, Mr. Bailey told him that whatever he had to say to Rose, flowers would most likely come in handy. Mr. Bailey also warned that he should listen to this prompting only if he thought it was coming directly from God. Daniel told him it had, although he couldn't prove it to anyone. There was no evidence of it. Mr. Bailey would just have to take his word for it.

Thankfully, he didn't ask a bunch of questions. Mr. Bailey mostly kept quiet when he told him the news, but he kept on dusting his hands on his pant leg and adjusting his hat a lot. Daniel hoped Mr. Bailey knew that his feelings and intentions were sincere and firm. There was definitely evidence of that. Hopefully, that would be of some consolation to him.

As he left, Mr. Bailey held up his hand and said he'd be praying for him. At this point, Daniel could use all the prayer he could get. But a thick line across Mr. Bailey's forehead gave away his deep worry.

Also, there was no guarantee she'd say yes. And, if she said no, that was probably confirmation he was a complete idiot, and the dream was only just a dream and nothing more.

On the drive over to her apartment, he wondered what she'd think of him. They'd only known each other for a few days, or more accurately, a few hours. He hadn't even held her hand. What if she thought he was a lunatic? What if she tried to call the cops? Daniel could think of a thousand reasons not to go through with it, but only one reason really mattered.

If it wasn't for this feeling driving him forward, compelling him, he probably would've tried to forget it—explain it away. But he needed, no, he had to ask Rose Dorset to marry him. He could barely believe it himself. *What was he thinking?*

When he arrived at her apartment, he got out of the truck and wiped his palms on the back of his jeans. They still smelled like bait. He took off his hat and fixed his hair as best he could in Sugar's side-view mirror. He gave himself a light slap in the face and checked his teeth to see if he had any food in them.

He bounded up the apartment steps two at a time and knocked on her door. No one answered. He knocked again with the side of his fist and still no one answered. Just as he was going to knock a third time, he looked over and saw Rose peek her head around the corner near the stairwell. The worried look on her face melted into a smile.

"Come up to the rooftop," she whispered over to him.

Daniel followed her up the stairs. The rooftop was peppered with discarded flowerpots and a few abandoned Christmas trees. A fallen clothesline lay in the corner. It was silent except for the occasional passing car on the street below, and he faintly heard classical music coming from her radio.

When he got there, it looked like she'd been watching the same sunset from an old beach chair facing the harbor. He thought she'd be more surprised to see him, but in a strange way, she wasn't. She asked if he wanted to sit down, but he told her he preferred to stand. What he had to say to her didn't feel like a moment he should be off his feet.

She had a blanket wrapped around her shoulders and next to her chair was a half-eaten cupcake and burned-down candle. In the twilight, with the lights of the town twinkling behind her head, she looked achingly beautiful.

Where should he begin? He dug his hands deeper into his pockets. He wasn't sure. He hadn't really thought it through. What should he say? Should he start with the dream? His moment of clarity? He couldn't decide. All of it would sound too hokey. He bit his lip.

How come everything had felt so certain only a few moments before, but now he wasn't certain at all? Without thinking, he reached out to hold her hand, and she let him. The certainty came rushing back to him.

"R-Rose, I need to ask you something. I know it won't make much sense to you," he started. "But I want to ask you to trust me. Can you do that for me?"

She nodded her head.

He took a deep breath and looked into her eyes. She stood silently looking back at him. The expression on her face a little uncertain.

"G-Gosh, I'm not sure I can explain it all to you right now, but I think—I think—I'm in love with you."

He spoke softly so he wouldn't scare her.

"There's something between us that I can't get out of my head. I-I think you feel it too. So, ah, I'm just going to say it. H-Here it goes."

God help me.

After a long pause, he bent down on one knee.

"Will you, will you marry me?"

Some words that are said linger in the air and you want to claw them back, but these words floated over to her from the depths of his soul. He didn't want these words back.

He'd brought the bouquet of flowers Mr. Bailey had helped him gather at the nursery before he left, but he'd put them down on the ground beside him when he proposed. All Daniel could offer Rose were his empty hands. Would they be enough?

He looked up at her and waited. He barely breathed. He had trusted the dream and followed his heart. Now the rest would be up to her and God.

Without saying a word, she helped him to his feet and drew him near. He'd never felt the curve of her hips or smelled the sweetness of her hair up close. He started to tremble, and she wrapped the blanket around them both. He leaned into her, pressing his whole body against hers.

"I, ah, can't believe I'm saying this, but—yes."

She looked puzzled by her own answer.

"Yes, Daniel, I'll marry you."

She put her arms around him.

Rose

She was up early the next morning, feeling like she was floating on air. She'd barely slept all night. Walking into the kitchen, she put on the kettle. Dark circles had formed underneath her hazel eyes. Gathering up her hair, she put it in a messy bun to get it out of her face and rubbed her eyes. *Was she still dreaming?*

Replaying the events of last night in her head, she laughed out loud to herself.

Duncan was taking his morning nap in the other room. She'd have a few minutes to herself, maybe enough time to let it all sink in. Rose picked up the phone to call Dottie and asked her to come over.

"I'll be over there in two flicks of a lamb's tail."

She barely finished her breakfast before she heard Dottie's heavy footsteps coming down the hallway.

"Hi, doll!"

Dottie's voice went from full volume to a whisper when she realized Duncan was still sleeping.

"I had an appointment with Grace over at the salon this morning at ten, but you sounded so desperate I just had to cancel."

Dottie must really love her because that was quite a sacrifice.

As Dottie walked into Rose's apartment, she stopped abruptly.

"Hold on! Hold on! Hold on!"

She held out her hands, feeling the air around her.

"Give me a minute, something feels new. It feels like there's been a change in here."

Dottie was good at picking up on things that went unspoken.

"I'm gonna be honest with you, doll. I'm not quite sure what's going on, but you look a little different too. Wait a second, are those new curtains? Did you get a new couch or something?"

She searched the room for a clue, like a bloodhound.

"No, no nothing like that."

Rose stepped out of her way as she walked around the apartment.

"Are you feeling all right? Come over here." Dottie put her hand up to Rose's forehead.

"No, I'm fine, Dott." Rose took down her hand. "I'm good."

"Trish at work was telling me there's something going around this summer. It's like a watery-eyes, stomachy, coughy-thing, and just about everyone is coming down with it. Is that what's going on here? Are you sick, Rosie?"

Rose shook her head.

Dottie paused for a second and then suddenly had a new revelation.

"Sugar, is it Duncan?" Her eyes got wider. "Is it my sweet baby? Is he sick?"

"No," Rose said, stifling a laugh.

"My feelers are twitching. I know there's been a big change. I'll get there. You just give Dottie a second to figure it out."

Searching for the right words to say, Rose took a deep breath.

"I'm not sure how to tell you this, so you'd better come sit down. Let's get you off your feet, Dott."

Rose guided her to the couch and pulled up a chair to sit in front of her. She took her hand. It was warm and soft, like her grandmother's used to be. She patted the top of it and looked in her eyes.

"What's goin' on?"

Dottie wasn't willing to beat around the bush any longer.

"Okay, here it goes." There was a long pause and then Rose spoke calmly—steadily.

"Dottie, a man named Daniel has asked me to, uh, marry him, and I've said yes."

She closed one eye, waiting for Dottie to start yelling at her, but all Dottie did was stare at her with her mouth wide open. She didn't speak or move. *Was she breathing?*

"I know what everyone is going to think, that I'm off-my-rocker or that I'm in shock from Carrie's death. But I want you to know, I'm not. I promise!" Rose started to tear up. "I don't think I can explain how I'm feeling in words, but I want you to know I believe I'm making the right decision."

She instinctively knew, no overexplaining would clarify the situation. Added words would only muddy the whole thing up. It was so off-the-wall she knew her arguments and defenses would only fall on deaf ears if she tried.

The apartment was completely silent for longer than she liked. It was so quiet, Rose heard Dottie's stomach gurgling.

"Dottie, can you hear me? Do you know what I'm saying to you?"

Rose was now worried she'd sent Dottie off the deep end. She waved her hand in front of her face. Dottie continued to blankly stare off into space, her expression frozen.

"I didn't know it was happening at the time or what to even call it. But I think I've fallen in love with him, if you can do it in that short of a time."

Dottie finally moved. Sitting back deeper into the couch, she squinted her eyes and put a finger up to her mouth.

"Honey, I'd have believed you more if you'd told me you'd been abducted by aliens!" She tapped her finger on her chin. "Just give Ol' Dottie a minute to catch her breath and think on this."

Dottie pulled out a portable fan she kept in her purse and held it up to her face.

"Doll, I'm gonna want you to start from the very beginning. I want to hear it all, and I mean all—everything. Don't leave anything out," she instructed.

"Sure, Dott, but we only have a few hours until the ceremony this afternoon and I was hoping you'd help me get ready."

"Well then, you're going to need to start talking fast."

She sat back into the couch and got comfortable.

Daniel

He strapped his watch around his left wrist, the one he only wore for special occasions, and ran a black toothed comb through his knotted hair. A strand that curled near his right widow's peak was turned in the opposite direction. He attempted to fix it as best he could, but it always fell back to the same location. He was dressed in his best navy suit.

He looked down, held on to the dresser with both hands and took a shallow breath, exhaling loudly. A single drop of sweat from his forehead fell onto his brown wingtip shoe. *God, be with me—and please be with Rose.*

The wedding was taking place near the flower beds at Bailey's Nursery in just a few minutes—at dusk, as the blue sky dissolved into blurry clouds of pink and orange cotton candy.

Mr. Bailey had agreed to perform the ceremony along with his friend, Father Callahan. The two men were acquainted through some ecumenical and volunteer programs around town and attended many of the same functions. Rose had requested Father Callahan's presence today and Mr. Bailey had no hesitations contacting him to attend the ceremony.

Earlier in the day, Father Callahan had gone by the nursery to drop off an antique mantel clock as a wedding gift. He'd bought it downtown in one of the antique shops on Main Street. The card was inscribed:

"Dear Rose & Daniel,

Some hours are long and some days are short. Find time to cherish the small moments. Best wishes on your journey as husband and wife.

Fondly, Father Callahan."

Hopping out of Sugar, Daniel walked past the shop and hanging baskets, past the koi pond and greenhouses, and saw Mr. and Mrs. Bailey arranging a few chairs for the ceremony. He caught a whiff of honeysuckle as he passed by it.

The plants and flowers were adorned with twinkle lights and the overhead lights in the greenhouses were turned on. Mrs. Bailey had planted foxgloves, lilies, irises, and peony in two large planters for a makeshift altar. The white chairs were laced with vines and pink ribbons. On a CD player at the front, a flute's high notes floated in the warm summer air like the seeds of a dandelion.

Daniel slowly walked down the aisle and stood next to Mr. Bailey in the front. Sinking his hands into his pockets, they were clammy. His heart raced in his chest and his legs slightly trembled. Playing with the rings in his pocket, Daniel stacked them on his pinky finger and twisted them.

Mr. Bailey occasionally leaned over and asked him questions, but he couldn't quite hear them. He smiled and hoped that was enough of an answer.

Drops of sweat rolled down his back and pooled at the bottom of his shirt. He wiped his brow with a white hanky he kept inside his coat pocket.

Watching a woman walk down the aisle with Duncan in her arms, he suspected Rose had arrived. A sweet little girl was carrying a basket full of flower petals and was practicing her technique at throwing them. The sun was still bright, but setting, as Rose turned the corner.

It looked as if she was walking out of the sun's rays. Raising a hand to block the sun from his eyes, he noticed she was in a beautiful white dress with small lace sleeves. In her hair, she wore a crown of braided flowers and ribbons. She held a small bouquet of pink peony in her hands. A string of white pearls fell from her milky neck.

The song changed on the CD player to *Clair de Lune*, and Rose walked toward him.

For the first time all afternoon, he took a slow, deep breath and wondered if he was dreaming—if this was all real.

As she stood next to him, her perfume, warmed by her body, smelled of orange blossoms. And even though there was a warm breeze, her arms were speckled with goosebumps and she shivered a little.

Looking down at her smallish hands, he'd never noticed a small scar near her left wrist. Her fingers were long, and her nails were painted with clear polish. Strands of ginger hair framed the sides of her face.

As Mr. Bailey spoke, he couldn't take his eyes off her. He held her hands through the entire ceremony, only letting go to place a thin gold band on her left ring finger.

When she said the words "I do" after him, he knew it had happened.

By some alchemy of words and sacred text, by some mixture of human and divine law, they were forever bonded. By earthly contract or heavenly covenant, at this moment in time, a unique compound was formed. The world felt a little different because of it. The air was charged all around them.

"Last but not least, you may now kiss the bride."

These last words came into crystal clear focus. He paused for a second, then took a small step closer to her. Taking her face in his hands, he kissed her soft lips twice.

"Please help me in celebrating, Mr. and Mrs. Daniel and Rose Goodman."

The small crowd applauded. She squeezed his hand tighter, and they walked down the aisle together.

If Rose was having second thoughts about the whole thing, she didn't show it. Daniel couldn't believe the first time he'd kissed her was at their wedding just a few minutes ago.

Rose was now his wife, and he was now her husband.

Mr. Bailey's words in the ceremony had still not left him—"then two shall become one." Not only were he and Rose stronger together, but they'd also created something new. Two people who were at first separate were now two parts of the same whole.

Mr. Bailey offered Sugar to them, but he and Rose wanted to walk home. They needed the extra time to get to know one another. A long walk would be good, but would it be enough? Because even though he was arranging a lot of this, much of it still seemed out of his hands.

Last night on the rooftop, he'd told her about the sober house and how he got there. It was the fast forward version of his journey, but there was still so much to tell. At least he wanted to get all the major stuff out there, so there were no big surprises. While Rose seemed startled at first, she was more accepting than he expected. She spoke of Carrie's struggles and of her notebook filled with the details of her own journey. It was now in the back of Rose's closet and was left unopened.

He was surprised at how well she'd taken his news. He didn't expect such compassion. She listened without judgment and didn't try to interrupt until he had finished. Placing her hand on top of his, she squeezed. And he thought, although he wasn't sure, that he saw a tear form in her eye.

Daniel didn't know the first thing about Rose—her favorite food, favorite color, or what type of music she liked to listen to. He knew it would all come in time, something they had plenty of. He just needed to be patient.

But the unasked and unanswered questions swam somewhere above his head, which both excited and unnerved him. In his fervor to know everything about her, he also worried if he'd be enough for her. He worried if his answers would satisfy her, and that in the fullness of time, she wouldn't stop asking questions of him.

Pushing the stroller home, he wasn't sure what Rose expected of him when they got there. He wanted to let her decide when she was ready to be with him. There was no way he was forcing this woman to sleep with him. He was willing to wait, if she wanted, for however long it took. He'd just be there when she was ready.

There was also Duncan to think about.

How could he forget that little guy? He was now a permanent part of his family. Before he got too carried away thinking about his possible wedding night, there were some practical things they needed to do, like change his diaper and give him a bath. It was hard to believe, but he was now a father too. The ceremony today made him more than a husband.

It got him thinking again. Today, three had become one.

Daniel wasn't sure how experienced Rose was with men. She was beautiful both inside and out, so he suspected she'd had at least a few boyfriends.

As for him, he didn't know if he was a virgin anymore. He thought back to the girl at the gas station. But he decided, if Rose asked him about it, he'd tell her the truth. He didn't want to lie to her. She deserved to know everything. She'd trusted him with her whole life.

At least he knew with Rose, it would be his first time in a lot of ways. But he was getting ahead of himself.

Daniel took off his jacket and draped it around Rose's shoulders as they walked home. When they arrived at the apartment, it was Duncan's bedtime. Rose gave him a quick tour of their apartment and pointed out all of Duncan's essential items. Before they could be alone, Duncan needed to be changed, bathed, and fed. She wanted to teach him how to do it tonight.

"I think you'll be great at it!"

Rose's enthusiasm gave him some much-needed confidence. He'd never really held a baby before, and especially one that was now his.

"What if I drop him?"

"You'll do fine."

Rose touched his arm for reassurance.

"Babies are slippery."

He looked at her.

This was going to sound crazy, but he enjoyed taking care of Duncan, even on his wedding night. It wasn't strange but felt natural. He felt close to Duncan in a way he couldn't explain. He loved him already—if that was even possible.

Rose was a good teacher. She made sure he got under the folds of Duncan's pudgy arms and legs, and then she let Daniel feed him. As he sat in the rocker, it sunk in how helpless Duncan really was.

Deep down, he was thankful Duncan was here with them. He acted like a buffer for the awkward moments that occasionally popped up between Rose and him. Instead of putting all their attention on what had just happened and what may possibly happen later, they could both just focus on Duncan for a little while. He made the stretches of silences less uncomfortable.

Finally, it was time for Duncan to go to bed and Rose showed him how to do that too. Daniel rocked him until his eyes were half closed, then quietly walked him over to his crib. He softly patted him on his belly to reassure him before he left the room.

Rose and Daniel were now alone.

It was quiet in the apartment except for the intermittent static coming from the baby monitor. Rose stood on one side of the living room and he on the other. They smiled at each other, and both looked at the floor every now and then.

As Rose twisted her hair around her finger, he knew it was his job to somehow break the ice. He'd only been to her apartment twice before, once to deliver the basket for Duncan and the other to propose. It must've felt odd for her to have him standing there.

Daniel wanted to hold her and tell her it would all be okay, but he knew he had to restrain himself. He didn't want to scare her.

Just breathe. Be patient.

"How—How are you holding up?" he asked.

"Good. I think I'm good. Maybe a little tired."

She played with her hands.

"A-Are you hungry? Did you get enough to eat?"

"Yah, a little. You?"

"Mrs. Bailey's red velvet wedding cake was pretty rich. I'm not sure how she pulled it off with such short notice."

He smiled awkwardly.

"She seems like the person to turn to in a pinch."

Rose smiled back.

"Y-Yah, I guess she is."

Daniel wasn't sure what to do with his hands. He shoved them in his pockets, then took them out and scratched the top of his head.

"Uh—"

Rose interrupted him. "Did you want to watch something? Or I could start setting up the couch."

She looked down at the carpet.

"No—No, that's all right. I-I can do that myself. Where do you keep the sheets and blankets?"

"They're in here."

Rose left the room to get the bedding. He waited in the living room. When she returned, it suddenly occurred to him they'd forgotten something important. Grabbing his cell phone, the baby monitor, and an empty glass, he walked up to her.

"Rose, come with me?"

He held out his hand.

"W-Where are we going?" she asked, tilting her head.

"You'll see."

She placed the pillow and blanket on the couch, grabbed the front door key, and followed him up to the rooftop.

"You're gonna love this trick," he said, and placed his cell phone in the empty glass, making it a makeshift speaker.

He plugged in the twinkle lights that were connected to a green extension cord around the side.

"Will you dance with me?"

They leaned into one another, and she put her head on his shoulder.

"Thank you," was all he could think to say to her. "Thank you, Rose."

And she raised her head to kiss his lips.

His heart ached in his chest. He'd never felt this way before. If she would have him, he wanted to be with her tonight.

As the song ended, she whispered, "I'm so happy to be your wife."

And she took his hand and led him down the steps to their apartment.

Rose

R ose let Daniel sleep as she quietly got out from under the covers. She heard Duncan stirring in the next room through the monitor. He was probably up for the day. Finding her robe on the back of the door, she slipped it on and couldn't help but notice a pile of clothes lying on the floor. She blushed.

It was strange to see a man's clothes on her floor. She noticed how big Daniel's shoes were and the length of his belt. Picking up his button-down shirt, she smelled it and placed it neatly on the chair in the corner of her room. Grabbing his pants, she folded them along the seam and noticed a small hole in one of his brown socks. His watch sat on her dresser.

Looking over at him lying in her bed, at his sandy hair on her pillow, she couldn't believe he was there. Was it a dream? And then she remembered how gently he'd made love to her, but also how totally unprepared she was for what happened. She'd never been with anyone before and had only kissed a guy at a junior formal. But when Daniel undressed her, she stifled a laugh. And when he tried to unhook her bra, she reached back and tried to help, although she could tell he wanted to figure it out for himself. When she saw him for the first time, all of him, she looked away and stared at the floor—her cheeks burned.

Under the covers, lying next to him, she'd trembled. Scared, she kissed his lips like they were an oxygen mask keeping her from fainting. And even though she was frightened, she also wasn't prepared for the pleasure. The feeling that grew insider her and left her shivering afterwards. And how she felt warm, salty tears tumble down her cheeks when it was all over. In the dark, she wondered if Daniel might be crying too.

After he'd fallen asleep beside her, she lay in the dark and touched all the places he had already been—tracing her own body like a map.

Walking out of the bedroom, she turned off the monitor and got Duncan from his crib.

As she changed him, she noticed he looked bigger every day. He had Carrie's eyes and the shape of her nose, even her forehead. Carefully taking off his onesie, she kissed him all over his belly. He giggled. His simple joy was intoxicating. She played peek-a-boo and gave him a squeaky toy to keep him occupied while she pulled on his pants and socks.

She also wanted to make Daniel breakfast before he woke. How strange it would be when he walked into the kitchen. Would he have a shirt on?

Duncan squirmed under her hand on the changing table. She stared at him for a moment and then bent to pick him up. And unexpectedly, like a rogue wave in the ocean, doubt crashed down on her.

Was this really what Daniel wanted? Was she what he wanted? Were his feelings for her real? Were they honest? Had she made a huge mistake?

Holding Duncan's body close to hers, she closed her eyes and said a small prayer for them.

"God help me," was all she could muster. "Please, be with me and Duncan." She rocked him gently in her arms.

Rose opened the refrigerator door and placed Duncan in the bouncy seat next to the table. She whispered over to Duncan, "What do you think he likes to eat?"

Duncan looked at Rose nonplussed as he chewed on his plastic squeaky toy.

"I suppose I'll make him a little bit of everything."

She decided on oatmeal, toast with jam, and scrambled eggs. Did he like coffee or tea? Milk or sugar? Strawberry or grape?

As she bit her fingernail, she noticed her hand still slightly trembling.

Daniel

He rubbed his eyes open and felt an unfamiliar mattress beneath him. There was a small dip in the center of it. He lifted the sheets and saw a small floral pattern against a white background. Dark pink flowers were tied with a light blue ribbon. He lay there staring at the little bouquets and remembered where he was.

Out of the corner of his eye, he saw a dark-maple dresser and mirror, a chair, a desk in the far corner, and a small white nightstand next to the bed. He still felt sleepy as though he was dreaming, but he was in Rose's room. He was in their room.

He looked over at a mirrored tray on her dresser filled with different shaped perfume bottles—some small, some big, and some that were old and ornate. Tucked in the frame of her dresser mirror was a small picture of Carrie when she was a teenager. In a pewter cutout frame was a picture of Rose and Carrie when they were little girls. They wore pink dresses and had big tooth-gapped grins and looked almost identical, like they could've been twins.

Staring up at the ceiling, it wasn't long before his mind wandered to the night before. Just thinking about her sent a shiver through his body. Turning over, he looked down at the hardwood floors and caught a peek of her white-lace bra underneath her wedding dress still lying on the floor. He remembered trying to undo the clasp. At the time, his hands were shaking, and he wondered if she noticed. Running his fingers up and down her milky skin, he didn't know a woman's skin could feel so soft. He moved her hair to the side and kissed the top of her shoulder. She turned her head to meet his lips. Everything about Rose felt soft and sweet and comforting—like coming home.

But he also remembered how clumsy they started out. He laughed a little thinking about how she knocked his chin with her elbow and how his body weight got too heavy for her, and she couldn't take a breath. She pushed him up with her arms and moved him to the side. And how her hair kept covering his eyes and tickling his nose.

But when the moment happened, it felt as if his heart would beat out of his chest. And a few seconds later, out of nowhere, tears came to his eyes. Before he fell asleep, he held her in his arms, and she rested on his chest. He wanted to protect her, comfort her—hold her until she fell asleep.

Looking down off the bed, Daniel saw Rose's heels on the floor. They were scuffed at the back. He remembered the color of her toenail polish that peeked through the top of her shoes when he carried her over the threshold of their apartment, while Duncan waited outside in the stroller.

After he scooped her up, he'd steadied himself. She wasn't heavy, but movie stars made it look easier than it really was. After he placed her on the ground, they looked at each other silently, maybe even a little awkwardly. Daniel's hands tingled at his sides. He felt the center of his cheeks heat up.

Putting one arm under his head, he turned to look at her alarm clock and saw the baby monitor. Rose's gold watch band rested on the nightstand.

Moving the clock toward him to see the time more clearly, he accidentally knocked over what looked like a bird's egg sitting on a pink-plastic toilet. The egg looked as though it had been broken before. There was a hairline crack around the center, but it was glued back together. It wobbled to the end of the nightstand. Just as it reached the edge, as it was ready to fall over, he caught it. If he'd let it fall a second time, it may not have recovered. Daniel put it back on the toilet and pushed it to a safer location on the nightstand.

He slowly swung his feet around and sat up naked on the side of the bed and yawned. Looking for his clothes, he found his shirt and pants neatly folded on a chair—his boxer shorts on the floor. He reached for them and stood to put them on. Finding his undershirt, he turned it right-side-out and slipped it over his head. Coiling up his belt, he placed it in his shoe and lined them up in front of her closet.

Through the bedroom door, he heard Rose talking to someone in the kitchen.

Making the bed, he pulled down the white-quilted comforter and pulled up the floral sheet. Straightening them out, he tucked them in at the sides.

Her wedding dress lay on the floor. Grabbing a hanger, he hung it up. Then placed her heels in front of the closet. He gently folded her bra and put it on top of the dresser and opened the bedroom door.

He cleared his throat.

Breakfast was being made in the kitchen, and Rose was singing to the radio while Duncan bounced in his seat.

As he turned the corner, the sun came in through the window. Turning to see him, he was stunned for a second time by his wife's beauty.

She walked over to greet him with a wooden spoon in her hand.

"Good morning, Daniel."

She bit her lip.

"G-Good morning."

He smiled out of the corner of his mouth.

Will

Waking up hung over, Will rolled over to check the messages on his phone. There was a text from Danny:

"Hey, Will. Do you have time to meet up today? I've got some news I want to tell you about. No rush if you're busy though."

Will dropped his phone on the nightstand and got up to use the bathroom. It was a good thing he and Danny were talking again. Fishing at Deer Pond had brought back good memories of the times they used to have together before everything went to hell.

He grabbed a cigarette and lit it, then took a long drag and coughed. Taking a swig of beer from a bottle on his nightstand, he spit it out because it was warm.

Before the O.U.I., they used to go dirt biking on a trail over on Jordan's Path. Will brought whiskey so they could look out over the cliff across from the quarry and get drunk. They always got pretty messed up together. A few times, they had to leave Danny's bike there and go back for it the next day. He was such a lightweight.

With Danny in his life again, Will hoped they could start all over again and be like brothers—like they were before. Hell, maybe Danny would consider moving back in with him, back into his old room. He'd clean it up for him. He'd get rid of all the dust and trash, get it back to the way it was before. It would be good to have a roommate again.

At Falls Tavern the night before, Will told Pat and Rusty about fishing with Danny. By the end of the story, and by the end of his fifth shot, he ended up making a toast to his brother.

"Here's to Danny," Will slurred his words a little. "Here's to Danny, my baby brother."

He raised a glass in the air.

"I love that little piece of shit."

Will texted back:

"You caught me on a good night. I'm free. Let's go fishing again. Deer Pond. Tonight. Tell me your news then."

Will pulled on his jeans and a t-shirt and grabbed his baseball cap. He had to go out and get some smokes and bait for tonight.

Rose

They made love for a second time that morning. With the bedroom bathed in morning light, Daniel stood at the side of the bed and kissed Rose's lips deeply. Looking into her eyes, he undid her robe and let it fall to the floor. She wasn't wearing anything underneath.

Pulling off his shirt from behind his head, he took off his boxers. He held her and she knew he wanted her. He laid her on the bed slowly, and, for a moment, the fear returned but then faded into the back of her head. She didn't feel like laughing this time. And when she looked at him, she didn't want to turn away.

Afterwards, they lay naked, sleeping in each other's arms, and Rose was shocked at how different her life was now. She never would have imagined a year ago being married and sleeping with a man.

In the past, she'd cringed at all the personal things at the store. Shy in a bathing suit, she remembered always needing to cover up. But how could she have gone from that to this in such a short period of time? And she wondered, for a moment, if her loneliness drove her to this place—to Daniel? Was the deep ache in her heart steering her decisions? Was what she'd done, marrying Daniel, just an excuse not to be alone?

Did she really love him?

With her head resting in the crook of his arm, she moved closer to him. Their breathing synced, rising and falling at the same pace. She gently touched the blonde hairs on his chest.

"Daniel?"

"Hmmm," he said, half-asleep.

"How did you know you cared for me? That, uh, we should get married?"

"I dunno, really. I-I just knew," Daniel said, and put his arm behind his head.

"Knew how…"

"I had this feeling, I mean, a thought. I still don't know what exactly to call it. It's hard to describe. I-I just knew this was what I needed to do. But had you said no to me, then I would've known it was only something I'd dreamed up. That it wasn't real. Love requires consent. It can't be forced. Even though I felt it on my end, didn't mean you felt it on y-yours."

"It can't be forced?" Rose repeated.

"No, love can't be forced."

He gently touched her hair.

"I love you, S.O., but you don't have to say it back."

He twirled a piece of her red hair around his index finger.

"Why do you call me S.O.?"

"Because."

"Because, why?"

"I'll tell you later."

He leaned down and kissed the top of her head.

A quietness settled into the room, and she liked feeling the warmth of his body next to hers. She snuggled into him and drifted to sleep—a surrendered sleep, a safe sleep—like nothing she'd ever experienced before.

But the stillness didn't last long. Duncan wasn't quite as flexible with his schedule and started to fuss through the monitor. Slipping out from under the covers, Daniel kissed Rose on the forehead.

"It's my turn. Take your time g-getting dressed."

Rose lay in bed listening to them both through the monitor. She heard Daniel greet Duncan with a warm hello, followed by a kissing sound. Rose also heard his failed attempts at changing his diaper.

"Oh g-gosh, Duncan. Stop p-peeing."

He fumbled for a diaper, as the monitor fell to the floor with a thud.

This morning they decided to take a walk with Duncan into town and, on their way back, stop by the nursery to pick up Sugar. Daniel needed to get some more boxes he'd packed up from the house.

The morning of the wedding, he was only able to pack a few and store them at the Bailey's home. There hadn't been a lot of time and a few things he'd left for later. Rose planned to come along for the ride.

Daniel

Driving up the gravel path to the house, Daniel couldn't help but wonder what his life would've been like if he hadn't met Rose or Mr. Bailey. Life had taken a dramatic turn in such a short period of time. It almost felt too good to be true. And usually when that happened, Daniel would anticipate the worst. If things felt too good, he always expected something to go wrong.

But he deserved some happiness in his life. Instead of second-guessing his blessings, he wanted to embrace them. He wanted to hold on to them with both hands. He didn't want to focus on the fear anymore, because doing that was making him feel trapped. He was determined to focus on the joy now, focus on Rose and Duncan—all the good in his life.

When they arrived, Rose said she would stay in the car with Duncan. The sober house was no place for a baby. Daniel agreed because he knew even the smallest changes at the house sometimes felt like a big deal to the men who were still living there. He knew it had felt that way to him, especially if someone took off without explanation and never came back. Daniel, out of respect for the other men, wanted to go in alone.

He opened the door and went inside to get the other boxes. He'd stacked them over by the front door yesterday. There were only a few to pick up. He'd brought very few personal items with him when he moved into the house, leaving most of his stuff at home with his dad and Will.

Grabbing two boxes, he turned to leave.

"You takin' off?"

Daniel's head dropped. He slowly turned to face him.

"Yah, my truck's outside."

He wasn't sure what to expect. He couldn't protect himself even if he'd wanted to with the boxes in his hands.

"Before you leave, I'm glad I caught you. Uh, I just wanted to say sorry for that night. I was completely out of line. I'm not sure why I got so angry, but I didn't want you to think I was a complete asshole. I do stupid shit sometimes. Didn't mean anything by it. It had nothing to do with you."

"I-I appreciate that." Daniel nodded but still felt cautious around him, despite the apology.

"Don't be a stranger, man. Me and some of the guys were talking last night and they wanted me to let you know that they wish you all the best. You've made it out—that's pretty cool. And, ah, now you're married. Congrats."

He put his hand on Daniel's shoulder. He tried not to wince.

"T-Thanks."

"Hopefully, this won't be the last we see of you. I mean, not here, but at meetings." He smiled.

Daniel finally let down his guard.

"M-Maybe you can come with me the next time I go o-owling." Daniel winked.

The man laughed.

"Let me help you with the door, wise ass."

As he walked out, Rose was waiting by the side of the truck trying to fix a stray hair that had fallen in her face. She was so beautiful. But her being there almost didn't seem real.

He'd never really believed in angels before, but she was the closest thing to one he'd ever met. It wasn't just her looks, there was something heavenly about her—her spirit was pure. She wasn't tough and cynical, but still soft and sweet. It seemed that no matter how difficult or how hard life got, she remained untarnished—untouched. Rose was so precious to him, he wanted to protect her in bubble wrap and never let her go.

"Ready?" she asked.

"I think so."

He looked up at the house.

Loading the last box onto the truck bed, he got behind the wheel and paused a second. He wasn't ashamed of his time there. He'd done some valuable work on himself. It'd been a literal lifesaver.

With the truck window down, the air was infused with the sweet scent of privet. A butter-colored sunshine blinded his eyes through the tree limbs, and the wind blew up old brown leaves long stuck under full green bushes.

Without saying a word, Rose reached for Daniel's hand and webbed her fingers through his. It was like she was reading his mind, and he wondered how so much happiness could come from such a small gesture.

"I'm glad you're here," he said, looking over at her.

"I'm glad I'm here too." She smiled and held her hair down from the wind blowing through the windows.

"I'm looking forward to meeting your brother tonight. I can't wait for you to introduce me to your family. I never had much of one growing up and I've always wanted to have more relatives living nearby. I'm excited to get to know them! I know you've had your troubles with them too, but hopefully this will be the start of something new."

She squeezed his hand.

"Are you sure about meeting him? It isn't too soon? We could always see him next week—next month. I don't want to rush things with us." Daniel grinned. "Not everything in our relationship has to be at warp speed."

They both laughed.

"No, really, it's fine." She reached out and touched his thigh. "He's your brother. I want to be there—help you build a bridge. Anyways, it'll be fun. Older brothers are always good at dishing the dirt. Maybe you're just scared he'll tell me some of your deep, dark secrets."

She nudged his side.

"You already know most of the skeletons in my closet. But don't worry, I'm sure he'll be able to scrounge something else up."

She smiled.

"It's really not *if* with Will. It'll happen. The last time I saw him, though, he said he wanted to meet the girl if I ever got one. I guess we're both trying to make a start of it. Thanks for doing this, Rose."

He squeezed her hand.

"Daniel, do you...do you think he'll like me?"

He lifted her hand to his lips and kissed it.

"How could he not?"

☾

1:00 AM

"Son, I want you to tell me what happened," the officer said, handing him a cup of water. "I want you to start from the beginning. We're gonna take it slow and if you need a break, just say so."

The officer pressed the record button on his device and placed it on the table.

They were sitting in the Plymouth Police Station located across from the county correctional facility on Long Pond Road. It was a brick building, recently constructed. Unfortunately, Daniel remembered it well. He'd been cuffed, sitting at a similar desk, while he gave his statement a little over two years ago.

Soaking wet and covered in mud up to his ankles, Daniel hung his head in his hands. Looking down, he saw blood soaked through his pant leg. He felt sick. Reaching for the trash can beside the officer's desk, he vomited, but there was nothing in his stomach left to bring up. He heaved again and wiped his mouth on his sleeve.

"I-I'm not sure where to begin, officer."

His head was spinning. He couldn't think straight.

"Would it help if I asked you some questions?"

Daniel nodded. The officer looked down at some papers on his desk.

"What were you and Rose Dorset doing at Deer Pond tonight?"

A wave of nausea hit him at the sound of her name.

"I'd taken Rose to meet my b-brother." He wiped tears from his eyes with his forearm. "Rose and I were married two days ago, and I wanted to introduce her to my family. I-I mean, my brother, Will." He choked on his words.

"What happened when you two got there? What was goin' on?"

Daniel's chest felt sore from crying.

"We drove to the pond in Mr. Bailey's truck, and Will was already there. I could tell he was drunk before we even got out of the car. I wasn't sure if we should s-stay. I'd warned Rose on the drive over about my brother. I'd told her he was a l-little rough around the edges, but to try to look past it. I'd told her I was trying to reconnect with him."

He stared at the wall.

"Since Will and I were starting to get to know each other again, I-I didn't want to back out. I thought we would stay just for a little while. We had to get back for our son, Duncan."

Daniel tried to take a deep breath.

"Getting out of the truck, I walked over to Rose and opened her door. She looked so pretty. I held her hand. But when we started walking over to Will, I noticed Rose p-pulling me back as though she wanted us to stop walking. Tugging hard on my hand—I-I was confused."

"Did you get the sense Rose and Will knew each other?"

The officer jotted down some information in his notebook.

"I guess. M-Maybe. I saw Will giving me a strange look as well. And Rose started digging into my hand with her fingernails, but I didn't know why."

Daniel held up his palm to show the officer the marks. Three red puncture marks were still imprinted on his hand.

"When we got over to him, he put out his cigarette butt in the dirt and f-finished off his beer. He threw the bottle on the ground."

Daniel thought he may pass out and leaned on the officer's desk.

"Go on."

"I said to Will, 'This is the someone I wanted to introduce you to. This is Rose Dorset. I-I mean, Rose Goodman, my w-wife!'"

Daniel shook his head thinking about what he'd accidently done to her. Tears burned down his cheeks.

"What happened next, son?"

The officer moved a tissue box over to him.

"Will started getting angry. Rose stood frozen beside me. And then he exploded, calling her names, saying crazy things, and y-yelled, 'What are you doing with my little brother?' Then Will stormed over to his truck. He got something out of the c-cab."

"And then?"

"And then, before I knew it, Rose took off into the woods around the back side of the pond. She started running. She ran so fast. There was no way to stop her. I-I called her name, but after a while I couldn't see her anymore. She disappeared into the woods. When Will got in his truck, I took off after her."

Will

Six hours earlier

H e got there before Danny to set up the fishing poles and start a small bonfire. He broke out the cooler with a few cold beers in it because it sounded like Danny had something to celebrate.

Maybe Danny was moving out and wanted to take him up on his offer? Maybe he was going to come back home? He wouldn't admit it to anyone, but he'd been lonely. The house was silent—void of life. After Danny's text, Will allowed himself a small speck of hope.

The humidity was bringing out the bugs and he looked in his truck for some spray. No luck. He unrolled his shirt sleeves and buttoned up. He noticed a storm approaching, but it was still far off in the distance. The gnats would drive them from the pond tonight well before the storm would. Dark clouds in the distance burst with flashes of light.

Danny pulled up in Bailey's red truck. It looked like someone was with him.

"Does this mean I'm gonna have to share my beers?" Will yelled over to Danny, as he watched him get out of the truck with some red-head in a bright orange dress.

"This is a change of plans, bro. I would've brought a date too had I known."

Already drunk, Will had to concentrate putting his words together. Maybe if things went right tonight, he would have a shot at the redhead too.

But as she turned the corner of the truck, and he saw Danny holding her hand, it was as if the world stopped.

"Hold up!"

Will shook his head, trying to refocus on the image in front of him.

"D-Dan, bud, what's going on?"

He couldn't believe his eyes.

"That looks like my fuckin' dead girlfriend? What the hell's happening? Is this a fuckin' joke?"

He threw his beer bottle on the ground and went to get a closer look. He approached her as if he was a tiger in a cage—stalking her.

The color of her hair was darker, but the shape of her face, as well as the color of her eyes were the same. Her mouth bent up on one side too, just like Carrie's. He clenched his jaw.

"She a Dorset?" he yelled so loud, people across the pond could've heard him.

Danny stood silent and looked confused.

"Danny, I said, is she a fuckin' Dorset?"

He couldn't believe what he was seeing. It was as though Carrie had risen from the grave and stood before him in his mother's orange dress.

The rage that lived so close to the surface began to emerge. And there was no way in hell he'd let another druggie like Carrie Dorset mess with a Goodman.

"W-Will, how did you know? This is Rose Dorset. I mean, Rose Goodman. This was the g-good news I wanted to tell you about. We got married."

"What are you saying? You're married to Rose Dorset, Carrie Dorset's sister?"

Will wasn't sure if he was going to be able to contain himself. He couldn't figure out how Danny and Rose knew each other, and now, how in the hell they were married.

What was Danny thinking? Will couldn't read his face, but, by the looks of it, Danny didn't have a clue he was being manipulated by this little piece of trash.

Will watched Danny put both hands behind his head like he was going to puke.

"Is this all about the child support? Did you marry my little brother to get at my money? Is that it?"

He spoke to Rose directly, totally bypassing his brother. She looked on the verge of tears, but he couldn't care less. Watching her start to tremble, Will didn't buy her act.

"It's all about the money. That's it, right? The Dorsets want my money and now you've married my brother to bleed him dry like she did me. Unbelievable. What scum suckers you both are—total lowlifes!"

He waited for her to answer, but she stayed silent—crying.

His first instinct was to tear into her. He made a fist at his side, but in a moment of calm, came up with a better plan and stumbled to his truck. He wasn't going to hit her and land himself in jail. Instead, he'd scare that little piece of trailer trash all the way back home.

"W-Will, where are you going?" He faintly heard Danny call behind him.

Will swung open the door of his truck and leaned in. Dropping open the glovebox, he searched under the manual. It was there—cold to the touch. He unclipped it from the holster and held it up.

This will get her attention.

He'd be doing Danny a favor—doing it for his own good.

Abruptly turning to face them, he showed her the gun.

Danny stood silent, but she took off running into the woods around the back side of the pond. Will watched her run and saw her fall in the sand and then trip on a tree stump. Her orange dress tore up the side of her leg. She clawed at the gravel to get back up and looked like a frightened animal. But as she reached the edge of the woods, Will knew he needed to make more of an impression.

Menacing black storm clouds formed in the distance high above the trees and slowly moved like a black blanket covering the sky. The light was fading. Scattered raindrops fell from the sky and the sun grew black.

Looking at Danny, he didn't anticipate him taking off after her.

Where the hell was he going?

"Get in the truck, Danny!" Will yelled, but it was too late. He was already headed into the woods.

Will stumbled over to the driver's side and fell in. Starting his engine, loud music blared from the radio. Switching it off, he slammed his truck into reverse, not paying attention to what was behind him. Will revved the engine.

He'd cut her off on Hatchet Pass and pick up Danny. He knew a shortcut down some old dirt bike paths—the ones over by the power lines.

Bolts of lightning crashed a few miles off and the edge of the storm was almost on them. It started to pelt heavy rain drops on his windshield, then buckets poured down. He could barely see anything. His windshield fogged up. Strong gusts of wind bent the scrub pines to the side, like California palm trees.

Slamming on the gas, he took off on an unpaved road. The tree branches scraped the side of his truck. He turned on his wipers, rolled up the window, and threw the gun on the passenger seat beside him.

The roads were uneven, laced with deep potholes. Swerving to the right and then left, his headlights only lit a few feet in front of him. The sky was pitch black.

Hitting a rock in the road, the handgun bounced off the seat and fell onto the floor mat below. Will saw it out of the corner of his eye and reached down to grab it. He swiped it with his hand, bending over—the brake handle digging into his ribcage.

Hitting another deep pothole, the uneven road inched the gun further back near the wheel well. He lifted his foot off the pedal and tried to grab for it again.

Daniel

Daniel motioned to the officer he needed a second. He was starting to feel sick to his stomach again. He leaned over the trash can and sat waiting for another wave of nausea to hit him.

"Where were you when this was all happening?" The officer continued to take notes.

"I took off after her, but I-I couldn't catch up. She was too far ahead of me. It was getting m-muddy because of the rain. I slipped. My feet wouldn't stay upright. The woods were dense, and I was having a hard time making it through the scrub brush. M-My clothes kept getting snagged. I saw her ahead of me, out in the distance. It looked like she was running toward the road."

"Hatchet Pass?"

Daniel nodded.

"I started y-yelling at her to stop. I called her name, but I wasn't sure she could hear me with all the thunder and lightning. It was cracking and b-booming all around us. It was so loud. She was soaking wet."

He tried to take a deep breath.

"I saw her make it to the road. She stood there, and for a second, I thought she heard me. She finally stopped running and looked back.

The rain started to ease, and I w-waved to her. She held up her hand. But before I could reach her, I saw headlights and Will's truck coming over the hill."

His teeth started to chatter, and he began to tremble.

The officer stopped writing and looked up at him. Daniel shook uncontrollably.

"I'm—I'm not sure I can finish, officer. I can't stop myself from s-shaking."

The officer took off his coat and put it around his shoulders.

"Son, is there someone I can call for you?"

Daniel handed the officer his phone. He directed him to Mr. Bailey's number. He felt like he was going into shock, like he may pass out. His breathing was shallow, and his heart raced. Was he dying?

"Daniel, it's all right."

The officer put his hand on his shoulder.

"I've called Reverend Bailey and he's on his way to the station. I think you'd better go lie down until he gets here."

He stood up and Daniel followed as best he could.

"Let's go into the lounge for a second and lie down."

The officer led him to the couch and shut the door. Daniel slumped down. He blankly stared at the wall. Leaning over, his shaking slowed but didn't stop. Exhausted, his heavy eyelids closed. He managed to fall asleep but woke a little later to muffled voices outside the door. He recognized one of them. It was Mr. Bailey. He stood and walked over to the door. Mr. Bailey reached out to him with a hug.

"Daniel, I'm here. It'll be okay, son."

Daniel tried to speak but couldn't. Mr. Bailey kept a tight arm around him.

The officer broke the silence.

"William Goodman is being charged with possession of an illegal firearm, felony drunk driving, and second-degree murder for the death of Rose Dorset Goodman. I'll need to question Dan further in the next few days, but for now, take him home and get him some rest. I'll be in touch."

He handed Mr. Bailey his business card.

"Let's go, Daniel."

He wasn't sure if he could make it back to the truck. They walked slowly. Mr. Bailey opened the passenger side door for him and helped him in. He buckled Daniel's seatbelt and closed the door. Daniel stared blankly at the dashboard.

"Son, I know you're exhausted but we need to stop by the hospital before we head home." Mr. Bailey looked over at him with tears in his eyes. "We, ah, we need to see Rose."

Daniel stared at a crack in the bench seat leather. He knew Mr. Bailey was taking him to say goodbye. He punched the dashboard with his fist. His yells turned to groans. Mr. Bailey drove and didn't say a word to stop him.

The nurse led Daniel down a bare, white corridor with shiny white tile on the wall and scuffed rubber baseboards. They'd taken the elevator one flight down in complete silence. He stared as the floor number flashed down to B.

Sterile lights in the ceiling brightly lit the hallway a shade of light green. His shoes shuffled on the linoleum and his legs felt like tree trunks that he had to drag along. Leaning over, he couldn't straighten his body. His muscles clamped down around his neck and his stomach was sore as though he'd just emerged from a fight. His body ached all over.

He saw the nurse's shoes stop in front of a door at the end of the hall. He looked up and saw her mouth move, but there was no sound. She spoke just above a whisper.

"She's right inside here. I've put a chair by the table for you. Take as long as you want. I'll check back in a little while."

Daniel barely felt her hand touch his shoulder. He waited for her to walk away before he opened the door. He was almost too scared to look inside.

Walking in, the door shut slowly behind him and locked loudly in place. Petrified, he wasn't sure he had enough courage to see her. He held up his hand to his eyes and looked through the cracks between his fingers. She was lying underneath a light gray sheet. Her hair was shaped like a half-sunbeam above her head.

"R-Rose?"

He spoke to her as if she was only sleeping and lifted his head above his splayed hand to see her in full view. He couldn't put his hand down and it stayed hovering in the air.

She was so still.

He looked at her chest to see if it would rise and fall, but the sheet remained flat and didn't move. A small air filtration unit hummed in the corner.

He stood still for fear of waking her.

A chair was placed on the right side of the table, and he imperceptibly moved closer to it—inching his way toward her. Looking down on her brightly lit face, the only evidence of the night could be found hidden in her hair. Small grains of sand were scattered on her scalp and there was dirt and dried blood near her temples. The rest of her face had been hastily wiped clean. A few strands of hair were dried to her forehead. He went to move them, but when he touched her skin, it felt cold. Yanking his hand away, he hadn't expected it to feel that way. Her lips were the color of the ocean during a storm.

The sheet covered her shoulders and rested just below her neck. She wasn't wearing any clothes underneath. It lightly rested on her body and rose and fell with each dip and mound. He watched her eyelids to see if they would open. They didn't move.

He slumped in the chair beside the table and bowed his head before her. The weight of the moment felt like a heavy yoke on his back.

"Where are you now, Rose? Are you with Him?" he asked the air and looked up at ceiling panels which were stained with old leaks. The room was windowless.

He bowed his head again and prayed, but not with words—only groans. Tears burned his cheeks.

When he heard footsteps in the hallway, he opened his eyes and stared blankly at what was once the temple for her soul. He stared at the flesh and bone and blood of Rose and wondered why her soul couldn't stay.

Rose's temple was so clean and uncluttered—unspoiled and sweet. It was the perfect dwelling place for something from God. But why God chose to dwell in things that would eventually die was beyond him. Why God chose to enter and live in broken places was a mystery. And the small speck of heaven which resided in her, and that he'd grown to love, was gone and would never return. It had secreted away to some place he couldn't get to just yet. It had floated away, like delicate cobwebs into the thinnest air.

Under the sheet, he saw the outline of her knuckles and he lifted just enough of the bedding to expose her hand. He wanted to touch her again despite the cold, but his courage was on the edge of collapsing.

But if he didn't touch her now, if he waited, it would be too late. He rested his hand on hers and stroked her long, lean fingers one at a time. They hadn't cleaned her hands yet and mud was still crusted underneath her nails. When he reached her ring finger, he stopped and felt the hardness of her thin wedding band. He twisted it once on her finger and carefully slid it off. He placed it on his pinky next to his own wedding ring.

Desperate to warm her, he stood up and carefully tucked in the sheet around her body.

In the few moments they had left together, before he'd never see her again, he leaned down and kissed her lips for the last time.

Tears appeared on Rose's cheeks, but they weren't coming from her eyes. His tears spilled down her face leaving wet streams. With a crumpled tissue from the police station, he dabbed them away.

"G-Goodbye, Rose."

He walked back toward the door and waited to see if she'd return to him. She lay there still.

Turning, he hesitantly opened the door and walked out.

As the automatic doors swung open, Daniel came into the lobby carrying a diaper bag over his shoulder and a car seat with Duncan in the other hand. Rose's blood stains were still dried through his pant leg.

"Was Dottie back there? The nurse told me she'd arrived," Mr. Bailey asked.

Daniel could only look at him and nod.

He grabbed the diaper bag from Daniel as they walked out the lobby doors. A warm blast of air met them on the other side.

When they reached the truck, Mr. Bailey buckled in Duncan's car seat and Daniel slumped in beside them. It was early in the morning and the sun was just stretching over the hills.

In the silence, Daniel's eyes drooped and the hum of the engine put him to sleep. He woke just before they reached the Bailey's house.

"Mr. Bailey."

Daniel's voice was hoarse and broken.

"Yes, son."

"Have you ever seen a snowy owl this far south?"

Daniel pressed his forehead into the passenger's side window. The cool glass felt good on his swollen eyelids.

"Yes, why do you ask?"

"I'm scared I may never see another one again."

☾

One month later

It was a cloudless day when he arrived a little before nine in the morning. Daniel walked in and registered signing their names: Daniel and Duncan Goodman. He took a seat and tried to keep Duncan occupied in his car seat.

A few people were reading magazines. One woman searched her purse and pulled out a pen.

Daniel's name was called, and a receptionist led them down the hall to an empty office. She told him to make himself comfortable and he took a seat.

Unstrapping Duncan from his car seat, Daniel fixed his slouching socks and bounced him on his knee. Holding him in the air, he gave him a raspberry on the cheek. It was already wet when he kissed him.

There was a knock at the door. Daniel wiped his mouth.

"I see you've brought a friend with you today."

Paul walked in the room.

"Yes, this is my son, Duncan."

"It's nice to meet you, Duncan."

Paul attempted to shake Duncan's hand as he sat down in the chair opposite Daniel.

"You look like you're getting the hang of it, of fatherhood, I mean."

"Mr. and Mrs. Bailey and our friend Dottie have been a big help. I didn't know the first thing about babies, but they're teaching me the basics. They take turns babysitting him when I have to work. Mrs. Bailey rotates night feedings with me, and he spends a lot of time at the nursery. He's like the store's mascot. He helps me feed the koi..."

He looked down and bit his lip, then gently bounced Duncan on his leg.

"How have you been doing? What's been going on with you? I know it's been difficult to connect with each other in person with everything that's been going on. I'm glad we've at least kept in touch over the phone."

Paul reached out to hold Duncan and sat him on his lap. Duncan looked curiously around the room.

"It hasn't been easy."

Daniel wiped his hands on the front of his pants and sat straighter in the chair. He cleared his throat.

"After Rose died, the Baileys closed the nursery for a week. There was so much to do and process. They helped me with the f-funeral p-planning."

Breathe.

"I wasn't sure what color Rose liked best. I didn't even know her favorite flower yet, so we got a simple casket and decorated it with a wreath of white roses and peony. Mr. Bailey performed a service in the chapel. It was a beautiful day. The sun streamed in through the stained-glass windows and colored her like a rainbow."

"That's beautiful, Daniel. Did any of her family attend?"

Paul leaned Duncan forward and patted his back.

"Her stepfather and mother flew in from Florida, but they didn't stay long. Her mother wasn't very interested in getting to know Duncan either. When I offered to let her mother hold him, she turned me down and walked away."

Paul held Duncan up in the air and smiled at him.

"I'm not sure what to say to that, Daniel. That's clearly not a normal reaction for a grandmother to have."

Paul imperceptibly shook his head.

And as if Duncan knew they were talking about him, he fussed, and Paul handed him back over. Daniel hiked Duncan over his shoulder.

He was soon fixated on something outside the window and drooled down his shirt.

"Mr. Bailey helped plan a lot of it and the pianist played *Clair de Lune* as the recessional. It was the music we had at our wedding."

Duncan let out a little cry.

"But the funeral felt surreal at the same time, like it wasn't happening to me. To be honest, I-I've had a hard time accepting she's really g-gone."

"Can you say more about that?"

Paul leaned forward.

"We packed up her stuff from the apartment. We ended up donating a lot of things to charity, which was her mother's wish. But I made a box of stuff to give to Duncan when he's older, and there's also a few things for me to remember her by."

He felt Duncan's body suddenly relax in his arms.

"I kept the crown of flowers she wore at our wedding, and Mrs. Bailey's going to help me preserve them. I also asked the funeral director if I could have a l-lock of her hair. When I delivered her burial outfit, he'd tied it in some pink ribbon and gave it to me. I'd forgotten how much it looked like the color of dark honey. I've also recorded her voice greeting from her cell phone so Duncan can hear her voice and know what she sounded like."

Paul gently lifted Duncan from Daniel's arms so he could wipe his tears.

"Dottie was kind enough to give me a photo of us she took at the wedding. I think it's the only picture I have of us together. W-We're both smiling. Dottie framed it and everything."

Daniel quietly blew his nose.

"But the one thing that matters the most to me is her wedding dress. I, uh, I can still smell her on it." Tears welled up in his eyes, and he bowed his head.

"I hear you, Daniel. I know this is hard. She was your wife and you loved her."

"I did… I do."

He tried to catch his breath.

"Daniel, you've done a wonderful job of preserving Rose's memory for both you and Duncan. I know in the future he'll appreciate your thoughtfulness."

"You think so?"

"Of course, it takes a special man to think of others when they're hurting—the way you have." Paul stood and gently rocked Duncan.

"But I want to ask you something important. It's a tough question. Have you been able to maintain your sobriety through all this?"

Daniel had been waiting for that question.

"It hasn't been easy. I can honestly say that not a day has gone by when I haven't wanted to drink. I've gotten really close a few times. The first week I just wanted to numb the p-pain. I even drove to Falls Tavern, but just sat in the parking lot."

Daniel looked out the window, too ashamed to look at Paul's face.

"I, uh, also drove to a liquor store with Duncan in the car but didn't stop."

He looked at the ground.

"What'd you do instead?"

"After I passed the liquor store, I found myself driving. I-I really didn't know where. I found myself at the cemetery. I needed to go and see her—maybe talk to her. I wanted to tell her about Duncan."

Paul gently patted Duncan's back.

"It was a pretty day, like today." Daniel looked out the window. "I searched in the back of the truck and found a mason jar where Mr. Bailey keeps his spare change. I emptied it out in the cup holder and went to the back of the truck and tore off two rose stems from a bush I was supposed to deliver that afternoon. I carried it all up to the top of the hill with D-Duncan in my arms. I found a spigot to fill the jar with water and I put the two roses in it and placed it in-between their graves. I-I sat there talking to them until the sky turned pink and orange and the wind picked up."

"You said—their graves?"

"Right, Rose and Carrie's."

"Yes, sorry, their graves."

There was a long silence in the room. Paul looked down at Duncan now cradled in his arms.

"This young man's lost his mother, like you."

Daniel felt a pang shoot through his heart.

"We have that in common, both in different ways, though."

"You're exactly what he needs, Dan. Someone who understands that sense of loss going forward. Hopefully, you'll be able to guide him on this pathway." Paul looked at him. "You'll know what Duncan is feeling. However, because of you, he'll never feel abandoned like you did. He'll only feel loved."

"I-I hope so."

Duncan started to wake up and rub his eyes. Paul handed him back over to Daniel.

"Paul, uh, there was something I wanted to give you."

He reached in his pocket and handed him a piece of paper.

"It's an invitation. It'll be over at Reverend Bailey's church in a few weeks. The service starts at ten."

"I've been there before." Paul put on his glasses and scanned the sheet.

Daniel started to pack up Duncan's things. He stuffed them into his backpack.

"I've really appreciated your help with everything. I'm not sure I would've made it this last month without you."

"We all need help every now and then, but I'll see you next week, right?"

Daniel smiled and placed Duncan in his car seat and handed him a toy to chew on. He grabbed a new bib from the front pocket of his backpack and fastened it around his neck. Duncan's t-shirt was soaked through underneath. Bending his arms under the straps, he buckled him in and adjusted the bar up his chest. Pulling the strap down tighter on the car seat, he readjusted the bar again.

"Paul, can I ask you one more thing?"

"Of course—anything."

He looked up from his notebook.

"Does the pain ever go away? Will it stop?" Tears brimmed in his eyes. "Part of me doesn't want it to because I feel if it stops, it'll mean I'm forgetting her. But then, I also can't stand the ache in my heart anymore. I'm not sure how long I'll be able to bear it."

Paul stood and put his hand on Daniel's shoulder.

"It will, Daniel, but not for a while. And no matter what you do or even who you end up loving next in the far-off future, Rose will always be with you. The memory of Rose will last a lifetime." He patted his shoulder. "Love lives on. It's a force more powerful than death."

Daniel could only nod, because if he spoke again, he'd only start to cry. And if he started crying, he wasn't sure he'd be able to stop.

"May I make a suggestion? You might want to write Rose a letter expressing how you feel. Some people keep it to look at later, some send it in a bottle and let it drift off to sea. Whatever you do, I don't need to see it. But it might help you sort through some of your feelings. I wonder if you feel some guilt that you're alive and she isn't, which would be completely natural."

Paul reached for his hand to shake it.

"And if you need me, Dan, I want you to reach out anytime. I'm always here for you. Don't hesitate."

Daniel walked into the hallway and out the double-doors. Duncan sneezed when the sunlight hit his face. Surveying the parking lot, he saw Sugar. He searched for his keys in his pockets. He'd parked under a tree, so the truck wouldn't be too hot for Duncan when they got back in.

Daniel placed Duncan's car seat on the ground next to Sugar and opened the door. Duncan squinted his eyes every now and then, as the sun peered through the leaves in the trees. The shadows from the leaves made a pattern on his face. Noticing Duncan's soft, curly red hair, he crouched down and rubbed the top of his head.

Daniel was still getting used to the soft indentation on the top where his skull had not yet fused together. Holding his hand on top of his head, Duncan smiled. All Daniel could think to say to Duncan was, "Bless you."

He hoisted the car seat into the truck.

☾

Dottie pulled up a chair next to him in the store's café. Daniel was there to clean out Rose's locker and she'd invited him to sit and have some coffee before he left.

"How are you doing, doll?"

"Not great."

He looked at the sunglasses he was holding near his lap and contritely bowed his head before Dottie.

"Me neither."

There was a long silence between them. The only sounds surrounding them were of customer's muffled talk and the pulsing grind of the coffee machine behind the counter.

For a moment, they both seemed content to sit in each other's company in silence. Dottie removed a tissue from her sleeve to blot beneath her eyes. Daniel bounced one leg up and down in rapid succession. Abruptly, he stopped and bent over in his chair.

When he looked up, Dottie was staring at the ceiling trying to stop the flow of tears, using gravity to keep them in her eyes.

The coffee remained untouched on the table. Steam rose from the cups, and he heard a child's cry in the distance coming from the back of the store.

"Why'd she have to go and leave us?" Dottie quietly sobbed. "I feel so lost without her. Every morning I hope she'll walk in through the front door. I sometimes think she's just late, and I can call her, but I can't find her number anywhere." She tried to catch her breath.

Daniel put his hand on her shoulder.

"I get so mad that she's not here, but I have no one to yell at. I just want to scream. My chest gets all fluttery. My doctor says I need to watch my blood pressure, but sometimes I feel like a pressure cooker just waiting to explode. It's so unfair. It's so damn unfair, Daniel."

Dottie clenched her fists as tears streamed down her red cheeks.

"He stole something so precious to us. He stole all the moments in the future I wanted to have with her. He stole our sweet friendship. It's like my love for her has nowhere to go. It's bottled up inside me and I'm just dying to let it out."

Dottie choked on her words.

"I just don't understand it." She banged her fists on the table.

"Dott, I'm so s-sorry."

"It's not your fault, Daniel. Don't go blaming yourself. How could you have known? None of us made the connection. None of us put two and two together. It just doesn't make any sense. How is she gone?"

She shook her head.

Tears tumbled from Daniel's eyes, and he quickly tried to swipe them away. Dottie unclenched her hands and rubbed his back.

"Sometimes I wish I could go back in time to the place I first saw her and do it all over again. I w-wished I'd asked her more questions about her family. I wish I hadn't tried to reconnect with Will. Why did I listen to that stupid dream? How—How could I have let this happen to her?"

He turned his face away. They sat in silence as Daniel's words hung in the air.

"Did I ever tell you how I first met Rosie?"

He shook his head.

"Well, I met her at the returns counter when she brought back an item to the store. I don't remember what it was. She was just a young thing, only about fifteen, on the verge of being sixteen."

A smile broke out on Dottie's face.

"You know what I said to her? I told her she was a peppy and perky person and that we could use someone like her at the store."

Dottie and Daniel couldn't help but laugh through their tears.

"She looked at me as if I had four heads. But we really did need the help and I was willing to recruit just about anyone. I said right there and then, 'Would you like a job?'"

"What'd Rose say?"

"She told me that she'd think about it. But then a few minutes later, she came back and took the job."

Dottie's smile beamed across her face.

"When she stood in front of me, I remember wanting to reach over the counter and fix a hair that was out of place. I wanted to straighten out her headband and tuck her little bra strap underneath her t-shirt, but, instead, I just told her how happy I was that we'd be co-workers and shook her hand. It was the strangest feeling, kinda instinctive for me. I just always wanted to take care of that little lamb. I felt as if I'd known her before somehow—for years. She found a way into my heart so effortlessly."

"I know what you mean."

"Of course, darlin'. Of course you do. I knew that you would."

Dottie blew her nose.

"Sweetie pie, my break is almost up. I should head back to work."

She reached down to grab her purse and stood up.

"We need to make this more of a habit. Don't be a stranger. I want to see you and Duncan more often. I also want to have you over to the house for dinner, with the Baileys, of course."

She kissed his cheek.

"It was good seeing you too, Dott."

He rubbed her hand on his shoulder and gave it a pat.

As she walked to the back of the store, Daniel reached down and grabbed the box with Rose's things from her locker. He stood to leave, and his heart ached a little—he felt dazed. Talking about Rose was never easy.

Leaving the café, Daniel noticed a woman with a yellow vest collecting carriages in the parking lot. She had long hair and wore white Converse high-tops and a pink hoodie. For a split second, his mind tricked him, and he thought it might be Rose.

Could it be? Was that her?

He rushed over to where she was standing. As he went to tap her on the shoulder, he abruptly stopped and remembered—that was impossible.

She wasn't coming back.

☾

Dear Rose,

When you died, I felt so alone. It was so dark. I've found life to have less meaning with you not in it, but I know you're in a much better place reunited with your sister. I'm happy you're free from tears and pain. I'm happy you'll forever be at peace.

I'm so sorry, Rose. I didn't know. I didn't know the connection between you and Duncan and Will, or I would've never taken you to meet him. Had I known, I would've protected you from him and kept you safe. Will preyed on women more times than I could admit to myself, and maybe that bridge to Will was never possible or never should be possible.

I struggle with the guilt of bringing you into my life, one that was filled with so much hate and pain. I struggle that I'm still here with Duncan and you're not. You looked back at me at Hatchet Pass and raised your hand. I hoped you stopped because you realized I'd never hurt you.

Can you ever forgive me?

What I do know is the sweetness and joy you brought into my life and that you have left with me and Duncan. I don't think I'd known love, however brief, but with you. I'd never felt tenderness or affection. I'd never felt peace or joy. I'd never known all those things until you showed up.

Now I have to live with the ghost of your memory. I have to go on breathing and living, never getting to hold you again, never being able to look into your eyes or hear you say my name. I have to live, when some-times all I want to do is die.

I wonder if it would've been better had we never met at all, then I wouldn't know this pain.

I will forever love you, Rose. I'll watch over and love Duncan. I'll forever hold you in my heart. The day I can see you again cannot come soon enough.

Peace be forever with you, but I'm not sure I'll be at peace until I'm with you again.

Love, Daniel

☾

Two weeks later

Arriving at the church, it was quiet, so quiet he heard the gentle call of a single bird outside on a nearby tree. The lights hadn't been turned on. The air inside the sanctuary was cool and musty, a dawn-like atmosphere—like dew evaporating from wet earth.

The pews were saturated with color from the stained-glass windows on the back wall. Greens and purples splashed the back of the seats. He turned to see where the colors were coming from. It was a depiction of Christ's first miracle, turning water into wine. He was standing beside his mother Mary. They were at a wedding.

"Daniel, is Duncan with you?" Mr. Bailey called to him from the front of the church. His voice echoed off the bare white walls.

"No, he's with Eleanor. They'll be here soon."

"Son, can you help me get organized? I need to put the bulletins in the lobby and turn on the lights in the sanctuary and the basement. The women who organize the refreshments will be here any minute."

Daniel gathered the programs and placed them in a tan-woven basket on a table. He unlocked and tested the doors to make sure they would open.

Looking down the center aisle, he saw Mr. Bailey change into a white robe with a royal blue stole. The stole was embroidered with gold thread in the shape of a dove on the left-hand side and had two crosses on either side at the bottom. His billowy sleeves, with three large blue stripes on each arm, fell to his wrists and his shirt and tie peeked out from an opening at the top.

Placing his weathered, black Bible on the pulpit, Mr. Bailey filled up a stone basin with water from a pitcher. Daniel walked to meet him.

"It's a beautiful day," Mr. Bailey said warmly, and organized some papers on the pulpit.

"Yes, sir. It s-sure is."

"Daniel? George?" Mrs. Bailey called from the lobby.

"We're in here." Daniel replied, noticing Mr. Bailey was now too preoccupied with the service preparations to answer. He was looking over some sermon notes he kept on a single piece of white paper under the front cover of his Bible. He mumbled to himself.

Mrs. Bailey was wearing a blue floral dress. Her heels squeaked when she walked. She was carrying Duncan on her hip. He'd been dressed in a white silk-embroidered dress with shiny white boots.

Daniel wasn't sure how she'd gotten his pudgy feet into them. He was sure it took a monumental effort and detected a small trace of perspiration on her brow.

When she reached them at the altar, one of his shoes spontaneously fell off. Daniel picked it up off the floor and tried to put it back on his foot, but it was no use. He put the shoe in his pocket and reached out to hold him.

"I think people are arriving, dear."

She patted Duncan on the back and made her way to the organ. She sat down at the bench and adjusted the seat.

"You'd better go take a seat in the front."

Mr. Bailey motioned Daniel over to the first pew.

After taking his seat, he turned around and watched the congregation enter at the back of the sanctuary. They dripped in, as each one carefully mulled over the right pew to sit in.

Daniel noticed one man hesitantly cross the threshold of the door at the back, as though he'd never stepped foot inside something sacred before. He watched him observing members of the congregation already in their seats.

Quietly, something stirred in Daniel, and he began to recognize the man's face. He thought it was familiar, but he couldn't quite put his finger on it.

Was it really him?

It didn't take long for Daniel to recognize the gentleman's distinctive mannerism, the constant checking of his wallet in his back pocket—a nervous tic.

It was his father.

He was twenty pounds lighter and had a beard, but it was his father all the same. They made eye contact and Daniel welcomed him by holding up a free arm above his head. He held his palm open in the air.

"I hope you don't mind me inviting him to this special occasion," Mr. Bailey whispered in Daniel's ear.

He looked over at Jacob Goodman and waved too.

"No, I don't mind. I-I just had no idea."

"I thought this was an important day for you both. I thought it'd be a shame if your father couldn't be here to share it with you. I'm sorry I didn't ask for your permission first. I hope you'll forgive me."

"It's okay, Mr. Bailey."

Turning back around, Daniel caught Dottie's eye as she walked down the aisle assisting Fran with her walker. Fran's neck and torso were still in a brace. Recently released from the rehabilitation facility, it looked like Fran was making good progress.

Paul was next to enter, and he waited patiently in the back as an elderly couple took a seat and folded their wheelchair like an accordion. Excusing himself as he crossed over the older couple, he took a seat and closed his eyes.

A few of Rose's co-workers from the store came too. He remembered their faces from the funeral, but still wasn't sure of all their names.

The breeze from the ceiling fans above blew Duncan's sparse curls on the back of his head. Daniel turned to face Mr. Bailey as the organ finished playing. He felt relieved that all the people who loved them were all in one place.

"Today we are gathered to do two very important things." Mr. Bailey's voice was welcoming and cheerful—upbeat. A feeling of warmth sparked in Daniel's chest.

"We're here to worship the Lord, as well as baptize young Duncan Henry Dorset Goodman into the family of God." He projected his voice so well that he didn't require a mic system.

Duncan sat in Daniel's lap sucking on his fist but began to rub his eyes and squirm by straightening out his back. Mr. Bailey was good at reading Duncan's cues now that they'd been roommates for a little while.

"And since the Lord in all his wisdom knows there's no soothing a cranky baby when he's tired, I'd like to start the service today with Duncan's baptism. Let's just cut to the chase, if that's all right with you all, and then we'll circle back to the first hymn."

He smiled at the congregation.

"Daniel, can you and Duncan please join me up front? Eleanor?"

Mrs. Bailey rose from behind the organ bench and came to stand on Daniel's right-side at the altar.

Duncan stopped fussing when Mr. Bailey reached out for him.

"Through this Sacrament, the Church declares its faith in the crucified and risen Christ and reasserts his claim to every human life. By bringing this child for baptism…"

Mr. Bailey dipped his hand into the font and sprinkled water over Duncan's head. He held his spread palm on top of his head as he finished the blessing.

Daniel looked down at the pink rose boutonniere on his lapel and took a long, deep breath.

After the church service, Mrs. Bailey sent him home to rest. Since Rose's death, he was exhausted—drained. It took all his strength to do the smallest things. It even felt like it took too much energy to breathe sometimes. And for some reason, lately, he couldn't think straight. It wasn't uncommon for him to find ice cream in the cupboard or his cell phone in the fridge.

Unbuckling Duncan from his car seat, Daniel picked him up and rested him on his shoulder. He walked Duncan into the bedroom and gently laid him on the bed. Getting a fresh onesie from the dresser drawer and a new diaper, he changed him before putting him in his crib for a nap. Sucking his thumb, Duncan never woke up.

Tiptoeing over to each window, he pulled down the shades to darken the room but let in a crack of sunlight at the bottom. He turned the overhead ceiling fan on low and slowly took off his blazer. Unpinning the rose from his lapel, he placed it on top of the dresser and draped his jacket on an overstuffed chair sitting in the corner. He unbuttoned his shirt.

Sitting on the bed, he untied his shoes and then loosened and took off his belt. Placing them neatly in the closet, he saw one of the boxes he'd labeled with black marker. It read, "Rose." He pulled it out and opened the lid.

On top of the pile in the box was the starling egg he'd carefully wrapped up in tissue paper when cleaning out their old apartment. He wasn't sure of its importance or why Rose had placed it on her nightstand, but he knew it had some meaning for her and he wanted to protect it.

Underneath the egg was her black, leather Bible. He picked it up and lay back on the bed. Touching the cover, he ran his fingers over the soft leather and outlined her name embossed in gold in the corner. It made his heart hurt, so he stopped when he got to the letter *s*.

Opening it up, he flipped through the tissue-thin paper and a bookmark fell out. He picked it up off his chest and smelled it. He wanted to see if her scent still lingered on it, but it didn't anymore.

That was the one thing that was the hardest to live without, not being able to smell her. He could see her in pictures and even hear her voice in old messages. He could touch things that belonged to her and feel near to her, but her scent was fading with each passing day. There was no way to preserve it. Clothes she used to wear, packed up in card-board boxes, started to smell like everything else in the closet.

The reality was, she was slowly fading away from him. He was left with only phantoms.

Internally, emotionally, he didn't have much room inside—only enough room to mourn her loss. Besides Duncan, Rose still filled most of his waking thoughts. And at the nursery, he often found himself working without thinking much of anything at all. Days passed quickly, but nights dragged on longer.

But just in the past few weeks, he'd found another thought lurking in the back of his mind. Strangely, he'd also been thinking about Will who was only a few miles away in the prison that was hidden behind the shopping plaza where Rose used to work. Even though Will was nearby, it felt as if he lived on another planet.

Will was housed at the Plymouth County Correctional Facility since being charged with Rose's murder. He couldn't come up with bail money or a private attorney.

A trial date had not been set, although Daniel read in the Old Colony Memorial that Will made a plea of not guilty. Daniel wasn't sure what to believe. He didn't know if Will was really telling the truth or just trying to save his own skin.

How could he think he wasn't guilty after running her over—after killing Rose? How could he proclaim his innocence after all he'd done? Will had killed her. He'd seen him do it with his own eyes.

Daniel picked up the bookmark again. On one side was a picture of Jesus in a long white robe holding a staff and herding sheep, and on the other side was a Bible verse from the book of Matthew. It read:

"Therefore, if you are offering your gift at the altar and there remember that your brother or sister has something against you, leave your gift there in front of the altar. First go and be reconciled to them; then come and offer your gift."

Go and be reconciled.

That was never going to happen, not in a million years. Those words could be written in stone by Moses himself for all Daniel cared, but the thought of reconciliation with Will made his stomach turn. It was hard for him to even read the word, let alone do it. No, reconciling with something as vile as Will, that was out of the question.

Fiddling with the tassel on the bookmark and listening to the rhythm of the fan above his head, he finally drifted off to a fitful sleep.

☾

One year later

Up early, Daniel went for a run down Jordan Road and found himself at a small stone bridge overlooking the Eel River. Two swans huddled together in a field of dense lily pads. As the sun rose in the distance and slowly heated up the air around him, he exhaled. The heat from the sun released the sweet smell of blossoms growing nearby. The rapid chirping of finches and the high-and-low call of tufted titmice woke up the trees. He stood there and felt overcome by beauty.

Mist rose off a nearby field and the world felt new again—reborn. Tempted to take off and run through the tall grass near a lane of stoic maple trees, he remained still. The somber call of a mourning dove perched on the other side of the stone bridge broke into his train of thought. He looked at his watch and ran back toward the house.

When he arrived, Duncan was being fed a handful of Cheerios in his highchair by Mrs. Bailey. He blew him a kiss, showered, and quickly changed.

It was a little before eight when he arrived at the prison. Visiting hours were from nine to eleven in the morning, but visitors needed to get there early to be prescreened and processed.

Getting out of the truck, he patted his pockets to make sure he had his wallet and locked the door. He then followed a small group of people making their way to the prison's visitor center. One woman held a little girl's hand. She was dressed as if she was going to church.

Walking into the lobby, he was instructed to sit on one of the blue metal benches until his name was called. He felt the cold metal through his pant leg. They would need to check his identification against the approved visitor list. He waited silently and thought about what he wanted to say.

The lobby felt sterile and antiseptic—not warm or welcoming. It was unlike any other visitor center he'd ever been to. He heard buzzers go off deep within the heart of the building and metal doors crash together, along with men's muffled voices. Signs on the wall instructed visitors as to what could be brought into the center and what conduct they were expected to adhere to.

Everything in the room was perfectly controlled and thought out. It was stripped down to the bare essentials—nothing superfluous. Daniel was aware that every move he made was being watched, maybe even scrutinized, which led to a slight feeling of paranoia. It also reminded him of his O.U.I. and the brief time he'd spent locked up.

Thankfully, he knew he could leave at any time. He could walk back out into the world unrestrained. He was free. He could go back to the stone bridge and see the swans and hear the morning songs of birds any time he wanted. He could run through the fields, then lay down and watch clouds form into different shapes all afternoon.

No chains, no rules, no people to rule over him. The only restrictions in his life were chosen—ones of his own accord. The confines he placed on himself were simple—whatever he needed to do to be a good father and whatever he needed to do to remain sober.

"Daniel Goodman."

His name was forcefully announced by an officer standing in the corner of the room behind a bulletproof glass booth. He stood up and wiped his damp hands on the back of his khaki pants and walked in his direction.

"Please sit in booth number one. The inmate will be along shortly. Use the phone at the side of the booth to communicate. You'll have twenty minutes. Do you have any questions?"

Daniel shook his head and walked down the small corridor to booth number one.

Breathing heavily, he checked for the paper bag in his back pocket. Wiping his brow with the back of his hand, he felt his heart rate pick up. He sat back in the seat and inhaled deeply, trying to calm the adrenaline rushing through his body.

The sectionals between booths made it difficult to see when an inmate was coming. Out of the corner of his eye, he caught glimpses of orange shirts.

Will, chained at the waist and ankles, walked clumsily to his seat. They sat in front of each other divided by a thick piece of impenetrable glass. Neither of them reached for the phone. Instead, Daniel looked at Will who was staring at the floor.

He hadn't shaved in a while and looked thinner. His hair was uncombed. There was an old, yellow bruise on the side of his cheek and the whites of his eyes looked red and irritated.

When Will finally looked up, Daniel looked toward the phone. They both slowly reached for the receivers.

"I'm here. What do you want?" Daniel said flatly.

The dark circles under Will's eyes indicated to Daniel that he hadn't been sleeping much. Will looked as if he was on the edge of completely breaking apart and he noticed a slight tremble to his shoulders. His head bobbed up and down. Was he having a small seizure? Did he need some help? Daniel slightly stood from his chair, thinking he may need to flag down an officer.

But then he heard it. Soft at first, then heavy sobs coming from the other end of the phone. Will was crying. Daniel wasn't sure he'd ever seen him do that before. It shook him.

"Brother, can you forgive me?"

At that moment, the visitor center felt strangely quiet. Daniel noticed a small tremor in his hands.

"I'm so sorry." Will took two breaths in rapid succession. "I really wanted to see you, but I didn't think I had the right to ask you to come. I was ashamed. I thought I'd lost you forever. You have every reason to hate me."

He watched as Will raised his whole arm to wipe his tears onto his shirt sleeve.

"I didn't mean to hurt Rose. I was drunk. It was dark. The storm. The gun wasn't even loaded. It fell and I picked it up. When I looked up, she was standing there—wet—in the rain—my headlights—her orange dress."

Will struggled to breathe.

"I slammed on the brakes, but it was too late. I couldn't stop the car. The tires skidded. I couldn't react in time. I'm so sorry."

Tears continued to stream down Will's cheeks.

"Ten minutes." An officer's voice boomed from the doorway.

"How—How are you h-holding up, Danny?" Will wiped his eyes and tried to lean in closer to the glass.

Daniel didn't want to feel sorry for him. But as he watched Will cry, old patterns emerged and part of him wanted to rescue Will from his own pain. However, this time he wouldn't. He couldn't. He wasn't going to enable him anymore.

Paul had taught him that word. It was a good word, because it helped remind him how he could become a part of the problem.

But Daniel knew he was wrong about one thing. Will wasn't breaking apart, instead, he was breaking open. He was being cracked open just enough to let in some light. Paul told him once, not all pain is bad. And no matter how much he wanted to rescue Will, he knew Will needed to face this alone. No rescuing, no enabling, no handholding. Will had to face what he'd done head on—like Daniel had had to do this past painful year.

"Some days are better than o-others."

He switched his weight in the seat and took a shallow breath.

"And this is the main reason w-why."

Daniel lifted off his chair and took out his wallet from his back pocket. Opening it up, he pulled out a picture. Staring at it for a second, he tentatively held it a few inches from the glass.

"Will, this is a picture of my son, Duncan."

He noticed Will stare carefully at the picture and then begin to raise his finger to try to touch it through the glass. Without thinking, Daniel pulled it back.

A voice sounded from overhead. "Visiting hours are over. Hang up the receiver and make your way to the exit, please."

"Is…is it?"

"Will, this is my son. This is o-our son."

There was a pause. Will looked up, and then his eyes went back to the small photo of Duncan.

The phones automatically shut off.

Will looked at Daniel. Daniel lifted his head and nodded. An officer came to escort Will out of the booth. Daniel watched him being pulled from his seat and then disappear past a heavy black door that slammed shut. A loud buzzer went off a few seconds later, then another one.

Placing the picture of Duncan back in his wallet, he stared at the empty seat where Will had sat. There was no beginning again or making a fresh start with him—no wiping the slate clean. That time was over—finished. But would it be another repair in the break, a joining of two loose ends, or just the end of the line? He didn't know yet, but he didn't need to figure it all out now.

Anyways, whatever it was, he was determined to enter into it with his eyes wide open and his boundaries rock solid. Will was not penetrating the fortress he'd built to protect Duncan. There was no way any of the stuff he'd pulled in the past would get by him now. His devotion to his new family was unshakeable—impenetrable, like Fort Knox.

The drawbridge was made, the moat dug. It was constructed of thick stone walls with small windows to fire at oncoming enemies. Daniel was grounded and steadfast. He was strong and stable. He was what a father was meant to be—a protector and guardian. He was the father he'd always wanted and the father both Rose and Carrie deserved. He was also the father that Will would never be.

Leaving the parking lot, Daniel made a right and decided to take the long way home. He drove down Warren Avenue, the coastal road, past beach mansions and old colonials. He passed by ancient white fishing shacks and an abandoned, dilapidated seashore restaurant weatherworn from past nor'easters. The silhouette of homes on a spit of beach perched out in the middle of the ocean gleamed in the sunlight.

Making a right onto Clifford Road at the top of the hill, he snaked along the Eel River past primordial fields blossoming with wildflowers mixed with hay—all sun washed. Occasionally, he passed by pods of sheep grazing and a handful of beehives sitting in the shade of mammoth Sycamore trees bordering the road.

Stopping at Old Sandwich Road, he made a left and parked Sugar on the side of the road. Transplanted Highland Coos with their long, red hair mooed in the distance. Dodging a passing car, he made his way over to the stone bridge. The same bridge he'd been to this morning. The swans were still there, but the tree birds were mostly silent. The morning serenade over.

Opening a brown paper bag, Daniel reached in for some small pellets of round fish food and dropped it in the water a few at a time. He watched it float on top of blue and green rippling water and in between long river reeds. Taking a seat on the edge of the wall, he watched as swans from across the way came over to investigate, followed by mallards trailing their water Vs behind them.

Getting back in the truck, he pulled out the picture of Duncan again and looked hard at it.

"I promise I'll do my best, Duncan," he said, rubbing at the corners. "I'm so sorry. I never expected all this to happen. I wish it'd never happened, but I want you to know I-I love you."

He kissed the photo and placed it down beside him. Shifting Sugar into gear, he headed back to the Baileys breathing in the sweet smell of hay as he passed by golden fields.

The back door creaked open and Daniel walked into the Bailey's kitchen filled with the sweet aroma of yellow cake baking in the oven. Mrs. Bailey was at the sink rinsing off batter from a bowl and wooden spoon.

"How was it?"

She turned and wiped her wet hands on her pink floral apron.

"Good, but can we talk about it later?"

"Sure, honey."

She smiled with her eyes and gently nodded her head.

"Where is he?"

Daniel dropped his keys and brown leather wallet on the counter.

"In the living room, in his Pack n' Play, watching *Curious George.*"

Daniel walked down the short hallway and stood at the living room door. Jumping up and down, Duncan tried to dance to the music and laughed at the man with the yellow hat.

The mantel clock struck twelve.

Daniel paused and took a long, deep breath.

"Hey Dunks, what'cha up to?"

Duncan quickly turned—a toothy smile beamed across his face. Reaching out his arms, he shrieked, "Dada!"

Resources for those in need

National Domestic Violence Hotline
800-799-7233

Suicide and Crisis Lifeline
988

The Samaritans Helpline: Loneliness/Isolation/Depression
877-870-4673

Substance Abuse and Mental Health Hotline (SAMHSA)
800-662-4357

Childhelp: National Child Abuse Hotline
800-422-4453

You are not alone.